Cahena

By Manly Wade Wellman

THE SCHOOL OF DARKNESS
THE VOICE OF THE MOUNTAIN
WHAT DREAMS MAY COME
THE HANGING STONES
THE LOST AND THE LURKING
AFTER DARK
THE OLD GODS WAKEN

Cah

By Manly Wade Wellman

THE SCHOOL OF DARKNESS
THE VOICE OF THE MOUNTAIN
WHAT DREAMS MAY COME
THE HANGING STONES
THE LOST AND THE LURKING
AFTER DARK
THE OLD GODS WAKEN

Cahena

A Dream of the Past

MANLY WADE WELLMAN

DOUBLEDAY & COMPANY, INC.
GARDEN CITY, NEW YORK
1986

All of the characters in this book
are fictitious, and any resemblance
to actual persons, living or dead, is
purely coincidental.

Library of Congress Cataloging in Publication Data

Wellman, Manly Wade, 1905–86
Cahena : a dream of the past.

I. Title.
PS3545.E52858C3 1986 813'.54 86-13470
ISBN: 0-385-19824-8

Printed in the United States of America
First Edition

To the memory of her who deserves to be remembered from the long ago;
How beautiful, how brilliant a woman;
Her womanhood and womanliness raised her to the heights,
Her womanhood and womanliness doomed her to the depths;
That queen, that prophetess, that goddess of war and love,

DAIA THE CAHENA

Foreword

A historical novel must be as historical as possible, but the almost forgotten history of the brave and beautiful Cahena, who for years blocked the Moslem conquest of North Africa, remains deeply shadowed. Today, her name has various spellings. Even the supposed dates of her rise and fall vary from work to work. Place names have changed over the centuries.

Most rewarding of available sources is Ibn-Khaldoun, the great thirteenth-century Arabian historian, whose monumental work, translated into French as *Histoire des Berberes,* cites many earlier commentators, now lost. Also helpful are Ch.-André Julien, *Histoire de L'Afrique de Nord;* E. F. Gautier, *Le Passé de L'Afrique de Nord; The Encyclopedia of Islam;* and William Muir, *The Caliphate.* Nahum Slouschz, *The Jews of North Africa,* gathers legends of the Cahena. Edward Gibbon, *Decline and Fall of the Roman Empire,* and Washington Irving, *Mohamet and His Successors,* notice with admiration her career and character. Germaine Beauguitte wrote a slipshod paperback novel, *La Kahina, Reine des Aures.* Some help comes from the works of travelers and historians such as Leo Africanus, Galbraith Welch, Amos Perry, E. Alexander Powell, Hendrik de Leeuw, Robert Graves, S. F. Scott, and, inevitably, Sir Richard Francis Burton. There are also fugitive newspaper and magazine articles, too numerous to list.

Perhaps H. Rider Haggard wrote *She* and Pierre Benoit wrote *L'Atlantide* because they had heard something about the Cahena.

—Manly Wade Wellman
Chapel Hill, North Carolina
1986

And now they wait and whiten peaceably,
Those conquerors, those poets, those so fair:
They know time comes, not only you and I,
But the whole world shall whiten, here or there;

When those long caravans that cross the plain
With dauntless feet and sound of silver bells
Put forth no more for glory or for gain,
Take no more solace from the palm-girt wells,

When the great markets by the sea shut fast
All that calm Sunday that goes on and on:
When even lovers find their peace at last,
And earth is but a star, that once had shone.

—James Elroy Flecker

I

When the two armed retainers marched the big stranger into the tent, Charles Martel sat and looked heavily at him. At last Charles Martel said, "Leave him here with me," and to the stranger when they were alone, "Sit on that other bench. If you can tell me how to fight those Moors I must soon face, I'll be glad to listen."

The tent was by far the biggest and finest in all the great sprawl of the Frankish camp. Woven of twisted sheep shearings, it could shed rain and fence out the October night wind. Black-oiled poles pushed the top high. By the light of heaped red embers just inside the doorway, the interior looked like a murky cave. Baggage and camp gear were cluttered along its walls. Between Charles Martel and the stranger stood a rough plank table on two trestles, with a big wooden trencher of cold roast venison, a torn loaf of bread, earthen wine flasks, and half a dozen cups of copper-bound leather. Furs and blankets were stacked to one side for a bed. On a rack hung mail jackets, a horned helmet, a lance, and a scabbarded sword. Among the shadows in the back of the tent stamped a big blond horse, tethered to a peg, with grain spread on a cloth under his nose.

Charles Martel was big and blond, too. His gold-worked tunic was thrown open to show his leather war shirt, sewn all over with lengths of iron chain. The ale-colored crescent of his mustache hid his mouth and clamped his hard, square chin, and from under his jeweled cap heavy braids of hair hung upon his shoulders. A fox-skin cloak draped him. On his legs were heavy boots, lashed at the knees. He studied his visitor again, silently and searchingly. With one yellow-fuzzed hand he fondled the haft of the great hammerheaded mace that lay across his lap, the weapon for which men had named him Charles Martel.

He saw a man fully as big as himself and perhaps twenty years older, in his mid-sixties anyway, with shabby garments and a massive cropped head. Thick, bowed legs showed cross-gartered beneath the stained tunic of brown cloth. The wide leather belt had clasps at the left from which a sword had been unslung, at the right an iron-riveted sheath from which a dagger had been plucked before the guards had fetched the stranger to speak alone with the chief of the Franks. Broad, sunburned hands bracketed themselves upon the square knees, and one big wrist was wound with a blood-spotted rag. The face was a weathered rectangle, set with three-cornered blue eyes and a nose that sometime or other had been smashed flat by a heavy blow. A scar squirmed down into the blunt, gray-laced tawny beard, like a dull river running among frosted autumn woods.

A stark old fighter, Charles Martel judged expertly, seasoned rather than burdened with his years. To fight such a man would be a fierce, violent joy, like a gulp of strong wine.

"They didn't say your name," Charles Martel addressed him.

"Wulf." It was a short growl.

"They did say you were English."

"English born, but I'm a Saxon, not an Angle."

A nice distinction, pondered Charles Martel. Maybe they understood it in England.

"And they say you came into camp after fighting the Moors and Arabs before us," Charles Martel prompted the old warrior who named himself Wulf.

"I've fought them for forty years," said Wulf. "In Asia and now here in your country."

Charles Martel scraped his mustache with his knuckle. "They also said that you had a band of stout men who stood in the way of this Moorish general—his name's strange, hard to speak."

"Abd-ar-Rahman," supplied Wulf the Saxon. "I had only twenty men, not enough to stand in his way. We stung his advance guard, but they killed half of us. We fell back and fell back until we found your army camped here, in Abd-ar-Rahman's face."

"Half of you got away. Did you have women with you?"

"My followers had one or two," said Wulf. "Lost them, I'm afraid. There was no woman with me. None." He snapped his hard mouth shut on the word.

"We've skirmished with the Moors for a week now," said Charles Martel, "waiting for them to give battle."

"Abd-ar-Rahman waits for you to give battle," said Wulf. "He's driven everything before him until now—driven them since he was a young man coming out of Africa. He won't go back unless you beat him."

"You talk as if you know him."

"I know him," said Wulf. "I've fought him more times than you and I have fingers and toes."

None of that was supple courtier talk. Wulf spoke respectfully but bluntly, in a deep voice. Charles Martel remembered Count Eudo, driven from his castle on the Garonne into the protection of the Frankish host. Eudo had been plaintive, even servile. Charles permitted himself to like the flavor of Wulf's speech, even while he was glad that no retainers heard their master so levelly addressed. Silence again, while the big war-horse stamped behind him and snuffed at its grain.

"No woman with you," Charles Martel harked back. "Don't you love women?"

"At my age, a man's nature gets past loving women."

"Ha!" Charles Martel barked a laugh. He leaned to pour wine into two leather cups and shoved one across the table to Wulf. "I'll warrant this wasn't always so with you, not loving women."

"I didn't speak of times long past," said Wulf, closing his corded fist around the cup. "I spoke of now, with Abd-ar-Rahman here in your country, his camp full of booty plundered from your people, his men swearing by Allah to wipe you off the earth."

That, too, was boldly blunt, but it was a wholesome reminder of why they sat together. Charles Martel drank and wiped his mouth.

"How do you swear, and by whom?" he asked. "I take it you're a Christian."

"England's been Christian for more than a hundred years," Wulf said, drinking in turn, and that was no real answer to the question. "My father wanted me to be a priest and put me to school at Canterbury. Abbot Hadrian was my teacher."

"Hadrian?" echoed Charles Martel, remembering that a Roman emperor had borne that name.

"Hadrian of Carthage. He taught me to read and write Latin and Greek and Hebrew, and I was good at those."

"I'd have thought your young mind would have been to war and weapons," said Charles Martel.

"It was, and Abbot Hadrian saw that it was. When I was seventeen, he sent me away from Canterbury, saying I'd be happier as a soldier."

"He must have been a wise teacher, and a kind one."

"He was as sharp as vinegar, but he understood me," said Wulf. "He told me cloisters and psalms were for some boys, but not for me. So I fought in an English war or two, and others among your Franks. I was at the battle of Tertry, forty-five years ago."

"Were you so?" Charles Martel wondered if Wulf had fought for or against his father Pepin, but did not ask. "Well, what then?"

"There was peace in these countries for a while. I traveled on and got into the imperial service at Constantinople."

"With the Byzantines. What sort of people were they?"

"Fairly proud. Fairly foolish. But the army was a good one. I was with it against the Arabs in Armenia and Syria."

"Was that good fighting?" asked Charles Martel.

"It was deadly fighting," said Wulf. "There was supposed to be a truce, but there was fighting. Then I visited Carthage, for Abbot Hadrian had come from there. I got there in time to be driven out by the Arabs in 695, but Constantinople sent a fleet, and we drove them out in turn. It was what you'd call good fighting."

"The Arabs destroyed Carthage next time."

"I was there when they started taking its stones apart," growled Wulf into his wine cup. "Some got away by sea as the Arabs closed in. I couldn't join those, but I managed not to get killed. I ran into the desert before the army of Hassan ibn an-Numan."

"Christ's soul, my friend, you seem to have done a lot of running before those infidels," Charles Martel could not help saying. "Back in Carthage and later, and now, too, they've chased you."

Wulf grinned, showing gaps in his teeth. "I didn't run long that time after Carthage fell. I came among the Moors."

"And the Moors are yonder," reminded Charles Martel, gazing into the night outside. "Deciding how to fight us."

"They weren't Moslems then," said Wulf. "We fought the Moslems, and I saw the Moslems do some running of their own."

"When did that happen?"

"Thirty-four years back, when I was thirty. I'd seen so much fighting by then that I thought I had no more to learn."

"There's always something more for a fighter to learn," pronounced Charles Martel. "Who was your Moorish general?"

"The Cahena."

"What sort of man was he?"

"The Cahena was a woman," said Wulf.

Charles Martel stared, he hoped not stupidly.

"She whipped Hassan and his bravest soldiers," said Wulf. "Drove them like sheep. Those who didn't run almost all the way back to Egypt, we killed or captured."

"God's rood, this is a strange story," vowed Charles Martel, filling their cups again. "I never heard of this war queen."

"There's always something more for a fighter to learn." Wulf gave him back his own words without mockery. "She was the only one who beat the Arabs, after they came from Carthage."

Charles Martel shoved the replenished cup toward Wulf. "Tell me how she did it," he said.

"That will be a long story."

"You'll have a long night to tell it," said Charles Martel. "Take your time to say what will help me fight them tomorrow. You say Carthage fell, and you escaped. How did you meet this Cahena?"

II

They had been riding after Wulf ever since the summer sun had risen behind sacked Carthage. Now that sun was a hot disk at the top of the pale sky. Its rays raked the sullenly scrubby plain and the hammered track that ran west by south toward remote hunches of mountains. Whenever he urged the tall bay horse to a canter, they picked up speed two furlongs behind. When he slowed down, so did they, but not quite to his slowness. They gained. Either their horses stayed fresher than his or they cared less for their horses than they cared about catching Wulf.

For the fiftieth time he peered over the broad cliff of his shoulder. Four of them back there, and somehow they didn't seem to be Moslems. What did they want of him?

Whatever they wanted, he'd better find out before his sweating horse fagged out in the hot, dry air. If he must fight four mounted men, he didn't want to fight them on foot. Reining around, he sat his saddle and let the horse breathe gratefully. He'd begun to love that horse since he had taken it from its Moslem master in a black hour before dawn, had taken, too, the Moslem's cloak and turban to look like something other than a fugitive resident of Carthage. A stolen horse carries you well, Wulf had once been told by a Hun of Constantinople's imperial guard. Weary as the beast was from carrying Wulf's big body so many miles, it knew a fight was coming and was not afraid.

Wulf loosened his straight sword in its sheath, and from a skin bottle he sipped water to churn inside his mouth. He looked this way, then that. The road had roughened to a sandy track across the rolling land with its brittle, dry grass. A mile or so to the left rose a tuft of palms with a little clay-brown hut beneath it. No hiding place, not even a big rock to set his back to, nothing except those pursuers coming nearer, while Wulf listened to his horse breathe. He squinted his eyes to see what he must face.

They weren't Moslems, they were Moors, coming at him. Wild Moors, he judged, none of the soft hangers-on he had seen in Carthage. They wore dull-hued capes with hoods thrown back from shaggy heads. To their left arms were strapped painted shields, and each right hand poised a javelin. Nearer still, and he saw their roughly made saddles and their clumsily booted feet stuck into leather stirrup loops. Their bearded faces scowled. Warriors these, ready for war.

They spread into open order to approach. Wulf wished he had a shield, too, but felt lucky to have a sword. If only they didn't cast their javelins all at once, if only they came to close quarters. Then a swift spurring charge to their right, outside the flanker's shield and a slash or thrust for the life. With one down, whirl at the others. He might get a second of them quickly and, with luck, a third—he didn't often need more than one fair chance at a man. With three down, the fourth would be no problem.

They had slowed their panting horses to a walk. They meant to take their time with him, savoring what they would do.

"I am Wulf the Saxon!" he shouted in the language they would know, braving his name at them in their own fashion. They came to a halt, fifteen paces away.

"He doesn't talk like a Moslem," said the swarthy, spidery man at the left.

"He has a Moslem saddle and Moslem clothes," said another.

"I took them to get past the guards around Carthage," said Wulf, glad of any chance to parley. "I'm a Saxon, I told you. I fought the Moslems at Carthage and, after they took the town, I sneaked around like a snake, looking for a chance to get away."

"He's lying," said the man at the left. "I've talked to people who watched from outside. The only Carthaginians who escaped were rich ones who got places on the ships before the Moslems closed in. Those Moslems killed all the men who were left, raped all the women."

"They didn't kill me," said Wulf. "I slung my sword behind and put a mantle over it, and I moved around carefully. When Moslems came frowning, I said, '*Allahu akhbar,*' and they thought I was a convert. It was like that for two days—no, three. Last night I got over the wall and started away on foot. A Moslem came riding after me. I got him by the leg and dragged him off his horse and put my sword into him. This is his horse and these are his clothes and this is his blood on them. But you're Moors, and I don't have to dress like a Moslem among you."

He raked the turban off with his bridle arm and shook down his tawny, sweaty hair. It was cut ear-length at back and sides and banged in front, to frame the flushed rectangle of his face. He shrugged out of the cloak, showing his embroidered tunic with a torn right sleeve.

"No, he's not a Moslem," said a man with red lights in his beard. "He's smooth-shaven, or he was a few days back."

The man nudged his horse's brown flank and came closer, staring at Wulf. His hard, bony face was chopped with scars. Its hairy chin narrowed forward from massive jaws. High cheekbones and heavy brows clamped blazing blue eyes. His nose was as lean as a knife blade. Jeweled plugs winked at his earlobes. "I'm Bhakrann," he said. "Stop calling us Moors. The Romans call us that."

"The Arabs call you Berbers," said Wulf.

"That means the voice of a lion, and we can be lions. We call ourselves the Imazighen. That was our name since the world began. Our tribe of the Imazighen is the Djerwa."

"I've heard some talk about the Djerwa," said Wulf, looking from one to another, his hand close to his sword hilt.

"He wears a Greek tunic," said the gaunt man. "I don't like Greeks either. They're too apt to change sides. I say he's a spy for those Moslem bastards, back there burning Carthage down."

"Can a Saxon fight?" inquired Bhakrann, as though he hoped so, and Wulf spread his hard lips in a grin to show his square teeth.

"Try me," he invited cheerfully. "One of you after another, or all of you at once if the Djerwa don't fight fair."

The gaunt man at the left hurled his javelin.

Instantly Wulf rocked to his right. As the javelin sang past, he shot out his left hand and clutched it in midair. All four of the Djerwa yelled. Wulf studied the weapon quickly. It was five feet long, and its wrought-iron head made up a third of that length. The point and both edges were rigorously whetted. The tough, oiled wood of the haft was clamped with turns of copper wire, about an inch apart. Into the butt was set a heavy iron spike. Poising it, Wulf grinned dryly at the man who had thrown it.

"Sell me your javelin." He spoke the worst insult a man of that race could hear.

The man's face knotted in fury, then went blank and open-mouthed. For Bhakrann suddenly roared with laughter.

"Greek or Moslem or Saxon, he's not afraid," Bhakrann whooped. "*Hai*, ready of hand and tongue!" His deep-set eyes twinkled. "I might approve of this Wulf—didn't you say that was your name? You make jokes in the face of death."

"That was no joke," snarled the one whose javelin Wulf had caught.

"You started it, Cham," said Bhakrann, still laughing. "Let's say he finished it, without feeding your javelin back to you. Maybe we'll all be friends yet." Again the red glint in his beard as he cocked his head. "Wulf the Saxon, eh? You're right, you'd hardly be a Moslem spy, wearing Moslem clothes and riding a Moslem saddle."

"I needed those to help me get away," said Wulf again, still poising the javelin. If they made a rush, a quick throw might pierce Bhakrann, then his sword against the others. But there was no rush, not while Bhakrann smiled like that.

"Tell us how you did get clear," Bhakrann invited. "You only said you killed one of them outside Carthage."

"I killed several inside Carthage, while they were taking it." Wulf began to feel easier, though not much. "I commanded some half-born, half-bred volunteers—shopkeepers, porters and so on. The enemy got in and my men ran and I couldn't fight all those people alone. So I ran, too, and hid awhile under a heap of baskets in a shed. Then I came up, holding up a finger and saying *'Allah.'* "

"And stayed several days," said Bhakrann, holding his javelin but holding it low. "Did you hear them talk? Do you know Arabic as well as you know Imazighen?"

"I've always learned languages quickly. I heard some officers talking with their general, on the street as I passed by. He said he wanted Carthage totally ruined, then he'd lead his army out to conquer the country. He questioned some prisoners."

"Their general," Bhakrann echoed. "Isn't his name Hassan ibn an-Numan? What does he look like, and what did he ask about?"

"He's middle-sized, with a gray beard," said Wulf. "He has a green turban —he must have been to Mecca. He asked those prisoners who was the greatest prince among the Moors."

"The Imazighen," Cham corrected him sourly.

"He called them Berbers. One prisoner said that the greatest leader, the most powerful, was a queen called the Cahena."

"That prisoner told the truth," said another rider, a man with a long face and a long beard.

"What else did he tell those Moslems?" asked Bhakrann.

"He said that the Cahena ruled all the tribes on Arwa, a mountain some days of travel off yonder." Wulf jerked his head westward. "That if they could conquer her and her people, no others would give him much trouble."

Bhakrann gazed at Wulf. "Do you know who the Cahena is?"

"I couldn't help but hear about her."

"Ahi," crooned Bhakrann. "What did you hear?"

"Cahena means sorceress in Arabic."

"It means prophetess in Hebrew," said Cham. "Priestess."

"I've wondered about that," said Wulf. "I've never heard that the Jews had priestesses."

"We're the Imazighen," said Bhakrann. "We know Jewish beliefs, but we have other beliefs, too."

"And I've heard that she's more than a hundred years old."

"Nothing like that old," said Bhakrann. "What else?"

"That she beat and killed other Moslem generals who came here—Okba ibn Nafa and Zoheir ibn Cais. That she drove the Moslems out of their holy city Cairouan. I'd heard that before, and the prisoner told it again. I don't think the Cahena's name was new to Hassan."

"Just what is her name exactly?" challenged Bhakrann. "She's called the Cahena—prophetess or sorceress or priestess, whatever you like—but what's her real name?"

Wulf shook his head, and his sweaty hair flopped. "I never heard it."

"I never heard it either," said the long-faced Djerwa.

"Her name isn't spoken," explained Bhakrann, sitting his horse easily by now. "She's called the Cahena, that's all. If anybody says her true name out loud, he dies." Bhakrann peered under a broad palm. "I see trees and a house yonder. Let's dismount and lead our horses there. They're tired. They can drink, and we can talk."

Wulf dismounted with the others and gave the javelin back to Cham, who grimaced. The four Djerwa slung their shields to their saddles, and Wulf took time to see that the shields were of thickened leather, rimmed in iron or brass and painted with geometric figures. The exposed left arms of the four displayed scabbarded knives strapped to the forearms. They tramped toward the cluster of palms, leading their horses. Wulf took time to study these, too.

They were all smaller than his own bay. They were lean and stringy, and would not have been lovely even if they had been well groomed. The saddles were high-pomeled, with girths both forward and to the rear. Behind each cantle rode a cloth-bound bundle.

"All right, what do you think of our horses?" asked Bhakrann, walking at Wulf's left. Cham moved at Wulf's right. Wulf felt escorted, perhaps guarded.

"I doubt if they could jump a wall or a hollow as well as a horse from Arabia," replied Wulf.

"But they can last longer on a journey," said Bhakrann. "They don't need much to eat, they've slept in the open all their lives. They run well—we kept up with you all the way from outside Carthage. By tonight they'll have gone about fifty miles, and tomorrow they'll be ready to start again. I wonder if yours will feel up to it."

Which meant that Wulf and his horse would be with them tomorrow.

"I'll care for mine," Wulf assured Bhakrann. "I wouldn't want to be afoot in this country," and he looked across coarse tussocks and scattered boulders.

"You've come far across the world," Bhakrann observed. "You escaped being killed by Moslems, then by us. Call yourself lucky."

"Call yourselves lucky, too," said Wulf at once, and Cham snorted, but again Bhakrann laughed.

"I say again, you're ready of tongue. You act like a fighter. If that's your trade, you couldn't have come among better fellow tradesmen. So this Hassan wants to hunt for us, eh? Well, let him find us. We've beaten his sort before this."

"Okba, then Zoheir." Wulf nodded. "Okba marched all the way west to the outer sea. Then he came back and got killed, with all his men."

"How do the Moslems think of Okba?" asked Cham.

"I gave him his martyrdom personally." Bhakrann grinned. "Killed him with my own hand. That's his sword on my saddle."

Wulf looked. It was a handsomely curved Arabian sword, in a scabbard of leather. Its hilt sparkled with jewels.

"Okba captured Koseila, one of our chiefs," Bhakrann elaborated.

"Treated him like a slave. Koseila escaped to where we were watching Okba's march—the Cahena directed us. We knew everything Okba did, every step and instant. A few days later we rushed him and martyred him, as you put it. But you can hear about that later. About you, how did you happen to be in Carthage?"

Walking with them, Wulf told how he had fought as a boy in the country of the Franks, as a young man at Constantinople against both Christians and Moslems, and again at Carthage when the Moslems attacked there. Bhakrann asked questions, and Wulf said he had been an officer to train diffident Greeks and Byzantines for battle, then to lead them in the slovenly defense. He described the sack of the cities, men butchered, women screaming in hysterical terror, children herded away like sheep.

"They're shipping those children to Damascus," said Wulf. "Abd al-Melik likes lots of slaves."

"Who's Abd al-Melik?" asked the long-faced Djerwa.

"Their caliph," replied Wulf. "Master of all Moslems and, he likes to say, of all the world."

"Not this part of the world," growled Cham. "We've showed the Moslems a short way out of here before, and we can do it again."

They led the horses among warty hummocks, tufted with coarse grass and thorny bush. Up ahead, the palms grew big and grateful in their sight. In the shade crouched a small, square hut of rocks and dried mud, from the door of which peered a grizzled old man. Bhakrann called out to reassure him, and asked for water.

The gray-tussocked face ventured out, then the scrawny body, leaning on a forked staff like a crutch.

"Trouble's coming this way," Bhakrann told him, "and you'd better let us tell you about it."

The old fellow limped toward him. "Trouble, master?"

"I am Bhakrann."

The name meant something to the old man, for he bowed respectfully. "What's happening?" he quavered.

"The Moslems have chewed up Carthage," said Bhakrann. "When they finish robbing and burning, they'll come here to take the land. But let us water our horses."

The oldster led them among palms and acacias to his well, stone-ringed and shaded. They dipped with a wooden bucket to fill a clay trough, and while the horses gulped gratefully the men passed the bucket from hand to hand. Wulf drank and doused his hot head. Three goats watched intently from a pen of poles. Wulf and the others dragged on the bridles to keep the horses from drinking too fast and too much.

"Could we have some food?" Bhakrann asked the farmer.

"But I don't have anything fit for great men to eat."

"We'll eat anything. If it's offered by a friend, we'll pay for it like friends."

They sat under the trees, holding their horses. Wulf studied the little homestead. There was a patchlike field of barley, a few date palms and almond trees. Grape vines straggled on rails. In the midst of the barley field a grinning donkey skull rode on an upright pole, its eyeholes staring darkly, to ward off devils. The old man limped out with a traylike basket. It held a stack of limp flaps of bread, some bunches of raisins, a patterned clay jug.

"Thank you, uncle," said Bhakrann. "One of you pay him."

"Let me," said Wulf.

He found a silver Byzantine coin in his belt-pouch and put it into the skinny hand. Eyes above gray whiskers widened. The old man put the coin to his mouth. Maybe he kissed it, maybe he bit it to make sure of its metal.

"You're too kind, master," he mumbled.

They took food and talked. Wulf broke a piece of bread. It was of coarse barley meal, probably stirred up with water and toasted on a clay tile. He ate hungrily, for he had had very little food in captured Carthage. His companions talked to him with casual goodwill, as though there had never been a thought of fighting him. Cham passed him raisins. The long-faced one said his name was Tifan. The fourth Djerwa was Zeoui, a short, thick-shouldered man with a brown beard. Wulf drank from the jug. It was goat's milk, nutty and fresh.

Bhakrann had flung off his cloak, showing a coarse-woven tunic faced on chest and arms with slips of iron. To his left wrist was strapped a knife, around his neck hung a copper collar set with uncut jewels. As he munched, he spoke to their hovering old host.

"When the Moslems come, hold up one finger like this." Bhakrann pointed skyward with a forefinger like a truncheon. "Hold it up and say, *'Y'allah il Allah.'* "

"What does that mean?"

"It means, there's no god but Allah. Say that and nothing else."

"They'll think I'm crazy," protested the old man.

"Better to be thought crazy than to be knocked on the head," put in Tifan. "I hear that the Moslems more or less respect crazy people."

"Yes." Wulf nodded. "Some of their chief saints seem to have been mad. Including Mohammed himself, as I judge."

"He's had able followers," said Bhakrann, red glints in his beard.

The farmer clucked at his goats. Wulf and the four Djerwa ate every crumb of the food and drained the milk jug. Then they filled their water bottles. At last Bhakrann pronounced the horses sufficiently rested, and they rode back toward the trail. The farmer leaned on his stick and gazed after them.

Bhakrann rode beside Wulf and asked knowledgeable questions about the Moslems. How many were at Carthage? Perhaps twenty-five thousand, Wulf guessed, with more coming from both land and sea. What were their arms? Wulf described scimitars, metal-faced shields, spiked helmets, lances and bows. What about their cavalry? It was splendid, a large part of the total force, much of it mounted on fine horses from Arabia. The Moslems conquered their nations on horseback. Wulf's captured bay was a fair example of their riding stock.

"And I still think that an Arabian horse is big enough to knock down one of yours at close quarters," he said.

"We have javelins to keep them from getting to close quarters," said Bhakrann. "They've come galloping after us before this, I told you, and some were lucky enough to gallop away again."

Wulf looked westward to the mountains. "When will we see your people?"

"Oh, some days yet. We started a march this way as soon as we heard of the siege of Carthage. We four were ordered ahead to have a close-hand look."

"How many can you muster against the Moslems?" asked Wulf.

"About what you say they have, twenty-five thousand or so. Of course, a big army means a whole nation of camp followers who can't fight. What we're bringing along now isn't like that—no women and children. They stayed behind to look after the cattle and sheep and goats, back beyond on the Arwa. But if we draft the men from all the tribes, lots of their families will come, too. No stopping them, worse luck."

Wulf gazed at the heights again. They seemed a trifle closer, but only a trifle, dun touched with green and shadows of blue.

"Is that your Arwa?" he asked.

"No, the Arwa's much bigger, and about two hundred miles on from where we are. Say two hundred and fifty from where Carthage is getting to be a thing of the past."

"Delenda est Carthago," quoted Wulf, more or less to himself.

"Huh?"

"Cato the Censor said that, nearly nine hundred years ago," said Wulf. "Carthage must be destroyed, he kept saying, and finally it happened."

"Did this Cato do anything but talk?"

"He was good at war and he was good at the law, and a good farmer," Wulf said. "He taught people how to make a good loaf of bread, better than what we had just now. And he wanted Carthage destroyed, and it happened, and now it's happening again. Meanwhile, that Arabian general Hassan wants to find the Cahena."

"I said she wouldn't be hard to find," said Cham from behind Wulf. "But she'll be damnably hard to beat."

They ambled along for some moments, thinking about that.

"The Cahena," said Wulf at last. "We talked about how that means priestess in Hebrew. And the name of your tribe, the Djerwa, sounds Jewish. Are you of the Jewish faith?"

"We have some of that," replied Bhakrann. "We respect a lot of various gods and keep their feasts and thank them when there's something to be thankful for."

"Like the Cahena?" suggested Wulf.

"Like her," said Bhakrann.

"She calls us her sons," put in Zeoui, "if we do something to make us worth calling that. About gods, I've heard the Moslems yell out *Allahu akhbar,* God is great. But there's also the Cahena."

"We've yelled that back to them," said Bhakrann. "There's also the Cahena."

"She must be a great queen," said Wulf.

"Judge for yourself when we show you to her," Bhakrann bade him. "She'll want to talk to you about the Moslems, hear the things you know about them."

"She's the Cahena," said Tifan. "That's enough for us."

"It will be more than enough for General Hassan," said Zeoui.

"Meanwhile," said Wulf to Bhakrann, "what's your Cahena going to think of me when we meet?"

"Probably she knows about you already, and is deciding what to think about you."

Wulf stared across at him. "You mean, she has second sight? Knows things in advance?"

"She knows everything, more or less, when she puts her mind to it," said Bhakrann weightily. "Spirits speak to her."

Perhaps that should not have put an end to the conversation, but it did. They rode on and kept riding on for some time, without any talk.

III

They passed other shabby little farmsteads with clumps of date and olive and almond trees and one settlement, a clump of mud huts; but they did not stop anywhere, and were alone on the road.

"We've not spoken to anyone since that old farmer," said Zeoui.

"Nobody's so witless as to ride toward Carthage," said Bhakrann. "The word must have spread about how the town fell, and everybody who wasn't caught is going the other direction, like us."

"Except that old farmer," reminded Zeoui.

"He doesn't think of anything except his barley field and his goats," said Wulf. "Poor old fellow, I hope he doesn't get hurt." He tipped up his water bottle to take a mouthful.

"Save what water you can," cautioned Bhakrann. "We may make a dry camp tonight. And the sun must be hot on your head, after you threw away that turban to show us you weren't a Moslem. Take this."

He sidled his horse over, holding out a big linen kerchief patterned brown and black. Wulf draped it shawl-fashion on his head.

"That makes you look more like a Djerwa," commented Tifan. "Let your beard grow, to be like us."

Far ahead, a gap was visible in the knobby westward range.

"When do we meet your friends?" Wulf asked.

"Another day, perhaps, beyond that pass." Bhakrann drew rein. "Let's lead our horses awhile. It'll rest them and stretch our legs."

They walked awhile in the evening light, holding the bridles. Bhakrann asked questions. Wulf told of being in the Frankish wars, then in border skirmishes around Constantinople, of the more recent fighting with Moslems outside and inside Carthage. He described the Frankish and Byzantine schools of arms and tactics. Bhakrann responded with talk of Imazighen methods, throwing or stabbing with javelins and using big knives at close quarters.

"Yet Okba got through you, rode all the way to the eastern sea," Wulf reminded him. "I've heard how he rode his horse into the ocean and mourned because he couldn't conquer lands beyond—he seemed to think there were lands beyond. You didn't stop him there."

"We stopped him when he came back," said Bhakrann. "I put my javelin right where his neck and shoulder came together."

"You told me that, but they said it was done by someone called the son of the Cahena. Are you her son, Bhakrann?"

"She calls me her son. How do the horses seem, friends? Let's ride awhile now."

A warm breeze had come up. Haggard rocks and knolls rose to either side of the way. The far-off range darkened under the sinking sun, with tints of sea green and russet and purple, with seamy streaks of gilt where the light touched ridges.

They reached a dry, jagged fold in the ground, with a fringe of scrubby trees. Bhakrann lifted his hand.

"We'll stop here," he announced. "See if there's water, Zeoui."

They dismounted. Zeoui slunk along the gully where a stream had run, his long beard thrusting down. He knelt, pawed at one place and then another, moved a few steps onward. He dug with his broad dagger. Cham tethered his horse and came to help.

"You thought there'd be water?" Wulf asked Bhakrann.

"We've found it here before this, even in dry times like now," Bhakrann raised his voice. "How does it look, Zeoui?"

Zeoui lifted a handful of dark earth. Bhakrann nodded.

"That looks damp," he said. "The horses already smell water. Tie them up until we make sure."

Wulf unsaddled his mount and patted the lather-streaked flank. Bhakrann attended to the horses of Zeoui and Cham as well as their own.

"Here it is," called Zeoui triumphantly, from where he had dug to almost the length of his arm into the stream bed.

Wulf tied his bridle to a thorn bush and walked over to see. Cham and Zeoui straightened from the wide hole they had scooped. A flow of milky mud churned there. Cham bailed it out with a brass basin and let more trickle in. Again he bailed. "We can drink it pretty soon," he said.

Saddles and wallets and blankets were carried to the shade of the thicketed bank. "Let's have a fire," said Bhakrann, picking up dry branches. Wulf, too, moved here and there, gathering an armful. Bhakrann struck flint and steel to ignite a scrap of tinder, laid on dry twigs, and fed larger pieces as the flame rose.

Cham and Zeoui brought the basin full of water to the fireside. Bhakrann drank, then Wulf, then Tifan. The water was only slightly clouded with silt. Back went Zeoui to refill the basin, while Cham and Tifan enlarged the makeshift well. It overflowed into a low place in the stream bed. Cham and Tifan skillfully built a dam of earth and stones to contain the water. Bhakrann leaned above them to inspect.

"Soon there'll be enough for the horses to drink," he decided. "You should see it here after the spring rains, Wulf; it runs deep enough to drown a man."

"Can you always get water by scratching for it?" asked Wulf.

"Almost always," Cham said.

"Then wells could be dug all around and the land could be farmed," said Wulf. "All this earth needs is water."

"Farm here?" Cham sniffed. "Not me."

Tifan brought the half-filled water basin to the fire, where big pieces of wood were burning down to coals. Zeoui took a slice of dried meat from a pouch, wiped the blade of his knife, and chopped the meat into the water. He set the basin on stones at the edge of the fire to heat. "Do you have any food?" he asked Wulf.

Wulf found a big wad of dried dates in the wallet of his captured saddle. His companions grunted their applause and broke off bits of the mass to eat. Zeoui watched the meat in the basin, and when it began to seethe he rummaged from somewhere an onion, which he minced up and added. Tifan brought a package of pale-grained couscous. He measured handfuls into the basin and stirred the whole with a peeled twig.

"What I'd like is an ostrich egg," he commented.

"That's for women and children," said Cham. "I'll be satisfied with what we have here."

"A cucumber would help it along," said Zeoui.

"You never had a cucumber in your life," Cham sneered. "You've always lived on the mountaintop eating couscous, and if you could get clabbered milk you'd think you were at a wedding."

The others laughed, and Wulf wondered why it was funny.

The sun had set behind the mountains to westward and the moon had risen, almost full. The air grew chill. Zeoui dragged the basin of stew away from the fire to cool. Bhakrann stooped above the tank where the water had collected and called for the horses to be brought to drink. After that, each rider noosed a line around his mount's neck and tied it where it could crop the scanty grass. Then the party squatted and ate from the basin, using fingers to pick out bits of meat and pinches of couscous. The mealy pellets had swelled and softened. They tasted good.

Bhakrann, sitting with Wulf, wiped his mouth. "That sword you wear," he said. "I haven't seen it yet."

Wulf rasped the blade from its sheath and handed it across. It was a straight, heavy weapon, longer than Wulf's arm, a good three fingers broad at the cross hilt and tapering to a keen point. Both edges were honed razor sharp. Bhakrann handled it respectfully.

"Is this better than a curved sword?" he asked.

"In some ways, yes. I'm used to it. It can stab to a heart or split a skull."

"These marks on it—writing, are they? I can't read writing."

"My name, in Greek. It was made for me in Constantinople."

Bhakrann passed it back. "I'll be interested to see you use it." He gazed at the moon. "That's light enough to travel by, but I don't expect any Moslems right away. And we can use some sleep."

"I'll watch first," volunteered Tifan.

"And I'll watch last, and wake us up at the first ray of the sun," said Bhakrann. "Our fire's pretty much down to coals. Keep it going, but not bright enough to make some stranger curious." He looked at Wulf. "If you've learned any prayers in all those places you've been, say them and sleep well."

Wulf hollowed out the earth with his hands, into a depression to fit his body, and wrapped himself in the captured cloak, with his head on his saddle and his feet to the fire. Looking up, he studied the patterns of the stars. Did they mean anything? He had heard astrologers talk about them, but he could not remember what the talk had been, or if it had sounded convincing. He drifted away into slumber.

He woke to a touch on his shoulder and sat up quickly, his hand on his sword.

"It's Zeoui," said a quick voice. "This is next to last watch, for you to stand. When the moon's moved far enough, wake Bhakrann."

Wulf rose. Zeoui moved away to his own bed. Wulf drew his cloak against the chill and mounted the brushy bank above the camp.

He peered here and there across the softly lighted plain. No movement. After a while he sought the well and slapped water on his stubbly cheeks. Then he returned to the bank and again he looked in all directions. Among the stones at his feet he found one that he liked and drew his great sword to whet it. He sharpened the whole front of the blade, then edged the back.

Swaddled in his cloak, he meditated on his present situation and wondered if it was good or bad. Bhakrann had called him lucky that he hadn't had to fight with all four of these Djerwa. But fighting would come with Moslems, and now that he was with the Djerwa he would be on their side. He respected Moslem warriors, but did not fear them. He'd killed too many for that, in Asia and here in Africa. As to that Imazighen chieftainess, the Cahena, Bhakrann and the others seemed to worship the very mention of her name. How would it be, fighting at a woman's orders? Probably he'd find out, and soon. The Moslems never let the road grow up in grass before they followed it.

He strolled over to see where his horse drowsed, its feet planted and head lowered. It had kept up all of a long day with the hardy animals of his companions. He and the horse had more or less learned each other, did well together. That horse would second him well against an enemy. He went to put wood on the fire.

The soaring moon flooded the plain and the heights with pallor. When he judged it had moved westward for two hours, he sought Bhakrann's sleeping place. "Bhakrann," he called, and at once Bhakrann woke, grinning up.

"Go back to sleep," he said, and came to his feet in a single swift motion.

Wulf lay down again and slept as soon as his head found the saddle. He felt safe with Bhakrann on guard.

He woke to hear Bhakrann shouting. They all rose, strapping on weapons and shaking out cloaks. Bhakrann dived into a leather bag and brought out fistfuls of flat, dull-colored biscuits. "I saved these for breakfast," he said.

Wulf's biscuit was the size and shape of a clay saucer and almost as hard to chew, but he managed with swallows of water. They filled their bottles and rode away toward the mountains that did not seem so far away in the dawn.

They had ambled for something more than an hour when Cham, riding at the rear, raised his voice:

"Look back there!"

Over a rise half a mile behind them came horsemen.

"Are they some of us?" asked Tifan.

"Hardly," said Bhakrann grimly. "We're the only scouts sent here to study things. Look, they're moving faster, want to catch up."

Wulf reined half around, but Bhakrann caught his bridle.

"You said you don't know any friends in a strange place," he reminded, "and we don't know those riders. Six, it looks like—no, seven. Head for the pass. Less room for them to surround us there."

They kicked the flanks of their horses and went swiftly onward. Behind them, the strangers also quickened their pace.

"You have good eyes, Tifan," called Bhakrann. "Can you make them out?"

Tifan set his bearded chin on his shoulder. "They wear turbans," he shouted back. "And green and yellow and blue cloaks. Moslems!"

"Make it to the pass!" thundered Bhakrann.

They galloped for it, but Wulf did not urge his horse to its utmost. He looked at the hurrying pursuers. One of them, perhaps the lightest rider on the fastest charger, drew ahead of his mates. He waved something like a purple banner on a stick. Wulf checked his horse, to fall back from his own companions.

"Faster!" Bhakrann bawled at him, but Wulf paid no attention.

That Moslem rider scuttled toward him at top speed. His fine chestnut horse ran like a gazelle. He had left his party behind by many lengths and gained on Wulf, waving that stick that now was recognizable as a lance, with a streamer of cloth upon it. Again Wulf slowed his retreat.

The Moslem had churned more than two hundred yards ahead of his party. He screamed some sort of shrill war cry. Wulf reined to leftward, circled, and came around to face him.

He saw the chestnut strive close, saw the rider, wiry and active as a monkey, poise the spear. That rider wore a white turban wound on a steel cap with a spike at the top. Wulf drew his sword to poise it on his thigh. He'd have to do this man's business quickly. They came at each other. Wulf saw the staring eyes, the tossing black beard beneath the turbaned headpiece. The spear lifted. Wulf nudged his horse's flank to slip to the side. The spear darted. He nudged his horse's flank to send it to the side. He struck the spear out of line, shot past, and whirled to come up on the man's left.

The Moslem, too, spun his mount, so swiftly that it turned on its rear legs. Wulf rode close and slashed off the lance's head with a sweep of his sword. He clamped his knees to his saddle and slid his point straight into the middle of the black beard.

As the Moslem tumbled in a flutter of garments, Wulf cleared his point. He heard a quavering cry. His comrades came racing back. Another whoop, almost like an echo, from the oncoming Moslems. An arrow sang past Wulf's head. He swiveled his horse to meet the onslaught.

At that moment the Djerwa launched their javelins in a single flight. Loud they yelled as two of the Moslems bounced from their saddles, transfixed. The others did not wait to meet Bhakrann's charge. They rode away, as swiftly as they had come.

Bhakrann pulled up and sprang to earth to drag his javelin free from a fallen body. The other Djerwa chased after the horses from which three enemies had been struck, heading them off and catching them. Wulf, too, dismounted to look at the man he had stabbed. That man was stone dead, his teeth clenched on a lock of his beard. A great gout of blood soaked his yellow tunic. The fleeing Moslems made speed for the high ground to eastward.

"*Hai,* they run from us!" exulted Tifan, bringing back one of the captured horses.

"We ran from them as long as they outnumbered us," said Bhakrann. "We'd have kept on running if Wulf here hadn't stopped to fight. Now they'll hurry back and report to their friends. Here,"—he beckoned to Cham and Zeoui, who led the other two captured horses—"come here where I can talk to you. You three take these horses of theirs, they're faster than yours. Their swords, too, and their food and water bottles. Cham's your chief, he'll give the orders. Head back yonder and see how many of them are coming."

"More than those we chased away?" asked Cham.

"You don't think that just seven were invading all by themselves," Bhakrann answered, withering him. "Those were the fastest and most daring scouts, out of a force that probably thinks it's big enough to wipe out anything this far from Carthage and beyond. See what's to be seen. Wulf and I will head through the pass, and you can catch up and report when there's something worth reporting."

Cham and Zeoui and Tifan plundered the bodies of the Moslems for weapons and steel caps and mounted the horses they had taken. Bhakrann and Wulf held the bridles of the animals they had left and watched them ride away.

"I haven't had time to say you reaped that fellow like a tag of barley," Bhakrann remarked. He gazed down at the body. "That's a good mail shirt under his tunic. You might like it."

"None of these three wore armor big enough for me," said Wulf. "Maybe some of your friends would like them."

"Help me get them off these carcasses."

They draped the shirts over the saddle of the horse Cham had left. Then they mounted, Bhakrann leading one spare horse, Wulf two, and rode away toward the pass.

They reached it well before noon. It was a good travelway through the chain of heights, and seemed to be much used. Ambling, they talked. Bhakrann told of the two battles in which Moslems had been beaten, in which Okba, then Zoheir, had been killed. His story sounded as if the Moslems had been considerably outnumbered.

"How did they form line of battle?" asked Wulf.

"They didn't. We struck Okba's camp before he could form anything. And as soon as Zoheir saw how many we were, he ran. But not fast enough."

"Didn't Koseila get killed?"

"He got into the fight too far ahead of the rest. Like that man you killed just now. You use a sword well."

"When you turn your head in the sun, your beard has a red light," said Wulf.

"Yes," Bhakrann growled. "Yes, it does. Speaking of beards, I see you're letting yours grow. You won't look so strange among us. By the way, you seem to think we had it easy in those battles."

"Easier than you'll have it now," said Wulf. "They'll bring a big army, and they'll have all the money and equipment of Egypt behind them, and behind that all the resources of the other places they've conquered."

"That's a long way to bring such a load of things," said Bhakrann. "Maybe we'll have their plunder when the fighting's over."

The road through the pass was hard-packed. Bhakrann said that trading caravans went through to Carthage and elsewhere. Wulf looked at the heights to either side. Eight or ten camels might have traveled the pass abreast, but no more than that.

"Good," he said aloud.

"What's good?" asked Bhakrann.

Wulf decided not to answer that at once. "I feel good," he said instead. "Maybe lucky's a better word. People have tried to kill me lately, and haven't managed it. How long does it take to go all the way through this pass?"

"At this rate, several hours."

"I doubt if a force of Moslem cavalry would move any faster."

"Not if they aren't sure what's beyond," said Bhakrann.

"You said that Okba captured Koseila, who got away."

"That's right," Bhakrann drawled, not admiringly. "He was one to be with what he thought was the strong side. He was a Christian for a while, then maybe a Moslem. Okba took him and treated him like a slave. We Imazighen didn't care greatly; we thought Koseila had more or less renegaded from us.

But he turned Imazighen once more, when Okba ordered him to slaughter a sheep for supper."

"That would be an insult. What happened?"

"He smeared blood on his beard. He told them that blood would make hair grow strong. But it's an old Imazighen custom. Blood on your beard means you're going to kill somebody."

"And he killed Okba," said Wulf. "No, I mean you did. But Koseila commanded you."

"The Cahena commanded," said Bhakrann. "Koseila just fought and got killed, and we didn't care much. We had the Cahena."

They rode in the shade of high pinnacles. Wulf sipped from his bottle.

"She must be remarkable," he ventured.

"That's an understatement. She has spirits to advise her, she has magic to serve her. And when you meet her, you'll probably think she's the most beautiful woman you ever saw."

Wulf thought of beautiful women he had known at Constantinople, at Carthage, elsewhere. He changed the subject. "Do I see the end of the pass up there ahead?"

"Pretty far ahead, yes." Bhakrann looked back the way they had come. "At least there weren't more Moslems behind that scouting party, or we'd have Cham and the others rushing to catch up with us. I don't expect any invaders to try this pass tonight."

"No, it'll be dark in this little furrow," agreed Wulf.

"You're quick to see things," said Bhakrann. "Keep that quickness. We'll need some quickness in the next few days."

On they rode. The far end of the pass became a patch of light, widened. They saw open country beyond. They came out at midafternoon, with the sun dropping down the pale sky ahead of them. The road was broad, without grass or bush on it.

"Doesn't this road lead to Bagai?" Wulf asked.

"Yes. Why?"

"That's where I judge the Moslems will want to reach."

"They won't get there," predicted Bhakrann grimly.

They found a wayside stream and let the horses drink.

"This is the first water we've seen since that well your friends dug last night," Wulf remarked.

"True." Bhakrann nodded, twitching a bridle to keep a horse from drinking too fast. "I've a theory that your main body of Moslems stopped at that well, to dig up more water for itself. Stopped to dig, while those fellows on the best horses hurried after us and then wished they hadn't caught up."

"Then your friends can see them a long way off across flat country and ride back to report pretty soon," said Wulf. "It's a good part of a day's ride from that well to this little flow. An army can get thirsty in a day, both horses and men."

"You're a real help," said Bhakrann.

"Probably it's a good thing you didn't kill me, there on the way out of Carthage."

"Probably," and Bhakrann flashed him a brief grin.

On they fared, leading the spare horses. The sun dropped lower and lower toward where the horizon rose in a distant ridge. An hour more, and Wulf thought he caught a flash up there ahead. He shaded his eyes.

"Is that a river?" he asked Bhakrann.

"Yes, and a fairly good one for this time of year."

"And a place for a camp. How soon will your people be in sight?"

"Take a good look," invited Bhakrann. "They're coming into sight now."

IV

Again Wulf saw riders coming into view over a horizon, though this time there were more than a handful. A score or so appeared, then another knot of them, another, more. As they advanced down the tufted slope, they fanned into a spaced line—two hundred or so, as Wulf estimated, trotting in a disciplined formation. They halted well back from the river as though on a signal, and sat their saddles. Behind came a dozen or more groups, larger and closer drawn, fifty or sixty in each. These, too, reined in behind the first line. Still others paused on the ridge, waiting like dark, low-lying puffs of cloud against the afternoon sky.

Bhakrann drew ahead. "Don't hurry," he cautioned Wulf. "They want to be sure who we are. I'll go in front and do the talking." He leaned back and handed the reins of his led horses to Wulf. "Can you manage these?"

"Of course," said Wulf.

Following Bhakrann, he let his eyes quarter the formation of waiting horsemen. As the intervening space grew less, he saw glitters from weapons and headpieces and bridle housings. At midpoint, a man on a gray horse held some sort of flag, oblong and deep red. It, too, flashed in the sun, as though with spangles.

Bhakrann uttered a prolonged, quavering cry and flourished his shield above his head, and trotted his horse at an angle to the left, then back to the right. The flag waved in answer. Half a dozen men rode clear of the line. The hoofs of their horses flung up flashes from the stream. Bhakrann rode toward them, shouting something. Then he beckoned with his shield for Wulf to come.

Bhakrann rode to the center of the group, talking to everyone at once. Those men frowned expectantly toward Wulf. They had tufty beards and hooded cloaks and ready javelins.

"His name's Wulf. He fought his way out of Carthage," Bhakrann was saying. "He can help us."

"Of what people are you?" challenged one of the waiting men.

"He's a Saxon," Bhakrann answered for Wulf. "Never mind wondering what a Saxon is. I said he's a good man. Here, take charge of these horses and ride back ahead of us. Tell her that I'm bringing him. Wulf, wait with me."

More questioning scowls all around from the men of the party as they turned their animals and trotted back across the stream.

"Give them time to get there and tell what I said," Bhakrann warned. "There, they're reporting. Ride with me, very slowly. You're going to meet the Cahena."

They walked their horses into the stream. On the far bank, the leader of the group that had talked to Bhakrann was talking to someone else. Wulf felt eyes upon him and silence along the line, except for a horse's whickering.

The water flowed brown and slow beneath the bellies of their mounts. On ground beyond, Bhakrann said, "Get down," and they dismounted.

Directly opposite, a dozen men stood around the flag, holding their bridles. Others came forward on foot, the flag-bearer among them. They were tall, crudely armored, bearded, all but the one who led the way.

That one was small and slim in a long, loose cloak of blue, with a head swaddled in a white scarf. A slender hand set the butt of a javelin to the ground with each step. Small, pointed boots of soft brown leather stirred under the robe's swaying hem.

Wulf pulled the reins over his horse's head and waited with Bhakrann. The group drew around them. The small one stood under the banner, casting a slender shadow in the light of the lowering sun.

"Kneel," whispered Bhakrann, and dropped to hands and knees. His bearded head sank to kiss the brown grass where the shadow lay.

"Stand up, Bhakrann," said the soft, slow voice of a woman. "Where are the others I sent with you?"

He rose. "They're still back there, Cahena, watching the Moslems move this way."

"I'll send others to help them watch." The veiled head moved. "I knew this stranger would come and help us, too."

Then it was the Cahena who spoke so softly, this woman with a face half masked in white folds. Wulf stood before her. She was one of those who somehow look taller than they really are.

"My name is Wulf, lady," he volunteered. "I escaped from—"

"I'm talking to Bhakrann," she cut him off, not sharply but authoritatively. "How did you meet this man, Bhakrann?"

Bhakrann told, in a voice more hushed than Wulf had ever heard him use before. He made much of Wulf's catching a javelin in midair, of Wulf's sure thrust that killed the Moslem pursuer. He declared his judgment of Wulf as a man worth knowing, and quoted Wulf's account of the taking of Carthage and the ordeal of escape.

"And he calls himself a Saxon," the Cahena said.

Her gaze fastened on Wulf. He saw her eyes between folds of the scarf. They were deep, dark eyes, set aslant in a face that seemed gently tawny, like the skin of some sweet fruit. Silently she looked at Wulf, the probe of her eyes almost like the touch of hands, while he counted five to himself.

"If you're a Saxon, what are you doing here?" she flung at him suddenly.

He kept silent long enough to count another slow five. "Lady," he said then, "I've been a soldier. I went where there was war, among the Franks, Romans, Byzantines. I fought the Arabs in Asia until the fighting got slack. I came to Carthage, and then the Moslems took the town."

"You think they'll come here?" she said.

"Yes. They want to fight you and beat you, Cahena."

"How many are there at Carthage?"

"Maybe thirty thousand. And I gather that an advance force has started this way. We fought a few of their fastest scouts. I judge they want a strong point to use as a headquarters and supply base. Like Bagai."

"Do you know Bagai?" she asked, her eyes ever at him.

"I've never been there, but the old Romans had an armed camp there. It must be a logical fortification site."

"We'll do something about that. Thirty thousand, you say they have? How big would such a force be?"

"Perhaps a tenth of their number."

"And how far away from us would it be?" she asked.

"I can only guess, but perhaps a day away just now."

She turned and looked up the slope at her gathered host. The movement of her body was silkily sure.

"Sunset," she said. "Plenty of water. We'll camp." Her javelin pointed. "I want a guard there where stream bends. Above the guard, water for drinking. Below him, water for the horses and camels and anyone who wants to bathe or wash clothes. You," she said to a tall man, "go and give that order."

The man strode quickly to his horse and rode along the line, beckoning others to ride upstream with him. The Cahena turned her slanted eyes back to Wulf.

"I knew you were coming," she said, with sudden music in her voice. "In a little while there'll be something for supper. You come—you, too, Bhakrann—and we'll talk some more."

She turned and left him, her companions with her. Their javelins fenced her like a clump of reeds. Wulf watched, his hand on the neck of his horse. He had time to see what shone on the red flag. It was a geometric pattern of glass beads.

"You should have knelt and kissed her shadow," muttered Bhakrann beside him. "You're ready enough to stay alive in most places, but you were in danger then. She might have had you killed offhand."

"Why wasn't I killed?" asked Wulf.

"If she'd pointed a finger, there'd have been half a dozen javelins in you—too many to dodge. But her spirits seem to speak for you. Anyway, remember you're with the Imazighen now. When we eat with her, bear yourself becomingly. I take it you've traveled enough to pick up good manners."

"I'll do my best," promised Wulf, and Bhakrann's beard twitched in a grin.

"*Hai*, and your best is pretty good. We'll camp here for the night, or maybe half of it. She might have us marching any moment."

The moon rose, broad and pale, across the flat land to the east, while the sun dived behind the western ridge. Horsemen were strung like pickets on the far side of the stream. Several others headed off into the distance.

"There go some to join the scouts we left," Bhakrann said. "Good men, with the sense to see without being seen. Let's go and see some people ourselves. You've been wondering what the Imazighen are like, haven't you?"

They remounted their own horses.

Far and wide over the sweep of the ridge, men were camping. They gathered in small bands, half a dozen or so to each, with horses staked to crop the scanty grass. Javelins were stuck in the earth, pair by pair. The men squatted without fires in the dusk, eating what they had brought with them and drinking from skin bottles.

Bhakrann hailed those groups, one after another. At last he paused where swarthy men with tufts or tussocks of beards sat in a circle. Several of them rose, and one spoke:

"Bhakrann, do you know when we're going to fight?"

"Not yet, but it's coming. Wulf, these men are Djerwa, which means they're the best we have."

Teeth glittered in the beards, like chips of quartz.

"This is Wulf," Bhakrann said. "He's a Saxon, from a long way across the sea and across the land beyond that. He and I are friends. Watch Wulf when we fight. Maybe you'll learn something."

"Does he fight our way?" asked another man.

"He fights his own way, and it's a good way," snapped Bhakrann.

He and Wulf rode to another squatting place, spoke to the men there, and visited more. At last Bhakrann wheeled toward the river again. The sun had set. Moonlight washed the landscape. The air grew chillier.

"I think she's ready to eat, Wulf," said Bhakrann, pointing to where a rosy hint of light showed beyond some sort of screen. "She doesn't want to be kept waiting for that, or anything else."

"Wouldn't it be good for me to meet a few more of these people?" Wulf asked.

"Those you've met are telling about you to others. The whole camp will get to know your name and that I've said you can fight. Let's ask somebody here to keep an eye on our horses."

On foot they approached the soft red light. It showed by the river, well away from the other little camps. It was shut in, Wulf saw, with cloaks or blankets fastened to javelins stuck all around, with the light winking above. As Bhakrann and Wulf walked toward it, they saw a ring of guards. One made a gesture of recognition and let them pass. Bhakrann found an opening in the makeshift wall of cloaks and led Wulf inside.

The enclosed space was a dozen yards across. Against one screening cloak was set up a little tent, made by propping a dark cloth on sticks. At the center a small fire burned down to coals, with several sitting figures around it. Directly opposite the entrance sat the Cahena, on a folded saddlecloth. The others were warriors, bareheaded, in jerkins strengthened with chains and slices of iron.

"Bhakrann," said the Cahena's rich, low voice. "Wulf. Come and eat with us."

Close to the fire were propped green twigs, strung with bits of meat to roast. The various diners held their hands in their laps. Wulf and Bhakrann found places to sit.

"Wulf, this is Daris," said the Cahena. "He's a Neffusa."

Daris was as gaunt as a rake, but sinewy. His beard looked brown in the light of the coals.

"This is Ketriazar," the Cahena introduced another. "A Mediuni."

Ketriazar sat, thick-chested. His face was pitted, as though by an old plague of boils.

"And Yaunis," said the Cahena.

Yaunis nodded. He had something of elegance about him, for all his patterned cloak was shabby. His dark beard was trimmed somewhat in a fashion Wulf had seen in Constantinople. His eyes were long and humorous.

"And Mallul," the Cahena said, looking at the one who sat next to her. "My son, a Djerwa like Bhakrann, like me."

"Wulf," said Mallul, the only one of the party to speak. He was young, perhaps twenty or so. His soft-bearded face was handsome. Across his knees lay a curved Arabian sword.

Now Wulf looked at the Cahena. She sat cross-legged, dressed in a loose dark skirt and tunic. Her scarf had been put aside, and her long black hair fell like great wings upon her shoulders. It was smooth, thick hair, with faint lights in it. Her face was a fine oval. Her nose was short and straight, with flared nostrils. Her strong, delicate chin had the slightest of depressions, not quite a dimple. Her slanted eyes held their own radiance. Bhakrann had been right, she was beautiful.

"Now let's have our supper," she said.

As though the others had been waiting for her word, they all reached for the twigs with meat skewered on them. Someone passed a loose-woven basket of flat cakes. Wulf took meat—it was goat, he saw—and a cake of barley bread. Ketriazar offered him a leather bottle and a brass cup, and he poured wine for himself. It was sharp but good. All ate hungrily, except the Cahena.

She took no meat. She barely nibbled at a handful of dried figs and broken morsels of bread, and sipped slowly at her cup of wine. Silence all around while they ate. At last the Cahena wiped her hands on a white cloth and spoke.

"Two scouts have come back," she said. "They say that three thousand or so Moslems are camped at the eastern end of that pass, with their own scouts into it. We don't have as many as that, but we'll face them."

"Yes," agreed Mallul, as though dutifully.

The Cahena turned to Wulf. "I knew you'd come to us," she addressed him. "I have voices to tell me things. I want to hear more about the Moslems. Meanwhile, you've seen a little of us Imazighen. What do you think about us?"

"I ask myself about your weapons," he said carefully.

"What about our weapons?"

"I haven't seen all your men, of course, but those I did see haven't enough javelins."

"Not enough javelins?" Yaunis half cried. "Every man has two and hits what he throws at."

"Which leaves him only one javelin to stab with," said Wulf. "The Moslems have bows, and they're good with them. But one missile to a man doesn't seem enough to me."

"We've always fought or hunted with two javelins," said big Ketriazar, shifting his pitted face in the fireglow. "We've beaten the Moslems with two javelins apiece before this."

"If I'm allowed to advise you—" began Wulf.

"You're here to advise us," the Cahena assured him. "You seem to know various fighting methods."

"I say that each man should have several javelins," insisted Wulf. "Four, perhaps five."

"Five?" repeated Bhakrann. "When we all hit our marks?"

"You don't all hit your marks," Wulf said flatly. "Yesterday we fought those scouts. Four of you threw javelins, and only two went home. That's only half of you hitting the mark."

"Hai!" cried Bhakrann. It might have been agreement, it might have been embarrassment.

"It takes time to make a javelin," put in Ketriazar. "It needs as much skill to make it as to use it. We can't make more just now." He drank wine. "You say they have bows and arrows. What else?"

"Swords," said Wulf. "Good swords."

"Here's a Moslem sword," said Mallul, baring his weapon to gleam in the firelight. "We've taken a number of their swords."

"How well do you use them?" Wulf inquired.

"None of us as well as you do," answered Bhakrann for them all. "My brothers, this Wulf's sword strikes like a snake. I've seen him at work."

"It will be javelins against swords," said Wulf. "Again I say, I wish we had more javelins to strike them and leave fewer to bring their swords close."

"You talk like one of us." Yaunis smiled. "You've been here just long enough to eat and drink, but you sound Imazighen."

"You want to beat the Moslems and so do I," returned Wulf. "That makes some kind of kinship."

"I'll vouch for Wulf," said Bhakrann. "I've liked him from when I first saw him handle weapons and heard him speak. Cahena, let me say that whoever distrusts him does the same to me."

"You don't have to say that, Bhakrann," her soft voice replied. "We need Wulf, to help destroy as much of this advance party as we can, leave only a few to run back and tell Carthage how badly they were beaten, and give us a chance to gather our own big army. I've already sent messengers to alert the men from everywhere on Arwa, from Thrysdus south of here, from the towns on the coast. Because the Moslems think that if they wipe us out, there'll be no more danger to them."

"I was there when Bhakrann killed Okba," said Ketriazar, deep in his chest. "I was there when we killed Zoheir. I'll be there when we beat them this time."

The Cahena's burning eyes roved around the circle. "If we're through eating, I'll say good night."

They got to their feet, Wulf among them.

"Stay here, Wulf," she bade him. "I want to talk more."

The others filed out without speaking. The Cahena motioned for Wulf to sit down again. She leaned intently toward him.

"Some of those chiefs were slow to believe you, but I believe you," she said. "My voices say that you are wise and brave. You're right about the javelins, though we can't get those just now. But tell me about the Moslem horses."

"You know by now that their horses are good," he said. "Horses from Arabia, better in most ways than yours. I know that your horses live hard and can travel, but the Moslems have bigger ones, stronger in a charge. I got out of Carthage on a captured Arabian horse, and it's better for war than any of those in Bhakrann's party that found me."

"What's the Moslem way of battle?"

"In the open, they like to form a long line of horsemen and charge, with more close columns behind, ready to gallop for any point where they can help the most. They close on the flanks if they can, to crumple the enemy formation."

"We'll keep them from doing that," she said. "We'll choose the ground this side of the pass and let them ride out to us."

"You're right, Cahena," said Wulf.

She smiled at him. "Then we'll start when the moon is high."

She rose. Her shadow fell close to Wulf. He bowed on his hands and knees and kissed the earth where her shadow was.

"Get up, Wulf," said her voice above him.

He did so. She smiled radiantly. He saw how white and small and even her teeth were, how beautiful she was.

"You didn't do that when we first met," she said with a hint of a laugh. "I knew you didn't know our customs."

Out came her slim hand. He took it, wondering if he should kiss it, too, but she laid her other hand over his, pressing gently.

"That's a warrior's hand," she said. "Strong for fighting, sure for thinking. You'll ride beside me when we fight the Moslems."

"Ride with you? You'll be in this battle?"

"I always lead my men." Her eyes swam in their own brilliance. "I've led in many battles, ever since I was a young girl. And I've always won."

"Bhakrann and the others say you have more than human wisdom, Cahena," he said.

"I can judge situations, foresee problems, and decide how to meet them." She looked at him all the time. "You speak Imazighen well, better than most foreigners."

That, he judged, was to stop his talking about her. "I learn languages quickly," he said. "Frankish, Greek, Latin, Arabic, Hebrew. And I can write those languages, too."

"You're a learned man. Good night, Wulf."

She turned and paced toward the makeshift tent. How gracefully she moved. He walked out of the enclosure.

She was like no woman he had ever seen. She had deliberately shown him her womanness, to awe him, maybe to overwhelm him. That must be part of why her men worshipped her, for the woman she was as well as for the queen and prophetess and commander she was. She had turned her light on him because she wanted him with her. For what?

The moonlight softly bleached the land. Wulf passed the silent sentinels. Up the slope to westward sprawled the little camps of the men. Someone was singing.

"Wulf."

Bhakrann came striding. Wulf turned his steps that way. Bhakrann stopped, half leaning on his javelin. His eyes caught a glitter from the moon.

"They picketed our horses where those Djerwa subchiefs are making ready to sleep." He pointed, and Wulf went with him in that direction. "What did she say to you?"

"Among other things, that we'd march when the moon is high."

"Didn't I say she'd order that? What else, if you're allowed to talk about it?"

"She didn't tell me to keep still about anything. She wants me with her when we fight. That pass where they'll come through, that's where she thinks to meet them."

"She's always right. She can choose a battleground better than I can." Bhakrann chuckled over that. "Maybe better than you. What else, now?"

"She said I was a warrior and a thinker."

"I told her that, but she'd know it anyway."

Wulf thought about the Cahena. "Does she always fight alongside her men? And doesn't she have women to tend her in camp?"

"At times like this, on a fast move, she looks after herself. She cooked that supper. She can do everything for herself. She's worth following. You'll find out."

"I'm finding out," said Wulf.

They came to where five men lounged, wrapped in their mantles against the cool of the night. Horses were picketed where there was grass to munch. Beyond that gathering, other men sang.

"What do they sing?" asked Wulf. "I can't hear."

"Who knows?" said one of the reclining men. "We make up our songs as we sing them."

"Maybe they sing about you, Wulf," said another. "About how the Cahena trusts you."

"Suppose we stop talking and get some sleep," said Bhakrann. "We'll move out around midnight."

Wulf tugged off his Byzantine half boots. He unbuckled his sword, cleared it from the sheath, and laid it where he could put a hand on it quickly. The others lifted their heads to study the weapon, but said nothing. Nobody had said anything since Bhakrann had called for silence.

Bhakrann lapped himself in his cloak, put his head on a saddle wallet, and seemed to go to sleep at once. Wulf lay with his hands clasped behind his head and gazed at where the moon swam among the stars, round and pale, with shadowy flecks. It might have been an Imazighen shield, complete with design. Wulf wished he had a shield.

How soon would the camp be awakened and marshaled, how many miles would be accomplished by the light of that moon? Those scouts who had been sent out, were they adroit enough to keep from being seen? How war-wise were these men he had joined, obeying the slightest soft word of the Cahena?

He could see her smile, could feel the touch of her hands on his. She had called him a warrior and a thinker, as if she knew what the words meant. She was beautiful in what she said and did. Thinking of her, Wulf wondered if sleep would come to him.

As he wondered, sleep came.

V

He half wakened in the moonlight, to what seemed the thud of heavy feet. He gazed to where, at another group of sleepers, moved a misty something. It was dark; it stood tall and knobby-armed. Its massive head seemed to have horns like a bull. A helmet? He could not be sure. He watched the shape tread heavily away, vanish. A dream, he told himself, and closed his eyes again.

The stir of the camp roused him. He was awake swiftly. He knew who he was and where he was. The moon blazed at the top of the sky. Near him, men pulled on boots or laced up sandals, buckled belts. Wulf carried his gear to where his horse drowsed, threw the cloth across its back, and set the saddle on that and drew the girth snug. Bhakrann was there beside his own mount.

"Here, maybe this headpiece will fit you," said Bhakrann.

An old Roman helmet, Wulf saw, rusted and dented, with a comb on top and worn felt padding inside. It went all right on his head.

"And here." Bhakrann handed him an oval leather shield faced with a gridlike iron netting and a brass rim.

"Thanks," said Wulf. "I had a strange dream. A sort of giant with a bull's horns, walking through the camp."

Bhakrann gazed at him. "Maybe that wasn't a dream. Did it stop beside you? No? That's good. That thing's name is Khro. He comes before a battle and picks out the men who'll die."

"A dream," said Wulf again.

"I'll show you it wasn't. Where did you see him?"

Wulf pointed to where other men roused. Bhakrann led him there and studied the ground. "Look," he said.

Wulf saw cloven prints in the earth. "An ox?" he said.

"We haven't a single beef animal with us," said Bhakrann, "and the prints are fresh as of last night. Khro was here."

They walked away again. Wulf shrugged off an uneasiness. "What are the marching orders?" he asked.

"Scouts went out an hour ago," Bhakrann told him. "The main body will follow, three columns about half a mile apart. We ride with the Cahena at the head of the middle column."

Wulf slung the shield to his pommel and mounted. He and Bhakrann rode toward the stream. Elements of the force splashed across. Murmurs of conversation rose. Wulf checked his horse to let it drink a few gulps, then pulled up its head and sent it wading over. Bhakrann and he trotted to where a string of mounted figures moved eastward in the half-light. A standard fluttered above the foremost rider.

"Bhakrann," came her voice. "Wulf. Ride at my right and left."

They took their places. The party moved at a brisk walk. Wulf recognized Mallul among the others, but nobody else.

"The chiefs are with their peoples," said the Cahena, as though she read Wulf's mind. "We're all Imazighen here, no Greeks, no Vandals. We didn't have time to prod them into coming along."

She wore her blue robe. The scarf was drawn back from her face. She looked young in the moonlight. Two javelins were slung behind her shoulder. She sat astride, confidently, like one who has ridden from childhood. Wulf saw her small boot in the stirrup.

"How far to that pass, Bhakrann?" she asked.

Bhakrann peered. "We'll be there before dawn, Cahena. We can push in —be right in their faces before they expect us."

"Won't they expect us?" asked Wulf.

Bhakrann looked across at him. "They don't know this country. Oh, maybe a few were here with Okba, but that was years ago. They won't know what to expect."

"Then they'll expect anything," said Wulf. "Try to prepare for anything. Especially prepare for us to come into the pass."

The Cahena smiled sidelong at Wulf. "How do you know they'll do that?"

"I only know that, before a battle, you prepare for anything the enemy might do."

"*Ahi,*" said Bhakrann. "How can we know, or they know?"

Wulf stroked his horse's mane. "I'm trying to think like their commander. You're right, Bhakrann, they aren't sure of the pass or the country this side, so they camped on the far side. But they'll have sent men up on the heights, scouts and observers and probably archers. He'll want to hold those points all the way along, while his main body comes through below. He doesn't want us up there, throwing javelins down on him."

"We could send advance parties to right and left," said Bhakrann, half impatiently. "It's easier to climb up from this side."

"They'd expect something like that," insisted Wulf. "Very likely they climbed up as soon as they stopped at the pass."

The Cahena gazed back at the column of horsemen. Then she looked to one side and to the other. Shadowy blotches paced out there to either hand.

"You think this Moslem commander is wise," she said gently.

"Hassan ibn an-Numan won't have sent a fool, Cahena. These people have fought all the way from Egypt to here. They're seasoned. Whoever leads them was chosen for competence and experience."

"So you don't want us up on the heights," said Bhakrann, "and you don't want us to meet them in the pass. Maybe you want to wait for them to come all the way out on this side."

"I think that's exactly what Wulf has in mind," said the Cahena.

"Not exactly, Cahena," said Wulf. "Not let them come all the way out. Let maybe half of them into the open. Then, before they can deploy for either a charge or a stand, strike them, demoralize them, before they can spread out into a proper line of battle."

"The other half would wait for us to come into the pass," objected Bhakrann.

"I don't think that will happen with those Moslems, chosen for a thrust into unknown country," said Wulf. "That sort goes to a battle like boys to a game. When the fight starts with half of them out on our side of the pass, the other half will rush to get out into it, come to close quarters. But by the time their rear elements get into the open, we can settle accounts with the first elements, then handle the rest."

The Cahena tilted her lovely head, smiling.

"I hadn't made a decision. But now I'm building on what you say, Wulf. Keep talking. Bhakrann and I will listen."

"*Hai!*" muttered Bhakrann. It didn't sound quite like agreement.

Wulf elaborated. He explained why he thought that the Moslems would explore the pass by night, in gingerly fashion, while the main body might well start slowly. No prudent commander, he said again, would emerge into strange and dangerous territory until there was light enough to see and fight by. He remembered that the opening of the pass toward which they now marched had jutting rocks and scattered boulders to each side. Even when the Moslem van could see, it could not change formation from column into line with any great speed.

"They'll rush us," declared Bhakrann. "Then we'll countercharge and drive them back in."

"Is that your advice, Wulf?" asked the Cahena. She looked at him with her full lower lip caught in her teeth, as though to keep from smiling. It gave her an expression almost coquettish.

"Not exactly," he said. "If they retreat into the pass, they can hold us off. Let our three columns come along. This middle one faces the pass, the others lie out to either side. As the enemy comes out, let this middle column retreat."

"Retreat?" Bhakrann barked his protest.

"It'll fall back but keep formation and spread into line as it retires. Those Moslems will gallop at us, calling on Allah almighty."

"There is also the Cahena," breathed Bhakrann, like a prayer.

"If we fall back, what then?" the Cahena prompted Wulf.

"Out come their first squadrons, thinking they've already won," said Wulf. "Our other columns strike from the sides, charge in close order, and, when they're almost there, throw javelins. This central force will charge, too, drive in, fight hand to hand."

"That sounds good," said the Cahena, nodding. "When did you think of all this?"

"While we rode," said Wulf. "Considered our possibilities and theirs, and tried to choose the best one. And you asked for my opinion."

"I did, and you gave it."

She laughed. It was her first real laugh that Wulf had heard. It was musical, like a flute.

"Bhakrann," she said, "did you hear what Wulf explained?"

"Very clearly, Cahena," replied Bhakrann.

"Then ride to the left column there. Yaunis leads it. Tell him and his subchiefs what's been decided. They're to approach the pass, not directly, but within sight and signal of us. When we, here at the middle, draw them into the open, Yaunis is to charge. Understand?"

"Very clearly," said Bhakrann again, and cantered away.

"Mallul," the Cahena called.

Her son hurried from behind. He listened as the Cahena told him the orders to carry to the right. "Ketriazar commands there," she said. "Say that this is my word, then come back to tell me that he will obey."

Mallul rode away, and Wulf and the Cahena continued side by side across a grassy level. Scraps of pallid mist showed, and Wulf had time to remember his dream, perhaps his vision, of the striding creature with its bull's head. Bhakrann had said he had seen something actual. He could still see it, in his imagination.

"Tell me what you're thinking of," the Cahena bade him, and he told her. She listened seriously.

"Yes," she said, "we know that one. He smells blood before a battle. We call him Khro."

"Do you worship him?"

"Not exactly, but we fear him. Yet you say he didn't come near you." Wulf heard the hoofs of their horses, stirring the grass. "Now, your plan sounds perfect. If we win, it'll be your doing."

"No plan's ever perfect," said Wulf. "They'll have the advantage of the rising sun in our faces. We'll have to make up for that by a quick, hard blow that will disorganize them."

"You think of everything," she said, not quite mockingly.

"Nobody thinks of everything. Any battle plan has mistakes. The side with the fewest mistakes will win."

"That's true. What's the worst mistake a commander can make?"

"Not having enough men at the right place and time," he said.

"If we could always have that." She smiled, but only faintly. "Maybe they have more than we do just now, but if we use your plan? You must have been a good commander, Wulf."

"I never had more than two squadrons at once, but I've always read whatever I could about battles. Julius Caesar, Tacitus, the reports of Belisarius—whatever came to hand."

"You can read and write," she said, impressed. "I never learned to do either. When we've won this battle, you can talk to my councillor Djalout. He's at home on Arwa—he's too old to come on campaigns. Sometimes I've thought him the wisest of men."

"As you're the wisest of women, Cahena."

"You talk like a courtier. Warrior and courtier, that's a combination. Luck rode into our camp with you."

"You overwhelm me," he said, and her laugh trilled.

"I doubt if you've ever been really overwhelmed," she said.

A scout trotted to them to report a stream just ahead.

"Stream?" repeated the Cahena. "Tell the other scouts to stop where they are and send to the other columns. We'll pause at the stream. The horses can drink and the men can eat breakfast, if they have food. Later, we'll have dinner from whatever we take away from the Moslems."

She sounded as if she counted it already done.

At the crawling thread of water, the horses dipped grateful noses. Wulf did not choose to drink where they drank, and sipped from his water bottle and ate morsels of stale barley bread. The Cahena talked to another scout, who said that the pass was directly ahead.

"It's not far from dawn," the Cahena said, gazing expertly at the stars. "Now we move forward slowly. Send to Yaunis and Ketriazar to come close, but keep distance for their flanking movements. Bhakrann? Wulf? Ride with me again."

Up ahead, the starry sky had a wash of paleness. The jagged, dark hunch of the high ground rose against it.

"We're almost there, and probably the Moslems are almost there, too," said the Cahena. "How do we maneuver now, Wulf?"

"Draw closer still, but not so close that we can't retire. When we fall back, do it quick in column, then spread out in line."

"Forward again," she commanded over her shoulder. "Bhakrann, ride to the rear and pass the word of what's to be done."

They moved at a walk. Wulf was glad that the horses seemed fairly fresh for what was coming. He touched the neck of his own horse, and it made a rippling sound with its lips.

As the sun showed rosy promise above the height, the Cahena halted them yet again. Wulf felt his heart race, as always before action. There was light enough to show Bhakrann's bearded face, tensely scowling. The Cahena gazed, as though she had ridden out to see the dawn. Behind her, a rider carried the red banner.

Time crawled. The sun's rim crept dazzlingly into view. Wulf saw the pass, a broad, dark jowly mouth. Bhakrann spat.

"All right, where are they?" he demanded impatiently.

"Wait," the Cahena said. "They want to be sure what they'll find."

"We're in plain sight as they come out, this middle column anyway," growled Bhakrann. "They'll see us before we see them."

"There they are," said Wulf, and there they were.

Tiny figures appeared, a scatter of them first, then more. They looked like little mounted chessmen with fluttering robes. As they emerged, they moved off to left and right, with disciplined rapidity. Wulf hoped that the Imazighen could act as purposefully. More emerged, hundreds. They spread into a close-drawn line that looked to be half a mile long.

"Look, a standard," said Wulf. It was green on a long staff.

"They're going to charge," said Bhakrann tensely.

"Let them," said the Cahena, not at all tensely.

She poised a javelin as though she knew how to use it. Mallul, behind her, also had a javelin at the ready.

The distant riders had formed their close line. Wulf judged that there must be four hundred of them. From somewhere at their center came a faint, tremulous note of music.

"That's a signal trumpet," said Wulf.

"They'll charge before they're all out on this side," said the Cahena. "Just as Wulf said. Mallul, ride back and get us ready to retire in formation."

Still other Moslems came into view behind the line, forming groups. Another faraway trumpet blast, a concerted cry of voices. The line moved forward at a well-controlled walk. Wulf watched for tense moments. Above either side of the pass appeared dark dots, dismounted men up there, those who had scouted the way. They wouldn't get into this fight.

The advancing riders quickened their pace to a trot.

"Fall back!" called out the Cahena, and the order was passed along. Wulf was now at the rear of the column. Riding, he watched the developing pursuit. Another cry beat up in the morning air, an exultant cry as of victory already won. He saw the wink of flourished blades. He urged his horse to a trot and looked left, then right. The other Imazighen columns were moving in.

"Our friends are charging!" he shouted his loudest. "Fall into line and counterattack!"

Wild cries, everywhere. The right and left columns of the Imazighen spread their fronts as they rode. From the approaching Moslems, a massed shout. Wulf heard it:

"*Ulululullallahu akhbar!*"

Back pealed a many-voiced response:

"There is also the Cahena!"

Bhakrann cantered past. "Let's get them!" he roared.

The far end of the central formation peeled out. Here they came, the savage Imazighen horsemen, into a moving line of their own. Wulf recognized gaunt Cham among them. They bent above tossing manes, their shields up, their javelins lifted. He wheeled his trusty horse and rode straight at the oncoming enemy.

A dozen leaps took him ahead of nearer companions. "Come on!" Wulf yelled back as he galloped. Behind him drummed the hoofs.

He must make them come on. Here was the time in a fight when you brought your men into it, hard and deadly. Then you were just another warrior yourself, trying to kill, to keep from being killed.

The Moslem horses flew at Wulf, bigger with every instant. To the front rushed a man on a bounding spotted horse with a tasseled bridle. A chief, anyway a champion, eager to be first to fight. First to fight could be first to fall, Wulf thought, like that enemy scout just days ago.

He tried to judge everything at once. This was a big man on a bigger horse than Wulf's. Black turban, black beard, square shield, flashing blade. As they drove together, Wulf kneed his horse's flank to veer right. They were close, close enough to strike.

Wulf felt the shock of a downsweeping blow on the metal rim of his shield, heard the ring of his own mighty slash on the other's helmet. The Moslem crumpled and fell flat among scattered tufts of coarse, thistly grass as Wulf reined clear of him.

"*Yallah—*" someone screamed, and another foe rode at him.

Something purred past Wulf. A javelin smote the charging Moslem's belly. Wulf saw the look of blank amazement on the shaggy face, saw the body fold in around the transfixing shaft, tumble to earth. He didn't know who had sped that javelin, whom to thank. He rode after the countercharge.

It had scrambled around him and past. The air was rent with shouts. He spared a glance to see the rear elements of the enemy force swerving leftward to meet the rush of the Imazighen right column. Even as they swerved, the other column swooped from the opposite side. The enemy had no shields on their right arms to guard in that direction. Wulf saw a streaky flight of javelins, saw men go down in swirls of garments. Then more adversaries here, and he must fight them.

Horses danced around each other, men struck at each other. The Imazighen were at stab-distance with their javelins. They rode through enemy ranks that were ranks no more, that frayed, fell back to defend themselves on three sides. Wulf chopped a turbaned man to earth. He saw the Cahena, close at his left, her blue robe streaming like a banner.

A Moslem made his way toward her. She moved her whole lithe body to launch a javelin. The man took it in his chest and toppled backward as though yanked by a rope. A dozen Imazighen saw.

"There is also the Cahena!" they howled all together, like a fierce declaration of faith.

She trampled over her fallen enemy. Wulf drummed his horse's flanks to speed up and join her. Another Moslem reined around in front of them.

Wulf saw his thicket of beard, the iron helmet-spike above his turban. He hewed at Wulf, who caught the blade's sweep with his shield and, at close quarters, dashed the shield against the Moslem's body, then drove his own point home. It rattled, it must be rending its way through chain mail. The man floundered to earth as Wulf tore his weapon free and got ahead of the Cahena to speed toward the main jumble of battle.

Writhing, furious faces came at him, dropped away as he struck, were replaced by other faces. He saw the Cahena among a handful of her followers, facing a press of Moslems. He rode in, with thrust and cut before anyone knew he was there. The Cahena's men plied javelins. Moments, and the enemies were cleared away.

Things had disorganized into swirls and knots of combatants, but everywhere the Moslems fell back to the mouth of the pass. Moslems attacked were never as deadly as Moslems attacking. Javelins stabbed and were wrenched clear. Wulf took time to exult.

"Hai!" blared Bhakrann's voice from somewhere near at hand. "Don't leave one of them alive!"

Others heard him, closed in savagely, striking, trampling. The Moslems fled, those who could still flee, who had not fallen before the murderous countercharge.

"Cahena!" a man bawled. "There is also the Cahena!"

Almost as the yell rang out, the fight was over. Into the pass scampered the defeated remnant. The field was strewn with bodies, slackly dead or writhing with the pain of wounds.

And from all sides, a great clamor of triumph. Wulf dabbed at his streaming face with his sleeve.

"Quick!" he thundered to those near him. "Hold everyone back from the pass—we've beaten them!"

VI

Half a dozen mounted men scurried to carry Wulf's orders. They'd begun to obey him, do what he said. Dismounting, he wondered how long this fight had lasted. Longer than it seemed, probably. His horse breathed deeply. Sweat lathered its flanks. He told it that it was a good horse, had borne him well, had helped him to kill.

Chiefs scolded their warriors away from the pass. Everyone shouted, exulted. No living enemies could be seen, only bodies. Men were off their horses, picking up javelins or plundering.

"Don't kill any wounded!" Wulf shouted. "There's a good reason for letting them live!"

"See that order is obeyed, Mallul," he heard the Cahena say.

Wulf raked off his helmet and let the wind stir his soggy hair. Another horse came near. The rider touched Wulf's shoulder. The Cahena leaned above him, glowing with a smile, her eyes starlike under the backflung veil. Her beauty, so close to him, was like a physical impact.

"We won, Cahena," said Wulf, catching triumph from her.

"You won, Wulf. It was your battle."

"I killed only a few of all these," he said.

"It was your battle," she said again. "You planned it. We had to beat them, and we did. We couldn't have failed."

He put on his helmet again. "Something can always go wrong," he said. "If that had happened—"

"If that had happened," rumbled Bhakrann, riding to join them, "we'd have felt that you'd tricked us into their hands."

Reining in, he gazed at fallen bodies, at riderless horses being caught. Wulf and he exchanged grins.

"If that had happened, several were ready to stick you full of javelins," Bhakrann said.

Wulf wiped more sweat. "Whose thought was that?" he challenged.

"Mine," said Bhakrann, grinning more broadly.

A warrior came cantering. He saluted with a bloody javelin.

"Cahena, we found their commander's body," he reported. "He's wearing a gold-worked coat and a jewel-hilted sword. He had a treasure of gold and silver in his saddlebags."

"Bhakrann!" cried the Cahena. "Ride and get those saddlebags, get any money they carried. Let the word go out, each man can take a weapon, but whatever food the enemy has is to be gathered and shared out to all of us. The money comes here to me."

Bhakrann loped away with the messenger.

"Wulf," said the Cahena above him, and he turned to her. "That was Bhakrann's thought, Wulf," she said gently. "About killing you. It wasn't mine."

"Then you trusted me."

Down came her slim hands. He put up his own big ones and she took them and pressed them.

"Yes," she said, more gently still. "I was told to trust you."

At the pass, chieftains still shouted their men back from riding in. Several horsemen came to where Wulf and the Cahena waited, bringing bags and parcels of bread and dates and raisins, strips of salted meat, skin bags of water. The Cahena ordered these things heaped together, with a guard beside them. She was joined by Yaunis and Ketriazar and Daris, then by Bhakrann. They dismounted and conferred intently.

Wulf thrust his bloody sword into the earth and wiped it with a rag torn from his cloak. Sheathing it, he stood with an arm across his saddle, watching here and there.

"What's to be done before we pull back?" the Cahena asked him.

"Get word through the pass for them to come get their wounded," he said. "Let them have the burden of them."

She studied him. "You think of the right things."

A close-huddled knot of unhappy men approached on foot, under guard. One guard sprawled to kiss the Cahena's shadow.

"These are prisoners, Cahena," he said, rising. "Shall we kill them or keep them?"

She surveyed the prisoners. They were a score, sullen and beaten.

"Neither one," she replied. "They can carry a message for us."

One of the group shuffled his feet and tried to readjust his turban, that must have been pulled off to take his helmet. His striped gown was smeared with dirt, as though he had been rolled on the ground. From his belt dangled an empty scabbard.

"Are you an officer?" the Cahena inquired.

"I led our first squadron into destruction," he replied dully, in passable Imazighen. "I'm Ayoub ibn Saud. I should have died."

"But you're alive. Go back and tell your general, the one who sacked Carthage and sent you here to be slaughtered."

"Hassan ibn an-Numan," supplied Wulf from beside her.

"You call him the good old man," said the Cahena. "If he's a wise old man, he'll pay attention to my words. Do you understand?"

"I understand," said Ayoub ibn Saud wretchedly.

"Say that this is the word of the Cahena, who rules here. As I defeated your advance party today, I'll defeat him if he dares come. Do you hear?"

"I hear." Plainly, Ayoub ibn Saud did not like to hear.

"He can have that country around Carthage," she pronounced. "But here, the land is ours." She straightened her slim body. "There's no room here for as much as the sole of his foot. If he'd been here today, we'd have killed him."

Her eyes stabbed at the captive like weapons.

"Your friends can come and gather up their wounded and bury their dead. Now go, you and these others who are lucky to be alive."

Ayoub ibn Saud gestured with a trembling hand. "Kill me now," he said. "I'd rather be dead than say that to Hassan ibn an-Numan."

A silent moment, while the Cahena studied him.

"Then I'll give you a letter to carry to him," she said at last. "Wulf, you write Arabic. Where can we get a pen and parchment?"

The things were found. Wulf spread the parchment against his saddle and wrote the message as the Cahena had spoken it, then rolled it up. The Cahena issued more orders.

"Give these prisoners one water bottle and some bread," she directed. "Start them for the pass on foot. But give the message carrier a horse to make speed with."

One of Yaunis's men led up a brown horse. Ayoub ibn Saud mounted it. Wulf handed him the letter. He rode away, his shoulders sagging in his dirty striped gown.

"A javelin thrown from here would straighten his back for him," said Bhakrann to Wulf.

"Ride with him, Bhakrann," commanded the Cahena at once. "See that nobody stops those Moslems. Watch them all the way to the pass."

Bhakrann trotted after Ayoub ibn Saud. His shoulders sagged, too, as though he disliked the assignment. The Cahena smiled, a touch of a smile. Her face was tawny golden in the sun.

"Did I do well to order that, Wulf?" she asked.

She looked at him, almost like a child waiting for praise.

"You did well," he said. "We handled about a thousand out here and killed and wounded a lot of them, but there are maybe twice as many in the pass or on the far side. Let their wounded hamper them. They won't come prodding after us."

"What next?" she asked.

"You've already said that. Stop to water the horses at that little stream, then on to where we left the baggage under guard. Leave scouts here to observe, though I doubt we'll be followed."

"You're confident," Ketriazar half accused. "You've been confident all along."

"Only fools are confident all along," said Wulf.

"Will they have mercy on their wounded?" asked Yaunis. "They seem like a merciless breed to me."

"Only to their enemies," said Wulf. "They'll carry the wounded all the way back to Carthage."

"We came out of it very well," Yaunis spoke up. "Their losses were heavy. They'll plan a long time before they try us again."

"Exactly," said the Cahena. "Let's start back."

The chiefs rode away to do as she said. The Cahena smiled.

"I wonder if I'll ever get used to you," she said.

He met her gaze.

"Just because I killed that man who rode at you—"

With that, she walked away to where two men were bandaging a prone wounded comrade. She knelt there, she seemed to shimmer for a moment. She leaned above the wounded man, put her hands on him, spoke something. Then she rose, and the man rose, too. He smiled.

Tifan came, leading a spotted horse. "You should have this extra one," he said. "I saw you kill the man off of it."

"Thanks," said Wulf. He remembered the man and the horse. "Tell me, does the Cahena heal wounds?"

"Yes, she does."

On all sides, a happy chatter rose. Warriors beamed at their spoils of swords or cloaks or helmets. Ketriazar bore the enemy's green battle flag. The wounded were helped astride captured horses, and those who were most badly hurt were lashed to their saddles. Other horses carried captured foodstuffs and water containers. The column moved westward at a walk, the Cahena at the head.

"Ride with me, Wulf," she called, and he joined her.

"You must realize that you've done a great thing," she said. "Your head is as strong as your hand."

"I killed a few," he said again. "Maybe wounded others." He rode in silence for a moment. "We'll have a bigger battle than this one. They'll come with ten times as many."

"Then we'll muster ten times as many ourselves," she said.

"And arm and feed them?"

"You think, four javelins each. We'll do it, if those invaders give us a little time. We make our own javelins, make them well. But food—that's a problem. It wasn't easy to ration this three thousand or so, even among good farms and orchards."

The sun rose hot and high when they reached the narrow stream and stopped to fill their water bottles and let the horses drink. The captured food was shared out. The Cahena ate a scrap of white Moslem bread and some dates.

"You don't eat," she said to Wulf. "You're not hungry."

"Not so hungry that I can't give my share to someone hungrier, Lady Cahena."

"Spoken like a chief," she said. "Mallul, carry the word that anyone who wishes to bathe may do so."

Everybody, it seemed, wanted to bathe. Wulf staked out his two horses, stripped, and waded in. The water was no deeper than his waist. He wished for the soap he had known in Constantinople and Carthage, and made shift with grating handfuls of wet sand. Bhakrann, also bathing, stared at Wulf's great body.

"Very few of us your size," he said. "You're muscled like a bull."

Out of the water and dressed, the men mounted again. They rode over land where they saw the hoofmarks of their earlier advance. Wulf looked back to the distant heights where the pass was. He saw tiny specks, probably riders left to see if the enemy would do anything. Men laughed and joked in the columns. The Cahena rode to where a wounded man slumped in his saddle. She spoke to him, touched him. He sat up straight as if he was healed.

There was a halt to rest at noon. The Cahena sat quietly in the shade of her horse. She beckoned Wulf and Bhakrann near.

"You two like each other," she said.

"We almost fought at first, Cahena," said Bhakrann. "That's a good way to begin, if it doesn't get to a fight."

"Now already, within hours, he's not a stranger," she said. "You and Wulf will be brothers."

"Cahena," said Bhakrann, "I already think of him as a brother."

"Think of Bhakrann the same." Her eyes stared from Wulf to Bhakrann. "I call Bhakrann my son, Wulf."

"Call me your son, Cahena," he ventured.

She rose. "If the horses are rested, we'll ride again."

At midafternoon they came to the larger stream, where baggage camels and spare horses waited under guard. Messengers had ridden ahead with news of the victory. Guards howled happy greetings.

As the Cahena dismounted among her chiefs, there was a rush to kiss her shadow on the ground. Wulf expected her to make a speech. But she said only that food for an early supper would be distributed and that they would camp, to start home on the following day.

"There'll be more fighting," she said, in a voice that carried over the listening warriors. "We'll do our share of it."

Bhakrann and Wulf rubbed down their horses well and found them a patch of grass to crop. Then they made a small fire to boil couscous and meat in a brass bowl. Bhakrann had secured a crockery flask of strong, sharp wine. Near them, other messes ate and chattered. At last they sat and stared at their fire. Night had brought a chill into the air.

"She said be brothers," said Bhakrann. "Think of each other as brothers."

Bearded chin in hand, he stared. "Who was your father? You had one, I suppose."

"His name was Fyr," said Wulf. "He was a farmer, raised grain and cows and some pigs, had two or three horses."

"Was he a good father?" Bhakrann asked.

"I think so. When the priest said I learned my letters quickly, he sent me to learn to be a priest, too. But I became a soldier."

"Your wars—you learned in them. I took a moment or two today to watch you cut those Moslems down. There's strength in your arm."

"In yours, too, Bhakrann. Now I've told you about my father, how about yours?"

"I don't know who he was."

Wulf stared into the savage, scarred face. Bhakrann looked back with raw blue eyes.

"My mother never knew who he was, either. My name's Bhakrann, son of nobody." His face drew into bitter lines. "Who dares call me that? I'll rip his tongue out."

His big, brown hands clutched at the sword taken from Okba across his lap. In his beard the flames woke a flash of red, like blood grown old without being avenged.

"If you don't want to talk about it, Bhakrann . . ."

"No, I'll tell you," Bhakrann said. "We're to be brothers. Listen, my birth was shameful."

Another moment of heavy silence.

"How I was born is my heart's shame, and it's been the calamity of some who reminded me." Bhakrann grimaced. "Who wants to die? All he needs to say is Bhakrann, son of nobody."

The hands shifted on the sword sheath.

"It was like this." Pain in Bhakrann's voice. "Fifty years ago, some of the Djerwa rode down from Arwa with donkeys and camels loaded with dates and almonds and raisins, to trade at the seashore for salt. They camped on that beach. That night a company of sea-robbers landed and rushed the camp. Nobody knows what people they were, only that they spoke foreign and had yellow hair."

And Bhakrann's gaze fell upon the tawny hair of Wulf the Saxon.

"I wasn't one of them," said Wulf. "I wasn't born fifty years ago, and my father never went to sea."

"Who knows who those sea-robbers were? They shouted and flowed over the camp like a wave. The merchants ran, those who could. The robbers killed those they caught—all but one. She was a girl." The bearded, battered face clamped. "They didn't kill her."

Wulf said nothing.

"Isn't that the way of conquered men with conquered women?" said

Bhakrann tightly. They tore off her clothes and tied her hands and feet to pegs in the sand. She lay helpless."

In his beard again, the red sheen of the old unavenged infamy.

"She endured them all night long, in terror and pain. And when the rovers sailed away on the morning tide, the merchants came back and found her pegged there—bleeding, fainting, bruised but still alive. They brought her back with them."

"Then she lived," said Wulf.

"Yes, she lived. In disgrace and scorn. She swelled up with a child bred on her by one or other of those robbers."

Bhakrann gestured with a clenched fist.

"Maybe it was bred by that whole band of them? She was despised among her people. She lived by drudgery, to support herself and her shameful son."

Wulf waited for him to continue. He continued.

"I'm that son. Bhakrann's my only name. How many men with how many names have I killed and trampled under my feet?"

"Yes," was all Wulf could say.

"The other children laughed and pointed at me and called me son of nobody. I'd run and hide, until I got strong and fierce, and struck back at them. When I was eight years old, I gouged an eye out of the head of a mocker. When I was twelve and my mother dead, a grown man laughed and called me son of nobody. I went for his throat, and when he drew his knife I caught his hand and turned his own point to drive into him and he was dead. That was the first of many I've killed, how many I don't know—I've stopped counting."

"You're a good fighter."

"Yes, but not a thinking fighter like you. Our tribes were at war then, before the Cahena joined us into one people. When I was still a boy, I went to those wars. I never thought of being killed, only of killing. When I was eighteen, I was thought the foremost killer of the Djerwa. Then the first Moslems prowled in, while I was still young. I was the chief of war parties. I fought whenever there was fighting to do. I got wounded, but I was never killed. I did the killing."

"Bhakrann," said Wulf, "you didn't have to tell me this."

"Maybe I did have to tell you. Maybe I had to talk."

"Isn't there any joy in your heart, Bhakrann?" Wulf half reached his hand out, then drew it back. "Do you have a heart at all?"

"No god I ever heard of would dare look into my heart," came the slow reply. "But I have a heart. There's even tenderness in it."

"Tenderness for what?" Wulf asked him.

"For the Cahena. She calls me her son. And she wants me to call you my brother. Now, don't you think I've talked enough for tonight?"

VII

On the move at pale dawn, munching scraps of barley cake as they rode. There was little discipline to their formation. They ambled in clumps and straggles, still loudly congratulating themselves and each other on their victory. Camels blubbered complaints under their burdens. The captured horses had mostly been appropriated by their captors, and many riderless Imazighen horses were herded along. Wulf heard that they headed for the Cahena's town on Mount Arwa.

The land looked rich, pleasant. Cattle and sheep grazed on grassy stretches. Here and there stood houses of mud brick and thatch, with fruit orchards and grape arbors. Streams flowed, enough water for grateful horses. Wulf reined aside once to study a closed structure of rough stones that rose to a cone. Zeoui said that it was an ancient Imazighen tomb, of someone once important and now forgotten.

A messenger summoned Wulf to ride with the Cahena and her chieftains.

They greeted him with noisy friendship, pockmarked Ketriazar, lean, pale-eyed Daris, the more elegant Yaunis. Bhakrann came, nodding cheerfully, as though he had never told his bitter tale of shameful birth. The Cahena beckoned Wulf with her riding whip. "Tell us more of this fighting you say we'll do," she said.

"Yesterday we defeated only a reconnaissance force," he reminded her. "Their main body will come, a great big main body."

"We ate them up like a relish of pickles," said Ketriazar.

"We ate up the ones who got out to us, and we outnumbered those," said the Cahena, easy in her saddle. "Wulf's plan. I saw at once that it would succeed."

"What would you have ordered?" asked Yaunis, and she turned a dry smile upon him.

"Why tell you what I'd have ordered?" she said. "Wulf had a good plan ready. I gave the orders, but they were Wulf's orders."

"Your decisions are always right, Cahena," said Yaunis.

"Which is why she is so great," added Daris.

Wulf had listened. "What makes her great is that her men hear her and obey her," he said.

"Lucky, Wulf says," the Cahena reminded them. "Luck is everything. I've been lucky in having my orders obeyed ever since I was a girl, fighting tribes that became allies, with Vandals and Romans and so on. And now with Moslems." Her eyes shone on Wulf. "You think they'll bring forty thousand against us."

"Hassan ibn an-Numan had that many to take Carthage," he said again. "Maybe he'll have more now. It'll be a big army to bring into strange country, finding rations and keeping fit for action."

"And stopping to pray five times a day," contributed Yaunis.

"They've done that all the way from the far side of Egypt," went on Wulf. "They'll come, as many of them as they can manage."

"We'll start gathering our own men as soon as we get to Tiergal," said the Cahena.

"Tiergal," Wulf repeated, and she laughed musically.

"It's nowhere as big as those old Roman towns on the coast," she said. "We Imazighen don't build big towns. We do things simply and try to do them well."

Wulf gazed at a string of nearby riders, tousled, sunburned, bare-armed. Their shocks of hair defied the sun. They wore daggers and javelins and shields as though they could use any of them, or all of them at once. Enough such men could win. But were there enough?

"We'll find the men," said the Cahena, as though yet again she read his mind.

They passed a mud-walled house with a hedge of prickly pear. A hoopoe fluttered close, speckle-bodied, yellow-crested. More houses showed ahead. The Cahena ordered men to ride to each.

"Offer them money for what food they have," she directed. "Here, take these coins we captured. Meat, grain, fruit, anything. If they won't sell, say it's for the Cahena."

The messengers jogged away to door after door.

"What if the food isn't given when they say it's for you?" Wulf asked the Cahena.

"I'm afraid it will be taken anyway. People mustn't refuse me."

Past the little settlement they marched, and bargained for food at houses beyond. The sun blazed high, then sank westward toward the distant ridge. When it set in a red blur, they camped in a broad hollow with grassy slopes and a swift stream at the bottom. Men unsaddled and made preparations for supper.

Wulf found Bhakrann and Zeoui and Cham exulting that an injured baggage camel had been slaughtered and was being cut up for roasts over a score of fires. As they licked their lips, Mallul appeared.

"The Cahena asks that Wulf eat with her," he said, and Wulf followed him to the enclosure of javelin-propped robes. Inside, she bent over a pot set on hot coals.

"You accepted my invitation," she greeted Wulf.

"People mustn't refuse you," he said, giving her back her own words.

She laughed, more merrily, perhaps, than the half-impudent jest deserved. Mallul served the food into bowls. It was a stew of mutton and green pods and couscous, seasoned with peppers. The Cahena poured cups of wine. The three ate and drank. The Cahena studied Wulf thoughtfully.

"Forty thousand of them," she said at last, putting a spoon between her full lips.

"Hard-fighting veterans," said Wulf. "Ready to die in battle and go to their promised paradise."

"So you said. But I asked you here to learn who you are, what you are."

Eating, Wulf told her at greater length the story he had told Bhakrann of his English boyhood, his studies of histories and languages, his service with the Franks and the Byzantines.

"We've needed you," she said, nodding her dark head. "You're learned and brave. Not all brave men are learned, not all learned men are brave."

"You flatter me, Lady Cahena."

"I tell the truth about you. I had a vision of you. I saw even the pattern of your tunic. I know what will happen."

"That's true, Wulf," said Mallul.

"Wisdom sees the future by indications of the past and present."

"You're a philosopher," the Cahena half crooned. She poured wine for them both and sipped from her cup as he sipped from his.

"You're kind to entertain me," he said. "To talk to me."

"We'll talk again, another time."

That was his leave to go. He rose and bowed, but did not fall down to kiss her shadow that still showed in the sun's last redness.

"How big you are, Wulf," she said. "We'll make you a coat of mail."

"Thank you," he said, reflecting that other women had praised his stature, ever since he was an upstanding lad in England.

"Good night, Wulf."

He went back to where Bhakrann and Zeoui and Cham were finishing their camel meat. Yaunis was with them, eating more daintily.

"We'll be fewer tomorrow," said Bhakrann. "Yaunis will lead his men off to the north at sunrise."

"I hope to talk with you again, Wulf," said Yaunis, wiping his fingers on the leg of his boot. "After all, I've been to Carthage. I went to the theater and the circus. My people are the Djerdilan. We have civilized traditions, we appreciate culture."

"That's meant for me and Cham and Zeoui, we're barbarous Djerwa," drawled Bhakrann without rancor. "You can fight anyway, Yaunis. We saw you fight this morning."

"This morning," Wulf echoed. It seemed long ago, that slashing hurly-burly at the pass. But far longer ago seemed his flight from Carthage. Had it been only four days back? Five?

"Did the Cahena tell you anything?" Bhakrann was asking.

Wulf reflected on certain things so carefully left unsaid at supper. "She wants to gather forty thousand men against the invasion that's coming," he decided to say.

"I'll have maybe four thousand Djerdilans, all who can sit a horse and throw a javelin," said Yaunis, rising. "Good night, Wulf. Come visit me among the Djerdilan."

He walked away with an elegance that may have been consciously assumed. Wulf and the others sat in the night, cool but comfortable. At last they slept. At dawn, the column marched again.

They moved on one slope after another, past knotty hummocks that, Wulf thought, could hide ambushes. Mounting rivers and crossing valleys, they pointed toward remote heights. With Yaunis's command gone, the force was smaller and even less ordered. Men rode out of the ranks without permission to javelin partridges and rabbits. One party returned with two deer. Others raided fig and date groves, and the Cahena gave money to protesting owners. Camp that night was among rugged hills, where horses and camels found grass. There were several streams. Wulf and Bhakrann stripped to bathe in one.

"You've quite a few scars," observed Bhakrann, surveying Wulf's brawny body. "Nearly as many as I have, and you aren't as old. What made that white mark on your shoulder?"

"An arrow, outside Damascus."

"We don't use those much—not grown men, anyway."

Wulf pulled his tunic over his wet torso. "You mean, children have arrows?"

"Oh, just to play with. I've seen little boys shoot at butterflies—hit them, too."

Mallul came to say that the Cahena would entertain them both at supper. She was in her little stockade of cloaks, with Daris and Ketriazar. The meal was a kettle of big snails, steamed in peppery oil. Again the Cahena ate only sparingly. Putting snails into his mouth, Wulf remembered how in Constantinople they were more appetizingly prepared.

The chieftains accepted war as inevitable, but when the Cahena spoke of forty thousand to fight it, they scowled and counted on their knobby fingers.

"That means women and children to tend the herds and crops," said Daris. "We'll need every man who can mount a horse."

"Wulf says the Moslems have better horses than we do," said the Cahena, half taunting the notion.

"Does he?" snapped Daris. "We ride better than any men on earth. Yaunis told me that the old Romans used Imazighen cavalry, all the way up there across the sea."

"Imazighen rode races in the Roman games," added Mallul. "Rode them and won them."

"The Romans didn't win wars with cavalry," Wulf said. "Their legions marched and fought on foot, and conquered everywhere. Even in England, where I used to live."

"How did they conquer?" inquired Ketriazar.

Wulf did his best to explain Roman military organization, the hardy legions of five or six thousand men. He described a legion's division into centuries and the groupings of centuries into cohorts, with efficient commanders. Taking a stick, he diagrammed a legion's harrowlike line of battle, with a second grouping of centuries to advance and relieve the first. The others asked questions. Wulf found it hard to put into words the way these units made themselves maneuverable, deploying or concentrating on command.

"But these tactics have deteriorated," he lectured. "Legions are smaller these days, made up of poorer troops. They've lost the old skill and spirit, they've been defeated again and again. The Byzantines sometimes go back to an older method—the Greek phalanx, hard to break but not really mobile. Yet phalanxes have defeated the Moslems."

"Old ways of fighting?" Ketriazar sniffed.

"When old methods have been forgotten they become new," declared the Cahena, and again her word put an end to arguments. "Didn't the Romans ever win with cavalry, Wulf?"

"Sometimes. A cavalry charge at the right moment can decide a battle's outcome."

"How should we train ourselves now?" inquired Daris.

"It's hard to say at once," Wulf felt obliged to reply. "I'm trying to think over everything I've studied."

"We don't have time to think," Daris said.

"We've days to think," said the Cahena, "and nobody had better talk before thinking."

"Wulf thinks as well as fights," added Bhakrann, sipping wine. "You saw him handle them at the pass, right on the spot. I say he'll do it again, against more enemies."

"Maybe," granted Ketriazar.

They waited for the Cahena to speak. Wulf watched their bearded faces and wondered if they dared look upon her with desire.

"I'll expect Wulf to think usefully," she said at last. "Now, we'll ride fast and far tomorrow. Let's get some rest."

Another authoritative dismissal, but she smiled at Wulf, a somewhat stealthy smile.

Back with Cham and Zeoui, Bhakrann sat and surveyed Wulf thoughtfully. "You're hard to believe," he said.

"I hope not," said Wulf, dragging off a boot.

"I mean how the Cahena listens to you, how she snubs others when they question you. Why? Is it because you're from so far away? She says she knew about you before she saw you. She knows everything."

"I don't know everything," said Wulf, stretching out.

The journey went on for days. The Cahena rode alongside wounded men, and they seemed to be better for that. Foraging parties went here and there. The way became steeper and rockier, curved here and there to mount rises or find passages among thicketed pinnacles and ridges. There were streams, where they refilled bottles and watered their animals. The sun glowed, wind stirred eddies of dust.

"I want to know how your people are organized and ruled," Wulf said to Bhakrann as their horses jogged together. "The Cahena wants my advice about war, but I heard so little about the Imazighen while I was at Carthage."

"You can say that they obey their fathers and their fathers obey something like grandfathers," said Bhakrann.

He went on to explain that, away from the half-ruined Roman and Vandal coastal towns, the Imazighen lived mostly in small settlements, grazing herds and growing barley and fruits. A community was made up of related households with a patriarchal chief. Several groups in the same area were further organized, with a commander to call local chiefs to council. The various tribes—Wulf had met their leaders like Daris, Ketriazar, Yaunis—all obeyed the Cahena. She herself lived simply, as Wulf had seen.

"You may laugh at our town of Tiergal," said Bhakrann.

"You haven't heard me laugh much at anything." Wulf watched some foragers driving in a flock of plaintively bleating goats. "There's not much to laugh about when you have to raise an army."

"She said it would be raised," returned Bhakrann. "Ask her how. She seems to answer your questions."

"And asks puzzling ones herself."

They kept riding upward on what, said Bhakrann, was the great eastern ascent of Arwa. The horses grew tired, and the Cahena ordered frequent rests and waterings. People emerged from clumps of dwellings to cry greetings. A number of women could be called comely, several might even be called beautiful. They were straight-standing, bright-eyed, with flowing hair and ready smiles. On the cheeks of some he saw small tattooed crossmarks. Bhakrann said that these harked back to some old pseudo-Christian belief.

In camp that night, among rocky points, Wulf and his companions ate stewed goat's flesh with their barley cakes. Nearby, warriors crooned songs. To Wulf, these songs seemed unwarlike. One in particular was melodiously minor, to celebrate certain appetizing features of a girl drawing water from a well.

"Do you like that music?" said a voice behind him. The Cahena stood there. Bhakrann lowerd his face to where her shadow fluttered in the firelight. Wulf rose to his feet. She smiled.

"An army needs songs, Lady Cahena," he said.

"They all sing at Tiergal. They play harps and flutes." Still she smiled, as Bhakrann rose and stood listening.

"I have you to thank for seconding me, when I didn't want to speak before thinking," said Wulf.

"You still have to learn that I see things far off, and things to come," she said, her voice musical. "I see things in you that I'm glad to find." She tilted her dark head. "For one, I see your beard's growing. That will make you more handsome."

She turned and paced away into the darkness.

"I've never heard her talk like that to anybody," said Bhakrann. "When I killed Okba she said she'd call me her son, but that was just praise. I'm not handsome, anyway. What are you thinking?"

"I'm thinking of how wise she is, how she leads her people," Wulf mused. "And how beautiful she is."

"Yes," said Bhakrann, sitting again.

It rained in the night. Wulf propped his cloak on sticks and refused to be miserable in the wet—how often in the past he had camped in the rain. They marched next day under foggy clouds.

"It's moving eastward," Cham pointed out. "It'll rain where those Moslems are. Good."

Once more the ascent of the mighty mountain, among cluttered rocks and thorny trees. Wulf looked to where the Cahena rode among companions. Ketriazar was there, and Daris and Mallul, but no word came for him to join them. At noon they paused by a stream where another mountain path crossed theirs. Ketriazar rode off south with his Mediuni followers, and Daris led his men southwestward. As Wulf and Bhakrann watched the departures, excited hails rose from men at the rear. A horse stumbled toward them, its rider bent above its sagging neck.

"Bhakrann!" the man croaked, tumbling to earth. It was Tifan, caked with sweaty dirt. His horse crept toward the stream.

"Water?" Tifan mouthed. "I've been short on that—and food and sleep. I've ridden days and nights. . . ."

He snatched the bottle from Bhakrann's saddle and swigged.

"Easy," warned Bhakrann, taking the bottle away. "Drink too much and you won't be able to talk. What's your news?"

Tifan managed broken sentences. The scouts had watched the Moslems carry their wounded through the pass, had cautiously followed. On the far side, the enemy had headed limply eastward. They had seemed to fear pursuit. Tifan said he had ridden one horse into the ground to bring the news, had traded a jeweled dagger for another.

"It's ready to drop, too, like you," said Bhakrann, studying the fagged beast. "Don't let it drink too much, Zeoui. Take another swallow, Tifan. Now you can walk—come and give the Cahena your report."

Wulf went with them. The Cahena stopped the tottering Tifan from kneeling to kiss her shadow and listened as he told, in greater detail, of how the Moslems were plainly in no case to fight.

"I thought that," said the Cahena. "Look after this brave scout. Sponge his face, get him a fresh horse."

She looked past Tifan and smiled briefly at Wulf, as though they shared a specific knowledge.

They marched on the hot, irregular road. The sun sank among western clouds as Wulf rose in his stirrups to peer ahead.

"I see houses, there among those crags," he said to Bhakrann.

"That's Tiergal," Bhakrann told him. "That's home."

VIII

Tiergal, once they reached it, was a collection of homes that huddled here, sprawled there, in a considerable depression in the mountain. In more distant stretches were grain fields and gardens, with clumps of trees among them. As many as twelve thousand people might live here, and there were other communities of the Djerwa. They were, he had heard, the largest tribe of all the Cahena's alliance.

Some dwellings were of stone or roughcast brick, or of dried mud spread over wattles. Here and there were simple tents with thatching on top. Other homes were dug into the rocky walls of the place, tier above tier. There were wells with curbs and sweeps. A brook flowed. Through the town ran its principal street, with thatched market sheds and chaffering merchants. Women sat at their doors, weaving. A hubbub of welcome rose up as the men rode in.

"The Cahena!"

"Cahena, there is also the Cahena!"

Riders left the column as though heading home. The Cahena sidled her horse toward Wulf.

"Wulf, Bhakrann, come to supper with me," she said. "I'll send for Djalout, too."

She rode away, attended by two warriors.

"Cham, Zeoui, will you look after our horses?" Bhakrann said, dismounting. "Look after Tifan, too; get him some hot soup and barley beer. We'll tell you later what's good for you to know."

He and Wulf walked a narrow passage between close-set houses. Men and women hailed Bhakrann from doorways, and he called back that the invaders had been beaten again. They crossed a busy street and on the far side climbed a sloping alley where roofs merged above them. Clouds thickened with the sunset.

The Cahena's home lay under a jutting shelf of dark rock. Its front seemed made of broken bits of carved stone, perhaps from forgotten Roman ruins. Bhakrann knocked at a red-painted door, then pushed it inward. A guardsman saluted with his javelin and gestured toward a dark curtain with light seeping from behind. They lifted it and passed into a broad, low-ceilinged room.

The floor was of great mortared pebbles, with rugs and blankets spread upon it. A low round table stood at the center, with a brass lamp upon it. The Cahena stood there. At her motion, Wulf and Bhakrann sat on the floor beside the table.

Someone else came in. He was a fragile old man, his body like a handful of sticks in his gray robe. A dark red scarf bound his head. A tassel of silvery beard hung below his seamed face. He raised his meager right hand. On its forefinger gleamed a ruby.

"Wulf, this is Djalout," said the Cahena. "Sit with us, Djalout, give us your counsel."

Creakily the gaunt body lowered itself to sit at the table. Djalout's brow was high and broad, his eyes deep-set and brilliant. His lean claw of a nose shone softly.

The Cahena, too, sat down and clapped her hands. Two handsome women came in with bowls and trays of food. There were partridges and doves, stewed with herbs and onions and quinces, and a mess of seasoned greens and hot barley bread. The Cahena broke the bread into fragments and passed them around. A servingwoman poured wine into cups. Her eyes studied Wulf demurely. The Cahena took the wing of a bird. The others helped themselves.

"What good wine," said Wulf.

"It's pressed from pomegranates," Djalout informed him. "Apples of Carthage. We grow them."

"Djalout," said the Cahena, "Wulf thinks the Moslems are better horsemen than the Imazighen."

"They conquered Syria and Persia and Egypt by riding, Lady Cahena," said Wulf.

"And you think they'll conquer us."

It was half an accusation. Bhakrann and Djalout watched.

"Not if we don't fight their way," Wulf said. "We might fight them on foot."

"You're joking," she said, "and it's no joking matter."

"I'm serious. I've told you how the Romans conquered whole horseback nations on foot, conquered even elephants."

"What's he saying, Djalout?" asked the Cahena.

"The truth," replied the thin old voice. "It happened and happened."

"Horses trample men," said Bhakrann, gnawing a drumstick.

"Not over close formations with spear points to the front," said Wulf. "The Cimbrians were big men on big horses, but Caius Marius and his infantry ate them up."

Djalout nodded. "That's in Plutarch."

"How did they do that?" Bhakrann prodded. "How?"

"With just about the weapons we have—javelins and shields and short swords," said Wulf. "The Romans could use them."

"I want to hear more from Wulf about it," said the Cahena.

"I'd meet a cavalry charge with close ranks on foot, four or five javelins to a man," said Wulf. "Throw javelins at close range, knock down horses, break the formation. Then stop them with the last javelin. That would be an extra big, strong one."

Bhakrann shook his head. "It couldn't be done."

"Could it, Djalout?" asked the Cahena.

Djalout crumbled bread. "As Wulf says, it's been done. What strikes me is that the Moslems wouldn't expect it."

"Who *would* expect it?" cried Bhakrann. "Not me. Don't tell me to get off my horse and fight a charge with javelins."

"You'd stay on your horse," said Wulf. "When the charge was checked, you and other mounted men would countercharge."

"It would take planning, but it could happen," said the Cahena.

"I'll have to be shown," insisted Bhakrann. "So will all the other men. They'll need a lot of talking to."

"They'll be talked to," promised the Cahena.

"Meanwhile," Wulf went on, "we must scout to see which way the enemy will try to come after us."

"They won't come at once," said Djalout. "The rains have started, and they'll want good weather to travel in."

"Giving us time to train," added the Cahena. "Experiment with formations, maybe choose a battleground."

She clapped her hands again. The servingwomen brought trays of figs and fresh dates and rosy grapes and a gourd bowl of honey. Djalout dangled a fig in the honey before biting it. Bhakrann, too, visited the bowl with a bunch of grapes. The Cahena dipped her grapes in wine, one by one, as she ate them.

"Choose where we'll meet them," she said again.

"As good ground as where we fought that advance party," offered Bhakrann.

"Ground that Wulf chose," reminded the Cahena, looking at Wulf as she spoke his name. "But I think closer than that. I'll call the chiefs to a council."

"Wulf can explain to them," said Bhakrann. "Or maybe I will. They might not listen to a stranger with foreign mud on his boots."

"Not you, Bhakrann," said Djalout. "Only the Cahena can explain and be heard. You agree, Wulf?"

"Yes," said Wulf at once. "There's nobody else this whole alliance will obey. Nobody else can get them out there in the face of death." He felt her eyes on him. "If she says to fight on foot, they'll do it. If she says to fight bare-handed, they'll do that."

"You have faith in me, Wulf," said the Cahena, putting a grape between her red lips.

"I've watched you with your men, and your men with you," he said. "They live or die by your word."

"Javelin throwers on foot," harked back Bhakrann, "and horsemen to countercharge. Is that your whole battle plan?"

"I've also thought of bows and arrows," said Wulf.

"We aren't a nation of archers," the Cahena objected.

"Bhakrann says that children play with bows," said Wulf. "Maybe we can train archers."

"I'll call the chiefs to hear," said the Cahena again. "Well, that's enough military planning for tonight."

They all rose. "Wulf," said Djalout, "I'd be glad for more conversation with you."

"Of course."

"When you're finished with Djalout, return here," said the Cahena. "I'm going to make you one of us."

"I'd hoped I'd proved myself one of you," Wulf said.

She smiled at him faintly, meaningfully. "I'll make you my son," she half whispered.

"You call all of us your sons," Bhakrann said.

"Wulf is different," said the Cahena, as though settling the matter. "He came as though I'd called him. He must be adopted by me." Her gaze kept on Wulf. "Come back when you finish your visit with Djalout."

Bhakrann scowled. Djalout stroked his lean beard.

"Whatever you ask," agreed Wulf.

From somewhere she had picked up a copper-bound hourglass—of Roman make, Wulf guessed—and set it on the table. The sand began to trickle from the upper bulge into the lower.

"Come back when it's run its course," she said.

Djalout sought the doorway. Bhakrann followed him, and Wulf followed Bhakrann. He felt the Cahena's gaze on his back, almost like the touch of a hand.

The sentry bowed them out. A foggy rain fell in the night. In the street stood a man in a hooded robe, bearing on his shoulder a great crude key. It was made of a slab of wood as long as his arm, with three metal pegs to the edge at one end. He bowed to Djalout and walked away as though to escort them.

"That's Gata," said Djalout to Wulf. "My servant."

Gata walked past several dwellings to another door set in the bluff. A span-wide hole showed beside the wooden portal. Gata thrust in his key and turned it. The lock groaned as it yielded. Gata opened the door, and Djalout beckoned Wulf in.

They came into a cubical chamber, lighted by two copper lamps in brackets. The walls were hewn rock, and on the floor lay coarse mats. Along one wall extended a low shelf of bricks, piled with rugs. Djalout nodded to Gata, who went out again. Djalout waved Wulf to a seat on the shelf and himself took the chair. From the stand he lifted an elaborately worked silver flagon and poured from it into two clay cups.

"This is better than what the Cahena served us," he said, handing a cup to Wulf. "Not all my tastes are as simple as hers."

Wulf drank. The wine was excellent.

"Bhakrann and I are two of her various upholding strengths," went on Djalout's thin voice. "Now she finds more strengths in you."

"You mean warrior and thinker," said Wulf.

"Bhakrann drinks the blood of whole tribes and smacks his lips. And yes, I think, I plan, rationalize dreams into realities." The curved nose stabbed into the cup. "Maybe you're as much warrior as Bhakrann, as fierce with the sword. And more, a strategist."

"Thank you," said Wulf.

"But maybe not the thinker I am."

"Probably not," conceded Wulf.

"I've been at the business of thinking for more than twice as long as you," said Djalout. "I've been successful at it. But I'm no fighter; I only think about fighting."

"So do I think about fighting," said Wulf. "I've had to."

Djalout's narrowed eyes raked him. "You agreed that the Moslems wouldn't hurry here. The rainy season will slow them up."

"And something else," said Wulf. "The Imazighen have defeated them—first Okba, then Zoheir, and the other day we whipped a strong advance party. Each time they were too headlong in unknown, hostile country. They won't keep making that mistake. Likely they'll consolidate their present holdings, refortify Carthage, organize carefully for any new advance."

"They're rich with the plunder of Syria and Persia and Egypt," said Djalout. "They'll use those things."

"Not at once," argued Wulf. "Not even Caesar outran himself. Alexander did, but war was simpler then. *Festina lente*—make haste slowly, says the Roman proverb borrowed from the Greeks."

"Caesar," repeated Djalout. "Alexander. Greek and Roman proverbs. You've been to school."

"When I was young, and I've always studied when I had time," said Wulf. "Mostly military matters and languages. I can read and speak in Latin, Greek, Hebrew, Arabic, and others."

"And your Imazighen is good," said Djalout. "You seem to catch languages as others catch diseases. You may want to look at some of my books. Maybe you've learned things that men like me—and we're few, Wulf—have always more or less known and used."

The fragile fingers of Djalout's left hand turned the ruby ring upon the right.

"You've known great men," said Wulf.

"Mohammed, for one. I sat on his knee seventy years ago, when I was a boy. He liked children, and he respected my father."

"Your father was a Moslem."

"A Jew of Medina, named Yakoub," said Djalout. "He left wisdom to me as a legacy. When he saw that Mohammed would conquer, he professed Islam. Allah's name was always on his lips, always lyingly."

Djalout refilled their cups.

"When I was old enough to keep my mouth shut—and I was old enough very young—my father taught me to be a hypocrite. He said, 'When a Moslem asks your faith, say you're a true believer and hold out one finger of your right hand. But lay it on your left palm.' "

The ruby-ringed right forefinger lay upon the open left hand.

"Can you read that?" asked Djalout. "One finger means one God, of course, but here's one finger with five more, six in all. The points of the Star of David."

"Yes," said Wulf.

"My name wasn't always Djalout, and I was born a Moslem by my father's profession of faith. But he taught me Judaism, and I've been of that faith and others. When Mohammed died and his companions quarreled, my father found the situation embarrassing. He took me to Egypt, and I went to school and began to know how wise you may become if you live long enough. I profess Christianity." Djalout smiled over the word. "Like yourself."

"There are many Christianities," observed Wulf.

"They fight among themselves, to no great purpose," said Djalout. "If they hadn't confused Mohammed, he might have become a Christian himself. But they don't confuse me." A smile in the beard. "They only amuse me."

"Are you married, Djalout?"

"I've had wives, but they died. I do well alone."

"You went to Egypt. The Moslems came conquering there."

"I got away to Carthage, lived there for years. Then I came here, for I'd heard of a young prophetess and queen who ruled a jumble of tribes and would go far."

"The Cahena."

"Yes." A slow sip of wine. "She saw my talents and usefulness, as now she sees yours. I've helped her, and she's appreciative. She might have succeeded from rule to rule without me, would have added tribe after tribe to her alliance; but maybe not so quickly."

"You said you weren't always named Djalout," Wulf reminded.

"Oh, that. When I left Carthage, I came first among the Djerdilan. They say they're descended from Philistines. Their hero was Djalout, the giant of Gath."

"Goliath."

"That's the one. Should I have told them that my true name was Daoud, like the shepherd boy who knocked their hero down with a stone?" The old eyes crinkled. "I called myself Djalout, and I didn't bother to change back when I settled here among the Djerwa, though they have Jewish associations."

"You were born a Moslem, Djalout."

"Yes."

"And you were secretly reared a Jew."

"Yes."

"Later on you were a Christian."

"Yes."

"In which of those faiths do you believe?"

"In none." The thin shoulders shrugged under the robe. "My mind demands proofs. Faith can't exist if it calls for proof."

"Then you don't believe in anything," said Wulf.

Djalout lifted his cup. "I believe in what I've found out, here and there in the world. And I believe in the Cahena. She's definite enough."

"What if somebody told her all about your adventures and attitudes?" Wulf smiled as he challenged.

Djalout smiled back, faintly. It was like the smile of a ghost.

"I told it to her myself, years ago," he replied. "She understood perfectly. She's tremendously understanding."

"Yes," agreed Wulf. "Yes, she is."

"Meanwhile, she expects you to come back to her. The sand in her glass must be fairly well run. Go to her now, and you and I can talk again some other time."

IX

Outside in the misty rain, Bhakrann fell into step with Wulf. He said nothing until they came back to the Cahena's door. Then Bhakrann caught Wulf's arm. His fingers bit like teeth.

"When you go in there," he said tightly, "when you go in, be sure you deserve to go in."

Wulf wrenched his arm free. "You don't need to talk like that to me."

They stared into each other's eyes. Raindrops ran on their faces.

"Be sure you deserve it," said Bhakrann again. "I don't remember anything like this. We've taken strangers into the Djerwa, but never one like this, alone with her."

Wulf looked at the red door.

"I'll try to imagine what happens," said Bhakrann. "Wulf! From this moment on, if you show that you don't prize—"

"Get away from me, before you and I fight," Wulf broke in.

Bhakrann swung on his heel and tramped off through the dark veil of the rain. His cloak snapped like a wet flag.

Wulf moved closer to the door, guiding himself with a hand on the rock. He felt the planks with his fingers and pushed the door open. He saw no guardsman, only a servingwoman who gestured him through the entry and to the curtain he remembered. He pushed it aside and stepped into the room where they had eaten.

It was dim; the lamps had been trimmed low. On the far side hung another curtain, one he had not seen before. Light soaked through, though not much. He went to it and stood.

"I'm here," he said.

"Come in," said the voice of the Cahena from beyond, and he pushed the curtain aside and entered another chamber.

A stone lamp stood on a narrow ledge just inside. The soft yellow leaf of flame sent up a thread of vapor to the hewn rock of the ceiling. On the chamber's far side, fully thirty feet from the curtained doorway, showed another light, red this time—coals in a brazier on a stand. Next to it he saw a blurred silhouette, head and draped body, sitting among heaped cushions.

"Take off those boots and put down your sword," the hushed voice said. "Your cloak, too. Leave them there by the door."

He dropped his wet cloak beneath the lamp and lifted one foot, then the other, to drag off his boots. Unbuckling his belt, he bent to set the boots and the sword on the cloak.

"Now come here," she bade him. "No, don't fall down and creep."

"I wasn't going to," he said.

"Walk here and sit down."

He paced toward her, trying not to seem too fast or too slow. His bare feet felt thick, coarse carpet. He came and stood above where she sat on heaped cushions that looked like dark silk in the dimness. Of dark silk, too, was the robe into which she had changed, the robe that clung to her body. Her black hair fell like a cloud upon her shoulders, to each side of the sculptured beauty of her face. How delicately straight her nose was, how softly pointed her chin. Under the sketched lines of her brows, her eyes gave back the glow of the brazier. Her mouth was ripe as fruit, and like carven pride flared her nostrils.

"Sit down," she said again, and Wulf sat on a cushion and crossed his big legs.

The Cahena held a tray, and from it measured a palmful of something. This she trickled into the brazier. A sort of steam rose from it, spicy to the smell. She lifted her head to look at him.

"Your name's Wulf," she said. "Djalout told me that that's the name of a brave beast in your language. Were you ever married?"

"No, Cahena," he said. "Ever since I was a boy, I've been going to wars. Warriors shouldn't take wives to wars with them."

"Don't you like women?"

He let himself smile in the red light. "Yes, I like women."

"You've had them?"

"Yes, from time to time, but I never married one."

"I was married once, Wulf."

"You were married once," he repeated her.

"Long ago, and I rarely talk about it, but I'll tell you. How old are you?"

"Thirty years old," he said.

"I'm forty. It happened when I wasn't yet twenty. His name was Madghis."

She said the name as though it was a bad taste in her mouth.

"He was a strong subchief of the Djerwa when my father Tabeta was head chief. My father died, and had no son, only a daughter—me. Madghis became head chief and said he wanted me. That he'd have me and rule over the Djerwa after my father. The other chiefs said it was all right. So he had me."

She paused as though to let Wulf speak, but he only waited for her to continue. She continued:

"It was night in his house, off among the hills west of here. It was like this house, dug into the rock." A gesture, perhaps to show the direction. "He had men on guard in front of the door in the dark."

"In front of the door," said Wulf, thinking of Bhakrann.

"Madghis had me then. It hurt, and he laughed and said that all his life he'd had whatever he wanted. The men outside heard him, and they laughed, too."

Again she paused and put a handful of whatever it was on the brazier. A thicker vapor cloud rose, and Wulf felt a ringing in his ears. He wondered if a drug were in that preparation.

"I can hear them laughing now," said the Cahena. "Right now at this moment, I hear them laughing. Do you hear them?"

"No, Cahena," said Wulf. "But if they laughed then, I don't think that anybody has ever laughed at you since."

"No," she said, "nobody ever has. Well, at last Madghis got tired of what he did to me and went to sleep and snored. I took his big knife and cut his throat to the neckbone and cut the neckbone, too, and took off his head."

She told it calmly, as though it had happened with strangers. Wulf thought of Judith and Holofernes, and wondered if Holofernes had had Judith before she killed him.

"Next morning," the Cahena went on, "I walked out and called the sub-chiefs together and showed them Madghis's head. They talked, they were excited, but they were afraid, too. Some of them seemed glad that Madghis was dead. I'd counted on that. Then I said that I was Madghis's widowed queen, that I'd rule the Djerwa, and told them to gather up the men who'd laughed outside in the night. They did, and I said to kill those men with javelins. Later on, when it turned out that I was pregnant, would have Madghis's child, the last objections quieted down. Mallul was born, my son by Madghis. After that, other tribes joined the Djerwa, and I ruled them, too."

"How did the other tribes join you?" asked Wulf.

"Two of them fought us, first one and then the other, because they'd heard that only a woman ruled the Djerwa. I beat those tribes and made them join us. After that, more joined, without my having to fight them. They all say I'm the Cahena."

"You're the Cahena and there's nobody like you," said Wulf. "Koseila wasn't like you."

"Koseila captured Cairouan because I told him how to do it. But when the Moslems sent Zoheir, Koseila retreated from Cairouan—he didn't understand fighting within fortified walls—and Zoheir caught him in the open and killed him."

"Then you ruled after him," said Wulf.

"No, Koseila never ruled the Djerwa and my other tribes. We were allies, that's all."

"Did he perhaps want to marry you?"

"Maybe, but he knew what had happened to Madghis. Whenever he and I talked, he usually let me do most of the talking."

Wulf looked at her intent face, at the lines of her body under the silk. "There's nobody like you," he said again.

"I'm what God made me and what I've made myself. If I weren't the Cahena, I'd be just a woman."

"The most beautiful of women," said Wulf, and her eyes shone again.

"The most wretched of women," she amended. "Sought out for my beauty, but never honored. Snatched from hand to hand like a fruit among apes. Violently boarded like a ship overhauled by pirates, boarded again and again, a hundred times by a hundred takers, until I broke to pieces under them."

That, too, she said quietly, as though it might never have concerned her.

"It didn't happen, Cahena," said Wulf.

"Only that once, with Madghis, and that was more than enough. What can I be but the Cahena? Before I cut off Madghis's head and became the Cahena, the prophetess, the queen, my name was only Daia." She looked at him, breathing. "Did you know that my name was Daia?"

"They said that anyone who dares speak your name will be killed."

"Are you afraid to speak my name and be killed?"

"Not greatly."

"Daia," she said the name again. "How does it sound?"

"Like the Latin word *dea,* for goddess. And like our Saxon word *doian,* for death. No, I don't fear death, but life isn't such a burden that I go looking for death."

She drew herself straight as she sat. The robe sank from her firmly rounded left shoulder, softly shining as if polished.

"But you're afraid of my name because it's like your word for death." She laughed, so softly that he barely heard. "Maybe Wulf is too brave and strong a name for you."

"You think you can sit there and laugh at me, Daia."

Her lips opened, then closed again without speaking.

"I've called you Daia," said Wulf. "Now you can stop laughing and call somebody in to try to kill me with his javelin. Maybe that's why you told me to put aside my sword."

She smiled, but she did not laugh.

"Call me Daia," she said, "and live."

"Daia," he repeated. He reached and took her hand. It was soft and slender in his.

"Will you kiss my shadow, here on these cushions?" she asked him.

"No. Not your shadow."

Her fingers stirred. He bowed his head and kissed them.

"Wulf," she whispered above him. "Brave Wulf, strong Wulf. Call me Daia. Tell me what you think of me."

"Daia," he called her. "Not the moon in the sky nor its light on earth is more beautiful than you."

"You're a poet."

"I say what I think. But why do you show me this favor?"

"Because you were sent to me. My spirits told me of you before you came. As soon as I saw you, I knew that this would happen. That it was destiny for us both."

She leaned forward and laid her other hand on his that clasped hers. The movement made the robe slide farther down. He saw her slenderly curved body and her full round breasts that swung like gently tolling bells. Her hands shifted to pull at the lacing of his tunic. He helped her unfasten it and cast it to the carpet behind him. His head sang with the perfume from the brazier.

"Your skin's so smooth, Wulf," she murmured, stroking his chest with her palm. "Not all grown over with hair."

His heart drummed. He put out his arms to take her, but she slipped away from him.

"Not like that yet, Wulf. Here."

Her hands took his head between them and drew it to her. He tried not to tremble. She shifted her bare body against his face. The rondure of a breast drew along his cheek to his mouth.

"I make you a son of the Djerwa," she was saying. "I nourish you at my breast. I suckle you. You're my man. Mine."

Her nipple throbbed between his lips. It tasted as sweet as honey; she must have put honey on it. She caught her breath as though she were sinking underwater.

"The other," she whispered in his ear.

He took the other in his mouth. She hugged his head against her, more strongly than he had dreamed she could hug. Then she sank back and down of her own accord and her thighs moved apart to receive him and he mounted her and his face came to her face and his mouth to her mouth and their tongues twined together more eloquently than speech, than any vow or prayer, and they mingled and somehow she was within him as he was within her with their breaths as one breath and their hearts beating as one beat, and their union was forever and ever with the triumphant torrent and thunder of the climax like the coming of Judgment Day when the mountains and islands shall be moved from their places and never never never had it been like this before, and he forgot utterly how it had been with any other woman all his life long in the countries where he had lived but never had known this or dreamed this or imagined this.

Afterward they lay side by side recovering, his left arm under her head and her left arm across his chest.

"Was that how you thought it would be, Wulf?"

"I hadn't thought how it would be. There can never have been a woman like you, Daia."

"There can never have been a man like you, either. Never anyone like either of us. Call me Daia, always call me Daia when we're like this."

"Like this, Daia?"

"Like this, Wulf, like this again. Wulf, Wulf, in beauty like this again, this again, like this again."

X

Late, late at night, Wulf came back to the clay-and-wattle bachelor home of Bhakrann and Cham and Zeoui and Tifan. Bhakrann was still awake but said nothing, only pointed to a bed of hay under the eaves. Wulf lay down but did not sleep for hours. He thought of the Cahena until it seemed almost as though she lay beside him, said soft praise in his ear.

At dawn they ate barley cake and drank goat's milk, and Wulf stepped out in the misty morning. He looked at the house's sun-browned mud walls and its strongly thatched roof and thought, That's how my father's house was made, of earth and thatch.

And he gazed along the sprawl of the street, where merchants dickered with robed women and men in tunics, and he thought, The market town in England where I was a boy was like that.

Mud for his father's house had been kneaded and then spread like plaster upon a framework of upright poles with withes twisted horizontally between them, with openings for a door and two windows curtained with tanned leather. Inside, the hearth where his mother slung a spit and dangled a pot. And there were pallet beds, woven cloths spread over crammed coarse grass that was taken out and burned every summer and replaced with fresh coarse grass. On the wall hung a wooden crucifix, with upon it the tortured figure of Christ in another sort of wood, showing the scrapes and fumbles of the knife that carved it.

The home farm was thought prosperous, with two gaunt little horses and a cow and a calf, a penful of pigs behind the house. Grain and hay grew in the fields around. It was a mile's tramp on a ruined road to the market town.

Nowhere near as big a town as Tiergal, but Wulf's neighbors had traded there, grain for cloth, pigs for calves, calves for pigs, hens for clay dishes, baskets of berries for strings of beads. A busy town at market time. Once it had seemed to Wulf the center of everything.

Girls had been there, with black hair and brown and yellow, smiling at Wulf, giggling at him, nudging him. Merchants greeted him as the sun of a good farmer and customer. And Father Thomas the priest, who taught him his letters and said Wulf should be a priest, too, helped him off on the long trudge to where stern, understanding Bishop Hadrian waited to say that Wulf would do better as a soldier than as a priest.

Remembering, Wulf forgot the sword he wore. Again he was the boy with a bag at his side and a staff in his hand, with a sheepskin mantle and cross-garterings on his legs, starting away into the world. His father and mother—did they still live, did they wonder what had become of their son?

"You frown," said Cham at his side. "What are you thinking about?"

"Just a place I knew once," said Wulf. "A long way from here."

"Want to walk out? I'll show you things."

They passed people working in their yards. Women ground barley in hand mills or wove fabrics. The younger women were comely, several even beautiful. Men whittled shafts for javelins. "There's Wulf," they told each other. "He showed us how to whip the Moslems."

Shops sold meal and fruits and cuts of meat, necklaces of bright stones, and clothes. Wulf stopped to find a zigzag-patterned tunic to fit him and paid for it with one of his few remaining coins. Handsome children played everywhere, black-haired, brown-haired, one or two red-haired. "Wulf, Wulf!" they shrilled at him.

Cham led him to a sturdy, smooth-shaven metalworker in a leather apron, and Wulf ordered a coat of mail. The man's name was Jonas. He said he was a Greek, a Christian, and that just then he was busy making javelin heads. He measured Wulf's chest and shoulders with a knotted cord. Jonas's daughter watched from inside the shop. She had sun-bright hair and a round face with a wide, happy mouth. Her body curved ripely. Her name was Daphne.

At the edge of town, men practiced with javelins. Their targets were outworn sandals, set upright. These men were highly accurate at various ranges. They invited Wulf to try, but he knew he did not have their skill and declined politely.

Boys herded goats and sheep and long-horned cattle in pastures among the slopes and hollows. Axmen chopped down gnarled trees. There were fields where reapers gathered grain into sheaves.

Many people wore patched or darned clothes, but were clean. Wulf commented on that to Cham.

"We always wash," said Cham. "There are two ponds past those ridges. Men swim in one, women in the other—swim naked."

"The women swim naked?" asked Wulf.

"I've often watched them," said Cham with relish.

Djalout joined them, leaning on his polished staff. Wulf asked him about religion in Tiergal. There were many beliefs, said Djalout. Christians like Jonas, others who professed Judaism—though very few could read and understand—and many who bowed to images of animal gods—lions, wild boars, snakes.

"How about Khro?" asked Wulf, but Cham flinched and Djalout shook his fine gray head.

"They say it's bad luck to say his name, and who am I to go against popular opinion?" said Djalout. "Ask me about other gods of wisdom and love and war and such things—most likely gods who were here from the first Imazighen."

Wulf looked at great scrawls on houses, crescent moons and coarse-toothed combs and, in one place, a huge spread-fingered hand.

"What about those designs?" he inquired. "Are they some kind of writing?"

"If the Djerwa ever had writing, it's been forgotten," said Djalout.

Wulf paid attention to men called doctors, caring for the wounded brought back from the fight at the pass. These doctors chanted spells and were diligent to keep their patients clean. They dosed against fevers with pungent brews of herbs.

A chatter of voices in the street proclaimed that the Cahena was there in her blue robe, attended by a single guardsman. The people thronged to her and talked quietly, gently, not at all as they had cheered her when she rode back from battle. Wulf and Djalout followed her.

Wulf saw her bend above a languid little child in its mother's arms. The Cahena's hands touched it, stroked it, she said something. The child laughed, stirred, was well again. An old woman hobbled up on a staff. The Cahena put hands on the woman's eyes and the woman shrilled out, "I can see, I can see!" She flung her staff down and scuttled away, stridently rejoicing.

"She heals her people," said Djalout.

"Like a saint," said Wulf.

"Or like a sorceress."

Back at the house of Bhakrann and his friends, Wulf was handed a leather pouch full of gold and silver Arabian coins.

"She sent it," said Bhakrann. "Your share of what we took from those reckless people the other day."

Wulf took the purse gladly. "I must thank her."

"Thank yourself," Bhakrann bade him. "You won for us. She's ordering a home made for you, in a cave near hers."

Wulf went to see it next morning. The cave was the size of a big room. Two plump women busily swept its stone floor. At the rear, a latticed screen set off a sleeping chamber. A small spring bubbled outside. More women fetched in a wooden bed, cross-woven with tough vines, and quilts for it. They smiled at Wulf. One, brown-haired and buxom, brushed against him and smiled to show that it was no accident.

Outside, two men put up poles for a stable yard. One was Susi, burly and short. The other, javelin-lean, was Gharna. They said they were honored to serve him. As they talked, a warrior came to say that the Cahena would give Wulf audience.

Wulf went to her home, along the passage to the council room. Entering, he saw light through the rear curtain, and went there.

She met him inside. She wore nothing but a gem-studded bracelet and two gold earrings. She was like the image of a slender, round-breasted goddess in a secret temple. "Love me," she whispered. "Love me, Wulf." And sank down on the cushions.

Undressing hurriedly, he lay down with her and thoroughly loved her. Afterward, they talked.

"If there should be a child—" Wulf started to say.

"I know how to prevent that."

They made love again, then dressed and went out into the council room. Wulf heard her tell a guardsman to call Bhakrann.

Business followed. The Cahena put Bhakrann at the head of a score of skilled scouts to ride eastward and spy on the Moslems. They would be gone for many days. Meanwhile, the Cahena sent for her other chieftains.

They rode in, Yaunis and Ketriazar and Daris. Wulf and Djalout and Mallul attended the council. The seven sat in lamplight and drank sweet wine brewed from dates. The Cahena told them to listen to Wulf's plan of battle.

He took charcoal and drew on the inside of a tanned sheepskin, a diagram of a dismounted open-order formation, four deep, like the teeth of a harrow. This, he lectured, would allow repeated flights of javelins against a charge. He sketched in a strong second line, which he said was cavalry to countercharge at the right moment. The chiefs asked questions.

"All this is new," commented Daris gravely.

"Hardly new," said Wulf. "Alexander's phalanx and Caesar's legion had elements of it. But extra javelins are important. Yes, and one spear bigger than a javelin. Say twelve feet long, on a heavy haft."

Daris stared. "What for?"

"When the enemy riders get close, plant those spears and let the horses stab themselves on the points."

"Good," applauded Djalout, and the others seemed convinced.

"I'll train my men to form and fight like that," vowed Ketriazar.

"I'll do likewise," promised Daris. "Speaking of javelins, why don't we go hunting when we're through talking here?"

The Cahena and the chiefs and Mallul and Wulf rode on, along a great grassy slope of the mountain. Near a trickling stream they chased a little herd of antelope. Ketriazar galloped to strike down a quarry. Expertly the Cahena transfixed another. Supper that night was of grilled venison. A choice cut went to Djalout, another to Jonas the smith.

"How many can we muster?" asked the Cahena as they ate. "I can speak for six thousand Djerwa."

"I'll raise five thousand," said Yaunis.

"Five thousand more," volunteered Ketriazar.

"The same, give or take a few," said Daris.

"We'll need more," declared the Cahena. "Yaunis, tomorrow I'll go with you as far as your place, then on to Cirta. Lartius is chief there. He's said he'd raise every man in his coastal towns if we need help. You come with me, Wulf."

That evening, Wulf walked out with Djalout to visit wounded warriors under the care of doctors. "Help nature heal," Djalout said, praising the treatment. "Nature heals better than science."

They talked of the nature of the earth, speculating on its great unknown reaches. Djalout remembered the raid of Okba to the very western sea.

"He swore that, if the ocean did not stop him, he'd carry the Moslem faith to lands beyond," said Djalout, stroking his beard. "I wonder if he knew how Ptolemy said the world was round, and if he believed that there were lands and peoples in the west."

"Are there?" asked Wulf.

"Someday someone will find out," said Djalout, "when they make a ship good enough to carry him."

"In Constantinople, wise men said that the world was flat, and if you sailed out far enough, you'd fall off."

"No wise man knows everything," said Djalout. "I don't, for one."

At Jonas's lamplit shop Wulf tried on the mailed jacket he had ordered. It was of stout leather, with lengths of chain sewed to the sleeves and overlapping iron plates on shoulders and chest. Daphne watched, bright-haired, bright-eyed.

"Well made," commented Djalout. "It will turn an arrow or sword."

Wulf bore the jacket to his cave. His horses whinnied to him from the stable enclosure.

Next morning, he mounted his spotted horse to join the Cahena and Yaunis. The Cahena joined four of her guards to the half dozen of Yaunis's escort. They followed a trampled trail down the northern slopes of Arwa.

Some miles along, they went through a village where people cheered them. Beyond, the slope became a strew of rocks. Scatterings of green grass grew here and there, and occasional hardy trees. There were evidences of humanity, too, old humanity. At one point stood three battered stone columns, supporting nothing. At another, back from the road, a conical structure of masonry.

"That's a tomb," said Yaunis to Wulf. "Maybe old Roman. I think there's something like writing on it."

More ruinous traces of building after that. At sundown they camped at a spring with fringes of palms. Yaunis grimaced, as though he did not like the place. Wulf saw scraps of white, scattered here and there on the sward. A guardsman built a fire and began to cook a brass basinful of couscous and smoked meat. Yaunis peered into the gloom.

"This is a good campsite," offered Wulf. "Wood, water—"

"A place of the dead," said Yaunis. "The water's all right, but a night here can be unpleasant."

Supper was dished up. "Place of the dead," Wulf echoed Yaunis. He looked at the scattered white things and saw that they were bones.

"Spirits come here," said Yaunis. "Many must have died here long ago—died violently. I've never heard when or why. But when it's dark, they walk. Let's pick up more wood, keep the fire going."

Wulf went to gather dead branches and paused to look at a scatter of pallid bones. They had belonged to a great wild boar, a beast that must have weighed four hundred pounds, with tusks like curved daggers. Even a lion might pause before attacking such a foe. What had killed it? High in the evening sky, vultures plied back and forth, their motionless wings spread wide.

The Cahena made herself a little tent of a cloak and a saddle blanket, propped on sticks. The others huddled close to the fire, wrapped in mantles. Men of both escorts took turns at watching and tending the fire. They sang softly, plaintively.

Wulf lay wakeful. A bird, or perhaps a big insect, chirped in a palm. The dark of night was not so dark. Small green lights showed in pairs, like eyes. The sentinels put more wood on their fire and one of them sang:

"What god may hear, help us;
Protect us, what god may hear . . ."

The eyelike green sparks gave back, but stayed in sight. Wulf dozed, wakened, again saw the lights prowling. Over him, close over him, fluttered a big bat, snatching bugs in midair. Those ribbed wings were what devils wore, in pictures Wulf had seen.

At dawn, the lights did not show. Wulf was glad of that as he ate a barley cake for breakfast and rode on with the others. He reflected that when he and the Cahena came back, they would have only half as many in their party. He hoped that they would camp somewhere else.

Noon, and Yaunis and his men ambled off on a side trail. The Cahena led on, and as the sun sank they saw where Cirta was.

Here was a town much bigger than Tiergal, built on a conelike height. It had neat stone houses up the slope and at the top. A river tumbled to bracket two sides of the place. An old, old road with troubled stone paving led in. Two armed guardsmen moved as though to bar the way, then saw the Cahena and fell down to kiss the shadow of her passing horse. The party entered the town. The houses were of cut stones, probably salvaged from Roman ruins. People recognized the Cahena and murmured applause. On the main street, past shops with canvas-shaded fronts, they came to a sort of palace.

It was a broad building, also of reclaimed stones, with hammered iron bars on the windows and a tall porch with ancient pillars. The guards at the door kissed the Cahena's shadow, then took charge of the horses. Inside, a portly eunuch made obeisances. He was the first eunuch Wulf had seen since leaving Carthage. Then a man strode into the hall and louted low before the Cahena.

"Wulf, this is Lartius. He is chief here and over other towns," the Cahena said, making introductions. "Lartius, Wulf is my military adviser."

Lartius looked to be in his forties, as tall as Wulf, but elegantly slender. His smooth-shaven face had slightly hollowed cheeks and a shallow jaw. His eyebrows made a single black bar above his nose. His tunic was liberally patterned with gold thread. His half boots were far more finely made than Wulf's own.

He offered Wulf a sinewy right hand with jeweled rings on three of its fingers. "Welcome," he said grandly. "We hear all the way to Cirta how you're a fighter and a planner." Again he bowed to the Cahena. "Will you come to my parlor? It's dinnertime. I'm honored to entertain you."

The eunuch led the Cahena's warriors away somewhere. Lartius conducted the Cahena and Wulf into a spacious chamber with lounges and polished tables, and wall-paintings of horsemen hunting bulls and lions. He gestured them to seats and clapped his hands loudly. Another eunuch appeared, and Lartius commanded him to send in dinner.

That dinner was fetched in by three serving-girls, all of them sleekly naked except for brief loin coverings and embroidered slippers. They swayed and giggled as they served hot roast meats and wheat bread. "Our wheat flour comes from Carthage," said Lartius. "When can we get more?"

"When we capture Carthage and open trade again," said the Cahena, eating a morsel.

The girls poured wine into silver goblets. They smiled at Wulf, were gravely careful in serving Lartius and the Cahena. Lartius lifted his goblet.

"Here's to our success against this invasion," he said. Now he looked at the Cahena, furtively admiring her. Wulf detected honey in the wine and did not feel that it was improved thereby. The swaying girls cleared away the dishes. Lartius watched them go, and drank again.

"War's inevitable, eh?" he said. "How do we fight them?"

"Which means, you'll help us," said the Cahena.

"Of course. My towns can muster maybe twelve thousand. I'll command in person."

"I'll command," corrected the Cahena, in the gentlest and most musical of voices. "Wulf here will tell you how we'll fight."

Lartius arched his fingertips together. "Go ahead, Wulf."

Wulf talked about more javelins per man and stout spears planted against charging cavalry. Lartius nodded approval, rather grandly.

"I have men who can fight on foot or on horseback," he said. "And some archers."

"Archers?" repeated Wulf eagerly.

"We've had good archers since earliest times. We hunt with arrows, even kill lions. Will bows be good in this fight?"

"Yes," said Wulf. "Formations of them on the wings to shoot into an attack, then to fall back and shoot over the front formations into the thick of the enemy. Bring archers if you can."

"I can," was Lartius's lofty promise.

More talk, about communications with all tribes, about scouts from Cirta to watch for possible Moslem moves toward the coast. Lartius named some of his followers as good scouts. Wulf wondered how good they were. They all drank more wine, and the Cahena said that she was weary from her journey.

Lartius rose and led them to broad stone steps, and up. Curtained doors lined the hall above. "Here is where I hope you'll be comfortable, Lady Cahena," he said, pulling a curtain wide. In the half-light beyond showed another curtain at the rear.

"An entry, with the main chamber behind," said the Cahena, peering. "I want Wulf to sleep in this entry as a guard."

Lartius blinked. "A guard, here in my own house?"

"I'll rest easier with one," she replied gravely. "Wulf is alert and trustworthy."

"Very well," said Lartius. "I'll send a mattress for you, Wulf. Then good night, and a pleasant rest."

Lartius strode away. The Cahena went in and passed the inner curtain. Wulf waited at the door until one of the fat eunuchs brought a wadded mattress and a quilt. Wulf put the mattress in the outer chamber and sat on it to doff his boots and tunic, and laid his unsheathed sword on the floor beside him. Stretching out, he relaxed his muscles and reviewed in his mind all the things that he and Lartius had said.

Then, a rustle from the Cahena's chamber. She came out and lay on the mattress beside Wulf. He did not know whose arms reached out first, his or hers.

XI

The Cahena and Wulf were dressed and out in the corridor by sunrise. They summoned their warriors and ate a hasty breakfast of hot bread in the big room downstairs. Lartius joined them, sleepy-eyed in a rich green robe. One of the eunuchs brought parcels of food for their homeward journey, and Lartius bade the Cahena a ringing farewell.

"What do you think of Lartius?" the Cahena asked Wulf as they rode. Her tone was utterly businesslike. Nobody could have guessed how tempestuous she had been with him the night before.

"I don't know yet. It was my first meeting with him," Wulf replied. "I wonder if he'll really fight."

"I wonder that, too. His people haven't fought much. Oh, maybe little actions against smaller chiefs, little clashes with robber bands. I hope our Imazighen can teach his men to fight."

"We might bring them down to us and see how they form up and act," Wulf suggested.

"Good," she agreed. "Now, if we make good time, we'll pass that campsite where things were uneasy. Just stop to fill bottles and water the horses, then on to camp a good way below."

Late in the afternoon they came to the water hole to replenish skin bottles. Vultures scoured the sky again. The party felt glad to ride on. At sunset it stopped at a hollow where grass grew for grazing, and sat down to eat what Lartius had provided. There were rolls of fine wheat bread, with slices of cold meat and dried figs and grapes. Wulf slept well.

Up at dawn again, breakfast on the remains of supper, and southward up the tufty-grassed slope of Arwa. As the sun dropped low, they saw the houses of Tiergal. Coming near, Wulf heard music. Some sort of flute wailed, drums beat, voices sang. "What's this?" he asked one of the escort.

"The people celebrating," was the reply.

"Celebrating what?"

"I don't know, but we'll find out."

The main street was thronged with people in grotesquely gaudy dress. There were cries and snatches of song. Wulf hurried to his cave, put his horse in Susi's charge, and walked back to the center of town.

People yelled at him through masks of garishly painted cloth or leather.

Some wore heads of wild dogs, bears, horned goats. Somebody in fluttery red and white draperies rushed to him, the hideous mask showing big wooden tusks. Up came two hands to pluck the mask from the smiling face of Daphne, the smith's daughter.

"We're having fun," she cried. "We're worshipping."

"Worshipping what?" Wulf asked her.

"Oh, everything. We'll dance. Come dance with me."

"Maybe in a while." He looked to where the Cahena had dismounted, people clustering to fall down and touch masked faces to her shadow. Her hands waved greetings. Suddenly all fell back to the sides of the street.

"There'll be a play," Daphne said. "A show, look!"

Women ran and screamed. They were pursued by long-robed men with turbans wound Moslem fashion. Other men rushed out to face these. That party wore hooded Djerwa capes. They threw toy javelins made of reeds, with feathers for points. The men impersonating Moslems fell and lay as if dead. A thunder of applause went up.

Daphne was gone. Djalout drifted close to Wulf.

"It's good to see them happy in their worship," he said.

"Somebody said they worship everything," said Wulf.

The music of flute and drum rose cheerfully.

"Perhaps not everything," Djalout said. "I doubt if you'll hear many addresses to Yahweh or Jesus, certainly none to Allah. There are plenty of older gods to invoke."

Someone with a long-beaked bird mask hurried past.

"Maybe those beast-headed gods came all the way from Egypt," Djalout was saying. "Yonder went something like Thoth, though probably not so well educated. The dog-headed one over there might hark back to Anubis."

The Cahena stood in front of a shop, smiling to her people. Couples formed in the street and moved to the music.

"I don't see anyone with a bull's head," Wulf remarked.

"And you won't, and don't say the name. Nobody wants to be reminded of that one, including me."

Daphne ran up, the hideous mask on her face again. "You said you'd dance with me," she hailed Wulf, and caught his hand and led him into the maze of posturing, stamping celebrants.

The music twittered and swirled. Wulf did not find it difficult to dance. He had often danced in other parts of the world. He and Daphne stepped it out face to face, swung around each other back to back, then face to face again. He saw the Cahena watching, not smiling now. At last he bowed himself away and headed for his cave again. Daphne was disappointed, he guessed. Surely the Cahena was not disappointed that Wulf had left the dance.

At home, he mended a worn bridle rein. A servingwoman brought him bread and goat's cheese and a vase of milk. He ate with good appetite. As he finished the last morsel and drained the last drop, Mallul walked in to say that the Cahena required his presence at a council.

He found her sitting in the big chamber with Ketriazar and Daris and two Djerwa subchiefs. Zeoui of Bhakrann's scouting party stood at attention to make a report. He told of being in wrecked Carthage, pretending to be a volunteer for the Moslem army. Hassan had addressed a mob of recruits to say that conquering the Imazighen—Maghrabi, Hassan had called them—would give the victors a whole generation of beautiful women. "Like the houris of paradise," Hassan had promised. Listening, Ketriazar and Daris and Wulf looked at one another, then at the Cahena, who was so beautiful.

"If they wait for women until they beat us, they'll go womanless forever," vowed Ketriazar at last. "Lady Cahena, what did Lartius promise you up at Cirta?"

"Twelve thousand men," she replied. "With what we can raise, that should be enough to beat this Hassan, this so-called good old man."

"You're sure, Lady Cahena?" asked Daris.

"I'll make sure. You can watch. Zeoui, go back to Bhakrann. Say that I thank him for the good spy work he's doing."

Zeoui departed. The Cahena rose.

"I'll make sure," she said again. "I'll call the spirits to tell me." She pointed to a black curtain at the far corner. "Mallul, go and lift that."

Mallul crossed the floor and tucked the curtain up. Wulf saw a deep shelf cut in the rock, set with faintly twinkling objects.

"Come close," said the Cahena.

They followed her to the shelf. She knelt at a brazier on the floor, scraped flint and steel for a spark to kindle a clutch of broken twigs. When it blazed up, she put on kindling, then handfuls of charcoal. They watched as a red glow was born, sending up a writhing thread of vapor.

"And now," she said, so softly that Wulf barely heard her. She had taken a skin pouch from the shelf and from it tweaked powder to throw into the brazier. Green flame sprang up around the edge.

"And now," she said again, and threw in another pinch. Red fire rose within the ring of green. A whisper came into the air, as of stealthily chanting voices.

The fire gave light to show the figures on the shelf. They were small, crudely modeled images of dried clay, with animal heads. One had a dog's head, one a boar's head, and so on. Wulf saw no bull's horns to be an image of Khro.

The Cahena cast in yet more powder. White, dazzling fire shot high at the center of the brazier. Its light showed more of the things on the shelf. At one end stood a rough model of a seven-branched candlestick. A crucifix of dark wood, with the white figure spread against it, hung on the rock at the opposite end. Judaism and Christianity, their symbols among the collection of gods.

The Cahena bowed above the brazier. The colored lights played on her face. The whispers were there, all around her. She, too, spoke, but Wulf did not hear her words. The green and red and white flames sank, and abruptly they died. The Cahena lowered the curtain over the images, and they all went back to sit on the cushions.

"We'll win," she said. "They said that we will."

"Is it to be a bloody battle?" asked Ketriazar.

"Yes, and many will die in it."

"Hai!" grunted Ketriazar. "Will I die in it?"

"Not you," the Cahena assured him. "Nor you either, Wulf."

"Shall I die?" asked a young subchief of Ketriazar's following, a sinewy, brown-bearded man named Uchia.

The Cahena stared at him. "Many will die," she said again, without answering the question. "But many will live and win."

She said it assuredly, as she might have said that the morning sun would rise in the east, off in the east where invasion gathered.

"We'll win," she said again. "They'll run, those who are lucky enough to be able to run." Her bright eyes were confident. "That's all for now. But stay here, Wulf."

The others bowed to kiss her lamplit shadow and went out. Wulf stood there and she stood before him. She took his hand in hers. She was as sure of him as she was sure of that victory to come.

She led him to the inner chamber. In the high moment of their embrace, she sang in his ear, "Wulf, Wulf."

Later, passion gentled, they lay side by side and she said, "We belong to each other." Wulf silently wondered about belonging. That meant possession, ownership. Did she own him, did he own her? All that he could think was that no woman he had ever loved had been like her. No woman could be like her.

She had said that he had come to her at the command of the spirits she talked to. Maybe that was true. Spirits must be everywhere, trying to talk to living people, and she knew the gift of hearing them.

"I want you to teach me Arabic," she said.

"Yes," he promised.

Next morning was foggy, but Wulf called the men of Tiergal and nearby settlements for drill. Jonas was there, and Wulf's men Susi and Gharna, all with javelins and a larger spear each, all with cudgels to practice swordplay. Djalout watched, heavily cloaked against the damp, leaning gracefully on his staff. Wulf formed the men three deep, the first rank kneeling, the second crouching, the third standing erect. At his command they slanted the big spears forward, butts rammed into the earth. They made a formidable hedge, those keen-pointed, deadly spears. Other ranks stood behind, javelins ready to throw. Wulf took them out of formation, brought them back again and again. They moved and took position well. They learned.

Afterward, there was fencing with cudgels. Jonas and several others were proficient, could serve to train smaller groups. The men liked the exercise and called for Wulf to fence with them. Smiling, he took a length of touchwood and competed with one after another, disarming them, threatening blows on head or elbow. They cheered him loudly. He was their master at arms; they loved him and at the same time feared his great strength, his dismaying skill. Later they threw javelins at targets, far better than he could have done.

When they sweated despite the morning chill, Wulf dismissed them and told them to report tomorrow. He and Djalout walked away.

"You teach them to kill," said Djalout, his smile in his beard. "To kill horses that don't deserve it, to kill men who sometimes do. How does that fit your peaceful Christianity? You're a Christian, I believe."

"A sort of loose one," said Wulf. "Yet Christ said he didn't bring peace on earth, but a sword."

"I know, I've read your gospels. But he spoke figuratively, religiously."

"The Moslems are religious enough about it," Wulf reminded. "They spread faith by the sword. They'll kill you if you don't accept their Allah."

"True." Djalout nodded. "Come have the noon meal with me."

They ate almonds, dried dates and figs, and barley bread with honey, and drank good wine. Afterward Wulf went to the Cahena's council chamber, where she and Mallul sat to learn Arabic. He taught them numbers from one, *wah,* up to a thousand, *alf.* He made them say simple words for hot and cold and fire and water and so on. Both were quick at learning a new language, though not so quick as Wulf himself.

"What's the word for surrender?" asked Mallul. "The command to surrender?"

Wulf told him, and Mallul repeated it. "I'll make them surrender to me," he vowed.

"Another lesson tomorrow, after I've drilled the men," promised Wulf.

The damp autumn passed in such exercises, and winter set in, chilly and sometimes heavy with clouds. Fires burned in the houses, the people wore heavy, hooded capes. Wulf repeatedly inspected the storehouses of grain and other provisions. He made a trip southward to Ketriazar's town, a place mostly of heavily woven tents with leaves and branches piled on the roofs. Ketriazar took Wulf to see his stark Mediuni warriors drill at planting spears for a hedge against cavalry, at throwing javelins, at riding headlong in attack formations. Gaunt, bushy-bearded Daris was there, too.

"My men work like yours," Daris said to Ketriazar. "They're trained to a hair."

"We could whip those Moslems tomorrow," declared Ketriazar.

"I'd say we need sixty or ninety days more," said Wulf.

The three ate supper in Ketriazar's tent, chunks of a roasted wild hog with an alelike brew of fermented grain. Ketriazar gnawed a rib and studied Wulf appraisingly.

"You organize and train well," he said. "The Cahena did right to make you a chief. What do you and she do these days?"

"I'm teaching her Arabic," replied Wulf.

"I'll wager that she learns well. She does all things well."

Wulf was back at Tiergal the following day, as another of Bhakrann's scouts reported. He said that he had gone all the way into the smashed streets of Carthage, and that Hassan was receiving reinforcements from Moslem strongholds to the east. Fine Arabian horses had been brought by ship. There were mountains of food and trains of camels to carry it.

"They talk as if they'd already beaten us," said the scout.

"Confidence is good in moderation," said the Cahena. "But overconfidence can mean disaster. True, Wulf?"

"That's always been true, Lady Cahena," said Wulf.

Glowingly she smiled at him. "Not an original observation, but a true one," she said. "Have you time to give Mallul and me a lesson in Arabic?"

With each lesson she and Mallul grew more proficient, and began to talk Arabic to Wulf and to each other. And she called Wulf to her now and then, to make love. It was always she who called. He kept himself from making an advance. He wondered what she would do if he made one.

Winter went on, now crisp, now soggy. The men of Tiergal and nearby villages drilled in all weathers, began to act like veterans. Everyone had a good sheaf of javelins, and some had captured Moslem swords. The Cahena kept couriers on the trails to her chieftains, carrying and bringing back news. Scouts rode in from time to time, with Bhakrann's reports on the great mustering of the enemy around Carthage's remains, Moslems from many nations, all the way to Persia. The Moslems prayed and prayed for victory.

So did the Djerwa in Tiergal.

Djalout accompanied Wulf to a sort of service held in the home of professed Jews, with kneeling listeners and a gaunt-faced man struggling to say some sort of ritual. Smiling, Djalout stepped forward to conduct the service himself. He quoted from what Wulf recognized as a psalm of David: "You will make them turn their back; you will make ready with your bowstrings against their face." When he had finished, the listeners loudly thanked him.

Outside, the Cahena joined them and they entered another house. The people gathered there were pattering prayers to a whole battalion of images. When they saw the Cahena they fairly howled welcome and prostrated themselves to kiss her shadow.

"Make your hearts strong," her voice rang out. "Be ready with your weapons. Where's a javelin?"

One was put into her hand. She carried it to the curtained doorway. "Here!" she cried. "Let this find their hearts!"

Fiercely she thrust the javelin into the open, brought it back and let the curtain fall again. "See!" she cried to them.

The javelin's head ran with blood. It dripped from the lashings. The onlookers moaned their awe.

"Be strong," she said again. "We'll win, my voices tell me."

In the street, Wulf asked, "How did you do that?"

She smiled her smile. "I just did it, Wulf. Don't you believe in my magic?"

"I have to," he said, with an air of confession.

Spring came, with early, rugged-seeming wildflowers, with new leaves on the trees, with blossoms foretelling fruits and nuts. The days grew warm, balmy, bright.

Bhakrann reported to the Cahena in her council room. Lamplight made bloodred sparks in his beard as he told of Hassan's marshaling of his forces. There were swarms of mounted warriors, columns of camels to carry supplies. Hassan had proclaimed the blessing of Allah and of the caliph in Damascus on his host, had named a day for the march westward.

The Cahena sat up on her cushions. Her eyes flashed like knives.

"I'll name the day for our own advance," she said ringingly. "We'll meet this good old man Hassan. Start messengers to all our chiefs, and to Lartius at Cirta. They must start at once. They'll meet us Djerwa—say a day's ride eastward from here. What place do you say, Bhakrann?"

"At that distance there's the valley called Chaiuta," said Bhakrann promptly. "Springs and a stream there, groves of trees."

"I know Chaiuta." The Cahena nodded. "There's a tomb there; nobody knows who's buried in it. We'll assemble here, move out as quickly as we can. Start those messengers at once."

XII

Two busy days and most of their nights were spent at gathering and organizing for the march to the rendezvous.

The Cahena directed everything efficiently. A squad of messengers hurried here and there with her orders. Wulf admired those orders, clipped and decisive, and he admired the promptness with which they were obeyed. Sinewy, hairy fighting men rode in from all the Djerwa communities, rode in on hardy horses, each man with what armor he had, with his sheaf of javelins. The Cahena assigned these contingents to camp tracts around Tiergal. Their subchiefs kissed her shadow and saw that her directions were obeyed. The area filled.

Trains of camels were assembled to carry bales of supplies. Some of the camel drivers were women and boys. Warriors were divided into thousands, more or less. The thousands were divided in turn into hundreds, each hundred with a self-important minor leader.

Women loudly insisted that they would follow the host. Those who would stay mostly had young children. Wulf ordered his own female servants to stay in charge of his cave. He thought that the Cahena disapproved of such a jumble of camp followers, but she did not forbid it. One who would go was Daphne, whose father, Jonas, commanded a pickup company of archers.

"What if the Moslems captured you?" Wulf asked Daphne.

"Let one come within range." She smiled, showing him a bow and quiver. "He'll wake up in wherever his paradise would be. I've used a bow ever since I was a little girl."

Djalout, too, would join the host. He chose a sturdy mule to carry him. "I'll be needed," he said to Wulf. "You'll see that. And a spring jaunt ought to stir up my old blood."

Wulf took both his war-horses. His servitors Susi and Gharna rode unshowy Imazighen mounts of their own.

The stars had barely winked out in a dim gray dawn as the Cahena formed her warriors of the march. All were mounted, and she mustered them in three long columns of fives, every man with two days' rations in his saddle wallets. The baggage camels formed other long columns behind. Women rode donkeys and mules and scrubby little horses.

The Cahena started at the front, with Wulf and Mallul and Bhakrann with her. Mallul flourished the red war banner for the march to begin. Bhakrann rode along the columns, calling out men he knew and trusted to trot out and form a line of scouts. Returning, he fell in beside Wulf. "If you like war, you'll like what's coming," he said.

"I don't particularly like war," said Wulf. "It never really proves anything."

"This one will prove that the Moslems can't beat us."

"You're sure of that," said Wulf.

"Isn't the Cahena sure? Look at her. She knows what these invaders are planning, knows it before they know it themselves, and she knows how to stop them."

Now and then a halt was called, to rest the horses. At noon the marchers nibbled food from their wallets. The warm sun slid low behind them as they came to the place where the Cahena had ordered her other forces to join them.

It was a spacious depression in the slope, with a sizable stream running its length and smaller rivulets feeding in. There were tufts and belts of trees, clumsy growths of cactus, which the camels ate, thorns and all. The Cahena posted guards at the smaller streams, to keep them to draw from for cooking and drinking, while the larger course would serve to water the animals and for bathing. Susi and Gharna found a camping spot well away from any stream and picketed the horses. Other groups of men made fires and cooked. Their gatherings reached as far as Wulf could see. The most distant of them looked like groups of tiny ants. Horses and camels were haltered to stakes.

Wulf, picking up firewood, suddenly straightened and stared. Up the slope and not too far away stood a sort of obelisk of plastered brown and gray stones, twice the height of a tall man, with a foundation almost twice its height in width. "What's that?" he wondered aloud.

"An old tomb," said Djalout beside him. Djalout seemed cheerful, almost jaunty, as though the day's ride had agreed with him.

"Whose tomb?" Wulf asked.

"Who am I that I should know? Let's go look."

They walked over together. The tomb was ancient, Wulf could see, incredibly ancient. Djalout pointed with his staff to a picture on the base, crudely but strongly chiseled into a broad stone.

"See that, Wulf? Something with wheels, horses drawing it, a man driving —a chariot. Once the Imazighen had chariots, I wonder how many lifetimes ago."

Wulf studied the picture. It was primitive but lively. The horses galloped. Almost, it seemed, the wheels turned. "The Imazighen must have been more civilized back then," he ventured.

"Yes. They had powerful princes and ruled this whole southern shore of the inland sea. They grew wheat for the whole Roman empire—no wheat these days, at least not around Tiergal. The Romans were glad to have them as allies sometimes, though other times they cheated and massacred them. When the Vandals were here, the Imazighen fought them." Djalout looked up at the spire. "I wonder who's buried here. We might dig for his bones, but that might be bad luck."

"You believe that?" asked Wulf.

"Well, I consider it. I consider everything."

Wulf studied the chariot picture. If the Imazighen had chariots now, would they help in this war? Something else was carved there, something ahead of the galloping horses, half obliterated by time. He bent to see better. Yes, a fleeing figure, on two striding legs like a man—but with the horned head of a bull. He pointed.

"Look. That chariot's after something that looks like Khro."

Djalout glanced quickly and turned away. "Don't say that name, Wulf. Now, may I invite myself to supper with you?"

They went back to where Susi stewed couscous and strips of smoked pork. Wulf poured from an earthen wine jug for all of them. Bhakrann joined them to accept a bowl of stew, a cup of wine. In the last light of day, the red glints were in his beard.

"I keep remembering what I heard in Carthage," he growled. "Hassan promising his men Imazighen women. He thought I was a volunteer. He made that promise to me." A fierce clearing of Bhakrann's throat. "I wish I could kill him with my own hand, the way I killed Okba."

"You like to kill," said Djalout, spooning stew.

"Yes, I like to kill," said Bhakrann. "Wulf says he doesn't, but he kills mighty well."

A shadow in the dim evening, there by their fire. The Cahena had come, silently, unexpectedly, as usual. Bhakrann and Susi and Gharna fell down to kiss her shadow. Wulf rose to face her. Djalout sat and stroked his beard.

"The other musters will be coming," the Cahena said to Wulf. "Where shall we camp them?"

She sat beside him. He took a twig and sketched in the dirt for various positions near the smaller streams. She looked at the diagrams and asked questions.

"We'll camp Lartius and his Cirta people here next to us," she said. "Close enough for me to inspect, maybe make a speech to them."

"Speech?" echoed Wulf, and he must have sounded stupid, because both Djalout and Bhakrann laughed.

"You've heard her speak," said Bhakrann. "When she speaks, people listen and obey. They follow her into the mouth of hell."

"You think there's a hell?" drawled Djalout.

"Yes," Bhakrann snapped. "I've been there in my time and back here again, and it's better here than there."

"This is enough talk for tonight, I think," said the Cahena.

Off at a level space upstream, a fire had been built. It glowed pinkly there.

Then rose the sound of instruments beside it. Drums beat a steady rhythm and some sort of flute or pipe joined in, shrill and weird.

"They're going to dance the blood dance," said Djalout. "A dance of prayer for victory."

"Who does it?" asked Wulf.

"Young women dance it, and warriors watch," said Bhakrann. "It hasn't been danced for years—no occasion for it. Let's go watch."

All rose and headed for the fireglow, the squall and thump of music.

"Do you know about this dance?" Wulf asked Djalout.

"Just that it's ancient among the Imazighen. Symbolic in some way that's hard to understand. Here we are, and a big circle of watchers."

Men ringed the fire, some squatting, others standing behind the squatters. In the firelight sat girls and young women, a dozen of them in patterned robes with hoods over their heads and faces. To one side male musicians beat painted drums while one drew wild strains from his flute. A woman entered the open space by the fire. Wulf recognized her as one of the Cahena's servants. She began to sing, and the audience of men clapped hands in time to the music. The woman pointed to a sitting girl, who rose to her knees and began to gyrate her body.

She moved lithely, her bare arms twisting like snakes, her hooded head darting forward and from side to side. So swiftly did she fling herself about that the hood slid from her dark hair, her pretty oval face. The mistress of ceremonies waved for her to subside, and another dancer performed. The music grew faster, the hand clapping speeded up. Again a hood dropped, and a third dancer went into wriggling motion on her knees. At last only one was left, and she stood erect and shook her hood down. It was Daphne, all smiling, her bright hair in disarray.

The onlookers raised joyous shouts. The music drummed and skirled. Daphne threw her cloak aside and stood there in a flimsy shift of light blue cloth. She danced, her sandaled feet flickering, her body swaying and undulating.

"Hai, hai!" Wulf heard Bhakrann yell, all enthusiastic approval.

Daphne postured, ever more agile, more alive. She shuddered with her whole body. Her hands flew to her shoulders, she whipped off the shift and danced in her nakedness. She was pinkly, chubbily symmetrical. Her opulent breasts tossed like billows. Clapping hands made an accompaniment that drowned the music.

The other dancers rose, tossed off their garments, joined in. There was a whole rhythmic spectacle of bare flesh, a drawing together in a bounding jumble, a spreading out into a living frieze of motion. All the dancers were pretty. They were such prizes as Hassan was said to have promised his Moslem warriors. The watchers struck hands together.

Then, abruptly, the music was silent, the dance stopped. The girls scrambled back into their clothes. Daphne glistened with sweat, as though she had run a race. The troupe ran out of the circle and into the dark.

Wulf headed back to his camp with Djalout and the others.

"What did it mean?" Wulf asked Djalout. "Blood dance, you called it, but I didn't see any blood."

"I think the name's symbolic," said Djalout. "Since they dance it before battles, maybe the beauty of the dancers reminds warriors what they're fighting for."

Wulf slept near his fire and awoke at first light. Susi and Gharna produced a breakfast of retoasted barley cakes and a pungent tea of herbs in boiling water. Afterward, Wulf walked out to campsite after campsite. He knew many of the warriors, and was glad to find them in good spirits. Daphne greeted him from among a group of women. Her nose was smutted from bending over a fire, but her eyes and smile were bright. He remembered her buxom nudity at the dance.

"Will you eat with us?" she invited him.

"I've eaten," he said. "I still think your father should have left you at Tiergal."

"He couldn't have done that, and neither could you." Boldly she eyed him up and down. "Wait, you'll be glad I came along."

Ketriazar and his Medusi arrived at midafternoon, and Daris's Neffusa just before sundown. The Cahena assigned them camping areas. The wide valley seemed to swarm with men and beasts. There was a council in front of the Cahena's low-pitched makeshift tent of brown cloth, with Ketriazar and Daris there, along with Wulf and Mallul and Bhakrann and Djalout. Scouts had brought word that Hassan was ready to start from Carthage.

"That's about ten days east from here," said Ketriazar. "When and where do we meet him?"

"Perhaps four days east from here," replied the Cahena. "If Yaunis and Lartius get here tomorrow, we'll start the morning after to meet Hassan. I want him beaten and well beaten."

"You'll have that, Lady Cahena," promised Ketriazar fiercely. "My men will go to this battle as to a feast."

"Mine, too," added Daris. "When can we expect Yaunis and Lartius?"

"Tomorrow," said the Cahena. "Yaunis, then Lartius. I see them coming, in my mind. Now, who's this?"

Zeoui interrupted, prostrating himself and then saying that the scouts had met a prowling stranger and were bringing him to account for himself. Two other warriors brought forward a lanky, youngish man with a short, dark beard and a hooded Imazighen cloak. He gestured protest as Zeoui accused him of spying.

"No, great lady and great chiefs, I'm a simple herdsman," he said in accented Imazighen. "I lived at the shore near Carthage. When Hassan, that

Arabian general, called for every man to join him, I got on my horse and ran away. I want to fight on your side."

The Cahena gazed at him. "What's your name?"

"My name's Barha, lady." He gulped nervously. "It was my father's name before me."

"Barha?" she repeated, her gaze burning upon him.

She took a twig from the pile of firewood and slowly drew a line in the sandy earth before her, then another line and another. Watching, Wulf saw that she made a figure like a skeleton. She studied it, then turned her eyes back to the man who called himself Barha.

"Is this a way to lie to queens?" she said, in the Arabic Wulf had taught her. "Isn't a lie hateful to your Allah?"

"I swear—"

"You're a Moslem and an Arab from Arabia," she cut him off. "You were sent to spy us out. Your true name is . . ."

Again she studied the skeleton figure she had drawn.

"Your name is Ali ibn Jafar," she pronounced. "A spy."

The fellow shook as he bowed almost to the ground.

"Lady, you have read me through and through," he quavered. "Nothing is hidden from you. Yes, I'm Ali ibn Jafar, in your hands. If you kill me, it's the will of Allah. But Allah is merciful."

Bhakrann scraped a laugh and dropped his hand to his hilt. "Lady Cahena, let me take off his head."

"No," said Ketriazar, teeth shining like a wolf's. "Let me."

"I speak here and decide here," the Cahena said coldly. "Did this man come on a horse? Give it back to him, let him go tell Hassan what he's spied out here. You Arab, what will you tell him?"

Ali ibn Jafar gestured, open-palmed. "That your men look ready and well armed."

"How many of us will you say?" was her next question.

The captive's eyes roamed over the great sprawl of camps. "Somewhere around twenty-five thousand of you."

"That's a good estimate," the Cahena said. "Bhakrann, go with him and see him safe through our lines."

"As you command," said Bhakrann glumly, and rose to depart with the scouts and the spy. The chiefs watched them go. At last Ketriazar spoke:

"Lady, your wisdom is great, but what wisdom was that?"

"Oh, I don't like to see unarmed, helpless men killed," she said. "Let him go and report what he has to report."

"Even our numbers here?" persisted Ketriazar.

"That's all right," put in Wulf. "He made his guess before Lartius and Yaunis got here. Hassan won't know about that reinforcement."

Ketriazar grimaced. "I didn't think," he confessed.

"No, you didn't," agreed the Cahena coldly. "Wulf thought. Wulf knew what was in my mind. It would do everyone good to learn how to think. Now you see, this Arab prowler will be of help to us, not to his own friends."

She closed her eyes. "Voices speak," she whispered. "I hear them—in Arabic." She looked up. "Will a good gift come to us from the enemy?"

The evening chill set in. Here and there was singing. Wulf heard the patter of drums, the minor wail of flutes, but not the wild music that had accompanied the dance of the women. He returned to his own fireside and slept with his feet to the warm glow and his cloak wrapped around him. Once he woke, because someone stood near him. The Cahena? No, Daphne, the smith's daughter. She stood silently for moments, then moved away.

Next morning, cattle and goats were cut up into steaks for the warriors. Yaunis and his men trotted in just after noon, were welcomed and assigned an area to unsaddle and camp. A scout came in to say that the Moslems were advancing from Carthage, a mighty host of them, with great camel trains of supplies. They were perhaps five days away.

"We'll march to meet them tomorrow," announced the Cahena. "What's keeping Lartius?"

Lartius arrived in the evening. His columns of horsemen wore finer garments than any of the other tribes, and Lartius himself displayed a fine coat of gold-mounted mail, which must have made him uncomfortably warm. With his personal retinue came two of his pretty servant-girls, and two pudgy, puffing eunuchs. He protested against marching the next day with but a night's rest for his followers, but the Cahena insisted and he fell silent.

In the first light of the next morning, the Cahena formed her army for a new advance.

XIII

The columns spread themselves, a hundred yards or so apart, and crept like great dark snakes. Their front reached miles, from horizon to horizon. Wulf, riding with the Cahena at the head of the Djerwa, looked right and left and reflected that never had he seen such a host. There must be thirty-five thousand men. Wulf had seen considerable military gatherings at Constantinople once or twice, but only in close-drawn, pretentious parades, never a purposeful going to battle across whole landscapes.

The Cahena's swift messengers headed here and there with orders. Lartius and his followers jogged next to the Djerwa. Once or twice Lartius made his way across at a summoning signal, to hear what the Cahena told him and to nod assent. Far ahead of the columns ambled the far-flung open line of Bhakrann's scouts, ever observing to where, at the east, Mount Arwa dwindled its slope toward level, grove-dotted open country.

They passed small villages of mud-plastered huts, where the inhabitants hailed them loudly. Several men in tattered tunics came on hardy horses to join them. There was a midmorning halt to rest the horses and mules and camels. Somebody told the Cahena that Lartius's men were drinking deep from skin bottles of wine and laughing raucously. The Cahena furrowed her brow as she listened.

"Ride over there, Wulf," she ordered. "Tell Lartius that wine drinking on the march must stop."

Wulf went. Lartius himself had a skin bottle to his lips. He shook his elegant head at Wulf.

"You're a good warrior and leader," Lartius drawled, drinking again, "but I'm chief of my people. I don't take orders from you."

"It's not my order," said Wulf evenly. "It's the Cahena's."

"Then I'll wait to hear it from her, not you."

"Come over to her with me," said Wulf, and Lartius did so. The Cahena spoke to Lartius apart. Wulf did not hear what she said, but apparently it was decisive. Lartius bowed acceptance and returned to his men to order no more wine drinking until camp was made.

There was a longer halt at blazing noon, and at midafternoon a short one again. Wulf dismounted to walk his horse part of the way. The Cahena sent him to visit the column from Cirta, to see that Lartius's followers left their wine bottles alone. Before sundown the whole widespread multitude was halted where there were scatterings of trees and brush, with springs here and there.

The warriors dug crude wells for more water, not too muddy for their beasts to drink. Wulf helped Susi and Gharna rub down the tired horses and picket them where there was grass. Djalout tethered his mule and dumped a roll of bedding next to Wulf's.

"The Cahena stopped drinking on the march, but we're not marching now," he said. "I've brought a jug of wine and a jar of honey."

Young Uchia, the Djerwa subchief Wulf remembered, also came to the fire where Susi toasted barley cakes and grilled strips of meat on green twigs. Uchia fairly beamed his excitement.

"War," he said, savoring the word. "I wasn't old enough for those wars the Imazighen used to fight among themselves, before the Cahena united us. I'm looking forward to my share of this fighting."

Wulf gazed at him and remembered that Uchia had asked if the Cahena foresaw his fate in the coming campaign, and that she had not answered the question.

"I hope you come out of it well," said Wulf. "We're having supper—will you join us?"

"I'll be honored."

Uchia sat down and ate heartily. "Where do we meet them?" he asked.

"I understand there's a river a day's march from here, a river the Moslems call the Nini," said Wulf. "Our scouts say it would be a good place to come face to face with them."

"Nini," said Djalout, dripping honey on a bit of barley cake. "Those Moslems keep giving their own names to our places. Maybe they think that gives them a title. Out there to the east there's Thrysdus, the old Roman town and circus arena. When the Moslems captured it, they started calling it El-Djem."

"Which I take to be the Arabic word for a council, a gathering," said Wulf.

"We'll scatter whatever gathering they've made there," declared Uchia. "Drive them out and take the place back."

Subdued songs rose from other camps. To Wulf, they sounded like hymns. Perhaps they were hymns, prayers to various gods. Supper was finished. Uchia thanked Wulf and departed to his own camp. Djalout and the others spread their bedding. As Wulf arranged his own couch, one of the Cahena's women came to tell him that her mistress asked him to come and join her.

He followed the woman to where the Cahena's small tent was pitched. "Come in," her soft voice called, and he entered and dropped the door-curtain behind him.

The ridge of the tent was no more than five feet above the ground, and he stooped beneath it. She sat on cushions, in her dark blue robe that clung so closely that he knew she wore nothing inside it. Her breasts stirred under the fabric. She took his hand strongly and drew him down beside her.

"Quick, quick," she whispered. "We don't have much time."

They hurried their lovemaking, were done, it seemed, before they had well begun. Afterward, she drew her robe back around her and sat and held his hand.

"I had to have you," she said, "to give me strength. Your strength is my strength. The voices I hear, they promised that."

Wulf kissed her long fingers. "I don't understand about those voices."

"I don't exactly understand them myself, but I've always heard them."

"Are they the voices of the dead?" he suggested.

"Who can tell? Don't the dead know everything? Maybe they're the voices of my ancestors. Or of spirits that don't exactly live or die like men and women. They say we'll beat the Moslems and drive them back all the way they've dared come. And we'll take from them something that will make us great. But now you must go. We can't be found here together. I wish you could stay all night, but go now. We march again at dawn."

As he tramped off in the dark toward his own fire, he felt as if he had been dismissed. She had needed him, had said she had needed him. But when lovemaking was done, when she needed him no more, she had told him to go. Obediently, he had gone.

But was it like that? She had said that they mustn't be found together, by some chance caller, some bringer of messages. She must hide her loves. Nobody must suspect. Did anyone suspect? Bhakrann? Wise Djalout? Wulf earnestly hoped not.

Lying down, he turned his mind to other things. He thought of young Uchia, so eager to go into battle and win. Wulf remembered his own first fight, long ago in his teens, somewhere in Frankish lands. He had looked forward to that adventure, but not as to a merrymaking. Wry, wise Abbot Hadrian, at home in England, had warned that war and violence were grim things, and he, Wulf, had learned at first hand that this was true. It would be true when they got hand to hand with Hassan's Moslems. Uchia would find out.

"Are you awake, Wulf?" came Djalout's voice from beyond the fire.

"Wide awake," said Wulf where he lay. "And so are you."

"Old men have a hard time sleeping. King Solomon notices that somewhere in his writings. I wondered what the Cahena told you."

Wulf grimaced to himself. "Why, as to that," he decided to say, "she's sure we'll defeat the Moslems. She spoke of her voices."

"And what are those voices?"

Wulf knew that Susi and Gharna were awake and listening. "She seemed to wonder if they're the voices of the dead," he replied. "She felt that the dead know everything."

"We won't know if they do until we're dead ourselves," said Djalout. "If we know anything then."

"Are you afraid of death, Djalout?"

"Me, at my age? If I'm to be afraid of death, I won't have time for anything but being afraid. If it so happens that I'm killed in this coming battle, I only hope it's quick and easy."

One of the others, Susi or Gharna, caught his breath sharply.

"Maybe death will be just a sound sleep," went on Djalout. "I'll try to sleep now. Conversation with you is always stimulating, Wulf."

Silence then. Wulf could not think of anything particularly stimulating that he himself had said. He thought of the Cahena, how silkily smooth was her skin, how soft was her voice, how abandoned her passion. Sleep came at last. It was sound sleep, such as Djalout half expected when life came to an end.

But he woke quickly, as usual, in gray dawn. Susi was building up the fire to toast barley cakes and heat water for herb tea. Gharna fussed with the horses. Djalout was up, too, talking to his mule. Wulf pulled on his boots and washed his face and hands in a pool of gritty water, then ate a hearty breakfast. He wiped his mouth and strode to report to the Cahena.

Her chieftains were there, Ketriazar and Daris and Yaunis and Lartius, listening to her orders.

"Choose all your best men on their best horses," she directed. "Form them in elements to ride ahead, make for that river, and form there ready for action. The slower companies will follow those faster ones and come to back them up."

"My slow riders will straggle," said Lartius.

"No they won't," the Cahena almost flung back. "Someone will bring up the rear and make the stragglers keep up."

"Who'll have that authority?" Lartius asked.

"You," she said at once.

His eyes started, his joined black eyebrows rose. "But I should be at the head of my men—"

"You'll keep the stragglers moving," she cut in. "If you can't, nobody can. We'll need every man in this coming fight."

Wulf listened. Who would think that she could be so assured at council and also so passionately tender at love, who but Wulf himself? Ketriazar spoke plaintively:

"Must I ride at the rear, too, Lady Cahena?"

"Not you," she said. "I know your Madusi people, you'll lead them and they'll keep up. The same goes for Yaunis and for you, Daris. Any more questions?" She waited, and nobody spoke. "All right, form up and start eastward."

The chiefs hurried away. Wulf waited. "Maybe you want me to be at the rear, to keep the elements closed up," he suggested.

She shook her head and smiled. How sweetly she smiled.

"You'll ride at the front," she said. "At my side. You'll comfort me by being near."

"And you'll comfort me," he felt compelled to say.

"Comfort," she echoed, almost inaudibly. "A beautiful word."

The columns formed across the stretch of the camping grounds. The sun was well above the far eastern horizon as they moved out. Wulf rode with the Cahena and Mallul in front of the first company of the Djerwa warriors. Those warriors looked ready. Wulf gazed to the men from Cirta at the left. Ahead of them rode someone in bright silver-mounted armor, on a black horse. He gestured importantly to those behind him. It wasn't Lartius; Lartius was behind the rearmost formations, where the Cahena had ordered him. Lartius would dislike that assignment profoundly. What would be the effect on his men from Cirta and his other towns?

They marched sometimes at a walk, sometimes at a trot, caring for the horses. Again and again scouts rode in to report no sign of the enemy as yet. There were occasional villages, scatters of houses with planted fields and fruit trees in blossom. As with the villagers yesterday, there were cries of welcome, of encouragement. The Cahena sent couriers to order several rest stops. At noon, as Wulf stood beside his horse and munched dried figs, Bhakrann trotted in from the east, dismounted, and spoke.

"They're coming," he said. "Not as fast as us—they stop and pray, five times a day."

"Yes," said Wulf. "At dawn, noon, midafternoon, sunset, and nightfall. That last comes when they make camp. Do their prayers take so long?"

"Throughout a march of days, quite a time. I've been right among them, I've bowed down with them so as not to attract any notice. But they're a big army, bigger than us, as I judge."

"The Cahena says we'll win, and so do I."

"You two should outnumber their Allah. Do you have any more of those figs? Thanks. It's been hard to pick up rations among the Moslems."

The afternoon was cloudy and the air somewhat close, but the advance kept on. Wulf's hair and beard were damp with sweat. To judge by their horses, those were getting weary when, in the late afternoon, wide, bright water showed ahead.

"That river is where we'll meet them," said the Cahena. "The Nini they call it; I don't know the Imazighen name. I don't see them approaching over there. We'll halt here and form for any action, we pick the place to fight them."

The stream was broad and shimmery and, from the way a horseman splashed across, it was shallow and firm-bottomed. The horseman was Bhakrann, sweaty and hard-panting as he reined in beside the Cahena and Wulf. He pointed across the water.

"Look there," he bade them.

The land beyond was fairly level, with coarse grass in bunches and tufts of timber. In the distance stirred a dark mass of movement.

"There they are," wheezed Bhakrann. "I was among them. I've been there so many times that Hassan knows me, thinks I'm one of them—once he saluted me as a friend. I heard him give orders that they ride to that opposite bank in battle formation and stop for the night, staying in their saddles."

"He's a fool," said the Cahena. "We'll dismount to wait."

"He promised them victory," went on Bhakrann. "I rode here as if I were his scout, then I outran other scouts and came to tell you."

The Cahena hurried messengers to order all elements of her force to halt a hundred yards or so from the river and to call the chieftains to her. Those chieftains came at a gallop and dismounted to kiss her shadow in the evening light. Wulf joined them in a group around her.

"We'll wait for their charge here, probably at first light," she announced. "Our line of spearmen on foot will sleep in formation, three deep. The mounted companies will camp behind them, unloose the saddle girths but not take the saddles off, and keep their weapons to hand. No fires anywhere, eat cold rations. And every fourth man will be on watch, with reliefs every two hours. I won't sleep at all myself, won't even pitch my tent."

"I won't sleep, either," Wulf volunteered.

"Nor I," said Daris. "Nor I, nor I," said Yaunis and Ketriazar.

"What shall I do with my archers?" asked Lartius.

"Group them at our far left, just behind the spearmen there," directed the Cahena. "The enemy won't have their shields to guard them from that angle. Send for Jonas; have him bring his archers to join those others."

She looked levelly at one chieftain after another.

"I suggest that everybody pray to whatever gods or spirits he worships," she said. "Send that word through the army."

All hurried away to do that.

Over across the river, the great blotch of the invading host had halted. It stretched left and right, as far as Wulf could see. The sun had set in the west. A tenseness crept into the dusk.

At the place where Wulf's camp was made, Djalout spread his bedding.

"Prayer, she's said, to any kind of god," said Djalout. "Do you pray?"

"Do you?" asked Wulf, without answering the question.

"Which god should I pray to? I was born a Jew, I professed Islam, I went to Egypt and was a Christian there."

He stroked his beard as he spoke, and Wulf stroked his own.

"Jews, Moslems, Christians," Wulf said. "They all worship what once must have been the same ruler of heaven and earth. Maybe there's just one god for all those faiths, under different names."

"Where those faiths rule, yes." Djalout nodded. "But what about out here? What god listens out here?"

"I don't know," said Wulf. He raised his voice: "Susi, don't worry about my horse. I'll make a little tour before I turn in."

He mounted and rode at a walk along the great extension of the spearmen. There were thousands of them, their three close-ordered lines extending for two miles or so. Those of Lartius's command chattered together, somewhat nervously, and here and there one of them drank from his wine bottle that had been forbidden on the march. Beyond, with the line formed by Yaunis, there was less noise. He heard murmurs, as though of the prayers urged by the Cahena. He thought of what Djalout had said about gods. To whom, to what, should Wulf pray? He hadn't prayed since leaving Carthage.

Turning, he walked his horse back to where the Djerwa had taken possession.

Those spearmen had lain down side by side, muffled in cloaks, except for those on guard. A hundred yards or so behind the triple line were gatherings of horsemen, riders and beasts at rest. He saw young Uchia, some paces to the rear of the prone spearmen, sitting with hands clasped around his updrawn knees, his head sunk between his shoulders. Wulf smiled in the dark. There sat a tired young man, drowsing after the long march that had brought him to the battle he craved.

And Wulf saw something else, moving down the bank in the shadows behind Uchia, a something itself strangely shadowy.

Wulf stared. It was a something taller than a man, a gnarled, angle-jointed body of a something, that stooped to brood over Uchia. Its massive head sprouted great curved horns. It was Khro.

Khro, attention riveted upon Uchia. Selecting Uchia. Khro, with horns like the crescent moon, with a jutting bull-muzzle, with gauntly splayed shoulders, with uncouthly straddled legs. Light from somewhere in the sky picked up a glint in the fixed eyes.

Wulf sat his saddle and watched. The Minotaur must have been like that in its Cretan labyrinth, when Theseus groped his way to it and killed it. Might Khro be the ghost of the man-devouring monster Theseus had killed, risen here to do more evil? But Khro could be faced and driven. There had been the crude picture on the tomb at last night's camp, the horned thing running from the charioteer. On sudden impulse, Wulf rasped his sword out of its sheath. He twitched his rein and rode straight in.

For one moment he saw Khro plain, horrible. Then Khro went blurred, vanished before his eyes like a puff of smoke. Khro was gone, would not face Wulf, would not choose him for death. Khro had faded to somewhere else, to choose others.

Wulf shrugged his big shoulders to keep from shivering, and sheathed his sword again. He was safe from Khro, but many would die in the coming battle. Wulf mourned those deaths and wondered if Khro visited the Moslem array, singled out victims there.

He dismounted upslope from where his companions slept, and loosened his saddle girth and stroked the horse's head and spoke soothingly to it. The other horses slept, standing with planted hoofs, like the good saddle horses they were. Wulf slowly paced on foot, behind the lines of recumbent warriors.

He had said, with the Cahena, that he would not sleep that night. And he could not sleep now. How could he, when he had seen Khro on the prowl?

XIV

Wulf sat on tufty grass for a space, sat in the dark not far from Uchia, half sprawled in his sleep. The warriors lay in their lines. They did not stir. They might have been lines of dead, struck down where they had stood in battle. It might be like that tomorrow, if the Moslems prevailed.

Nobody made a sound. If the men on guard prayed as they had been ordered to, they did not pray aloud. Wulf thought again of what Djalout had said, how perhaps other gods ruled here than the civilized deities of Israel, Christianity, Islam. There was Khro, for instance, Khro the messenger of death, who might have been a god once, who now crept in the dark before a battle to choose those who would die.

What happened to gods when their peoples perished, or turned away after other faiths? Did gods die then? What had happened to the gods of Greece and Rome, of Babylon and Canaan, what about the three hundred and sixty grotesque idols at Mecca, one for every day of the Arabian year, before Mohammed cast them out? It might be unchancy to be a god when worship stopped, when prayers were chanted no more, when the odor of incense, of sacrificial blood died out of the air above the altar. In Wulf's England the church was strong, but here and there the people still built the Beltane fires, stayed awake all night to welcome midsummer, trembled in fear of the spirits out and wandering on the eve of All Hallows. And what about here, with the Imazighen bowing to gods of all sorts? How long could those gods live and prevail?

Wulf's eyes were wide awake in the night. He did not feel weary, not even when he got up on his feet and paced here and there. He looked off to where the Cahena must be awake, too, thinking of what dawn would bring. She knew, she said, that her people would triumph, that from the Moslem host would come a gift of help, of inspiration. She was sure of victory, and Wulf was sure, too. But the fight would be terrible, spreading far over the land, a greater battle than any he had ever seen, had ever imagined.

Wulf had said to Bhakrann that he did not love war, and he had said the truth. War was ugly. But when it came upon you, you'd better be good at it.

To pass that long night, anticipating and preparing, was an exercise in endurance. It was like wearing a way through rock. Wulf glanced to where Djalout slept, remembered that conversation about gods. The Christian

Deus, the Hebrew Yahweh, the Moslem Allah—all of them somehow the same to begin with, all of them versions of a spirit all-powerful and all-knowing, perhaps with a blizzard of beard, with hands that could hold the sun and moon and stars. Perhaps with a smile caught deep in that beard, with kind, understanding eyes. No need to tremble before such a presence. But here, Djalout had said, other gods reigned, obscure, grotesque, dubious. Would they, those strange and terrible ones, decide the victory tomorrow, the defeat tomorrow?

Wulf cursed the thought away. He would be fighting men, not gods or devils. Moslems were strong in war, but he had killed Moslems in his time and would kill Moslems when morning came. The Cahena had sworn that he, Wulf, would live through whatever happened. Uchia, slumbering yonder, had been given no such promise. And Khro had focused fatal attention upon poor young Uchia.

"You're awake," said Bhakrann, strolling up to stand beside Wulf. "So am I. You and I don't need to sleep before a fight."

Wulf had taken a leather bottle in his hand. "Have some wine," he invited, and Bhakrann took the bottle and drank, and Wulf had a swallow himself.

"There's an iron taste to your wine," Bhakrann said. "Many will taste iron pretty soon. I'm ready. I wish it was happening now."

Wulf strained his eyes to peer across the darkened river. He saw red glows here and there—the enemy had campfires, while the Cahena's host lay in deep night. "I'm as ready as you are, Bhakrann," he said, "but I don't particularly look forward to it. I've come a long way across the world, fighting. It's lost whatever novelty it might have had when I started out twelve or thirteen years ago."

"You're bored with it," suggested Bhakrann.

"Not exactly. I'd better not be bored when I'm going to have to fight for my life."

Bhakrann chuckled. "You've been seeing too much of Djalout," he said. "You're beginning to talk like him. Now, I'm going to walk around here and there. Care to come along?"

They strode, side by side, between the close-drawn triple rank of sleeping spearmen and the silent bivouac of men and horses up the bank to the rear. Here and there moved javelin-bearing men on guard, craning their necks to look beyond the river.

"Our Djerwa will fight to win," said Bhakrann. "What do you expect from all those city people with Lartius?"

"I'll have to wait and see," replied Wulf. "Anyway, he brought archers, and maybe they'll do something. The Cahena sent the few archers from Tiergal to form up with the ones that Lartius brought. Jonas is with them."

"And so is his daughter Daphne," said Bhakrann. "She's a fine-looking young woman, have you noticed?"

"I have."

Wulf fancied he heard a murmur of voices somewhere. He had heard that sort of murmur before, when the Cahena had called it up in her inner cave at Tiergal. He frowned. Did he imagine it?

"We'll win," he said fiercely, to Bhakrann and all the world. "Whip them, show them a quick way back from here. The Cahena says so."

Bhakrann showed his teeth in a smile. "You believe what she says about it, then?"

"Yes," said Wulf.

"You believe everything she says about anything?"

"Yes."

"Then you've become an Imazighen," said Bhakrann. "A Djerwa. I believe, too. We'll win, and you and I will live to see it."

Djalout's talk about deities here in their own land—Wulf remembered that talk.

" 'Happy he who knows the country gods,' " he quoted aloud. " 'Pan and old Sylvanus and the sisterhood of the nymphs.' "

"What did you say?" asked Bhakrann.

"It was Virgil who said it," replied Wulf. "I read it in his *Georgics.*"

"That's right, you can read. I told you I couldn't."

Wulf smiled, feeling relaxed for the first time that night. "Maybe when this war business is over, I'll teach you your letters."

They dawdled along to the flank of the Djerwa formation. A young officer of Lartius's following met them and asked what they thought the morning would bring. A mounted scout came to join them. It was Zeoui. He reported that he had been across the river and that the Moslems were waking up.

"They're forming in three big bunches," said Zeoui. "They're thicker than fleas on a goat and a lot more dangerous. They'll try to hit us all along our line."

"We'll be ready," said Bhakrann, and he looked up at the stars. "It's almost morning. You from those Cirta people, better go get them on their feet. Tell them not to be any more afraid than they can help."

The officer headed away. "Look after your own men and their fears," he said over his shoulder.

Wulf made swift strides back toward the center of the Djerwa position. The Cahena was there, surrounded by aides. He knew her robe-draped outline, even in the dark.

"I know what they'll try to do, and where," she said when Wulf told the news brought by Zeoui. "Their middle force will come straight across here." Her eyes were bright in the darkness, her face seemed to be carved skillfully, nobly, out of stone. "Get the men ready," she said.

Wulf shouted orders. He heard Uchia and other subchiefs repeat them, all the way left and right. The dark shapes of the spearmen rose, holding their triple line. Wulf ran to his horse, tightened the saddle girth. "Good horse," he said, touching the sleek neck. He hurried into his mail jacket and put on the helmet Bhakrann had given him. Susi and Gharna readied their own mounts, slung their sheaves of javelins at their backs.

"The sun's coming up," Bhakrann roared somewhere. "They'll be coming up, too. Let's all get at least one of them apiece."

Rosy light showed far to the east. Wulf saw the great spread of the enemy force on the far shore of the stream. He reined over to take a leader's place in front of a ready formation of the Djerwa cavalry. Swiftly he slung his shield to his left arm and loosened his great sword in its sheath. Over yonder, the Moslems had drawn into great, clotted masses. Many Moslems, many.

"*Ulululallahu akhbar!*"

That war cry thundered up from thousands of throats. There they came, at a gallop. They were at the brink, they splashed across. The sun's bright rim had risen off there behind them. Wulf could see individual riders in the charge, close together, weapons flashing above their heads.

"*Allahu akhbar—*"

God is great, they yelled, they believed. Here they came, the crowd of them, straight at the waiting line.

"There is also the Cahena!" roared back the spearmen, into the hurrying faces of the enemy.

"Stand to it!" Wulf heard the excited cry of Uchia, there on foot with the triple line. Here came the rushing horses, and then up rose the stout, slanted spears, each with its butt driven hard into the soil, a sudden deadly hedge. And the horses came upon the points with a crash like falling timbers, and they screamed with agony as they impaled themselves.

Hoofs and heads and manes tossed. Gray, brown, and black bodies crashed down. Riders flew from their saddles. More riders clattered from behind, and the second and then the third lines planted their weapons to meet that headlong assault. Here and there the men on foot were borne down, but the charge had been thrown into a bloody confusion. Fallen men and horses built into a floundering wall. Rear elements stumbled and broke against it.

"It worked!" cried Wulf. "Now—"

He lifted his sword high and urged his war horse forward. Spearmen fell away to right and left before him, running to find their own mounts and join the counterattack. A wordless howl beat up from the men riding behind Wulf. He saw Uchia on foot to one side, and even as Wulf saw him Uchia went down under the frantic blow of a Moslem scimitar. Riding in, Wulf sped a swift slash and down went the slayer, across Uchia's body. Wulf put his horse to a mighty jump over two chargers that struggled in crippled pain on the ground, and drove in among the discomfited Moslems beyond.

Most of those were splashing back across the river, but some made a stand against him. He blocked a blow with his shield and slid his own point into the adversary's shaggy throat. "Ohoy!" yelled Wulf, the Saxon battle shout. His companions hurled javelins with deadly accuracy. Enemy riders swung away from that tumbled press of death and terror. They ran, they were demoralized. They fled across the river. Wulf led his men after them.

"There is also the Cahena!"

That was Bhakrann, cutting down a Moslem. Wulf, speeding past him, spared a look to the left. Over acres of ground, Moslems retreated. Lartius had managed to turn them back. It must be happening everywhere. Hassan's army, put to that overconfident charge, had been stopped, was being routed.

Wulf sent his horse churning across the shallow river. Here and there on the far side, Moslems held up their hands in token of surrender. Imazighen warriors snatched the weapons from such captives, pushed them from their horses, herded them toward the river, away from the battle that suddenly was not so much of a battle.

"Don't kill any prisoners," Wulf shouted to one group.

"We won't," came back a cheerful bawled assurance. "The Cahena says not to."

Others spurred to join Wulf. They rode toward a knot of Moslems that had stopped, trying to oppose the pursuit. Wulf was the first to charge into that party, hewing as he charged. But he had ceased to be a commander, had become just a death-dealing warrior. Fighting thus, with one and then another, he had lost touch with the main aspect of the action. Anyway, the enemy was running again, and he checked his panting horse to watch. This battle, what was it all about? Why had these strangers come all the way from Carthage, come all the way from the east beyond, intruding into the very mouth of hungry death? Senseless, senseless. Now they ran. Senseless the battle had been, like all battles.

He and his followers reached a little cluster of farmhouses. Past that, the Moslems flogged their horses to a lathery sweat, with miles of level ground ahead, ground dotted with groves and strung with little streams. Up overhead soared vultures, their wings motionless in flight, looking for the dead meat provided them here. Wulf pressed his men after that retreating army. Wulf sweated, too. He steamed inside his mail and under his helmet, and his beard felt clammily wet. He spared a look to either flank. Moslems ran everywhere, except for those who would run no more, who lay motionless and waited for the vultures. The Cahena's forces harried the retreat.

The sun glowered, well up in the eastern sky. Wulf wondered how long this confused violence had gone on. He had been so murderously busy that it had seemed only moments. But he was tired with it; his horse was tired, too. Near at hand trotted a riderless gray horse, a big animal that could bear his weight. He caught its bridle and turned his own fagged beast over to Susi, who came up behind. He swung into the saddle of the gray. That was a handsome saddle, silver-mounted, it must have belonged to a Moslem officer.

Ahead of him, the pursuit had lagged somewhat. The wide level of ground was strewn with bodies, like sheaves of grain on a harvest field. He rode near two of them, lying on their faces with javelins jutting upward from their backs. Victorious Imazighen scurried here and there, plundering dead and captured Moslems of weapons, armor, purses. Bhakrann rode near Wulf and waved his sword, which ran red to its very hilt.

"I don't know how many I've killed," he said. "I don't count the ones who were running. By now, they're all running. Look up there, we've captured some of their supplies."

Yells of self-congratulation rose where a line of baggage camels had been overtaken, each beast laden with food. Wulf rode there, rummaged in a pannier, and brought out a scone of wheat bread. Gratefully, he bit into it. Beyond him he saw Lartius, exploring a captured bundle of dried fruits. Munching, he hailed Wulf.

"These Moslems didn't bring along any wine," he complained. "Too bad, my men are running low on wine."

"From what I could see, your force did very well against that attack," said Wulf, and Lartius smiled.

"Our archers more or less slaughtered them," he said. "Ours, and some from among the Djerwa. One of those was a young woman, a very handsome young woman. I think her name's Daphne."

"She's Grecian. Her father is an armorer among us, an archer, too."

Lartius ate a fig. "I wouldn't mind taking her with me to Cirta, to have in my household."

Wulf only half heard him. He looked ahead. Off in the distance, near a grove of scrubby trees, moved a horse with a man walking beside it.

"Who's that?" he wondered aloud, and shook his reins and rode to see.

Trotting briskly, he narrowed the distance. Neither that horse nor that man moved faster than a walk. Both must be weary. Closer, and Wulf saw that the man wore a white turban. A Moslem, then, an enemy, left behind by the retreat of his fellows. Wulf kicked his horse's flank to make it canter and closed in, sword in hand.

"Surrender!" he shouted in Arabic.

The man dropped the rein of his horse and turned. He was slim and young, with a rich scarlet cloak. He wore a gold brooch at the front of his turban. His pointed beard was like black silk. He drew a scimitar that shone like silver, and fell on guard.

Wulf reined in at close quarters, leaned, and with a flick of his own blade sent the scimitar bounding and flashing across the grass-tufted earth. He swung out of his saddle.

The young Moslem flung out his slim, empty hands, palms up.

"I am Khalid ibn Yezid al-Kasai," he said. "A companion of General Hassan ibn an-Numan, an officer of his army. Go on and kill me. I'm not afraid to die."

XV

Wulf smiled in his sweaty beard. He felt like smiling. Far away to the east the rout of the Moslems was being harried, and he found himself relaxed, the easiest he had felt all morning. At the girdle of the young man he spied a jeweled dagger hilt, and, still holding his sword ready, he shot out his left hand and drew away the weapon. It was beautifully keen. Quickly he bent and shoved it into the top of his boot.

"Why should I kill you?" he asked genially. "I've never yet killed a helpless man. No, you're my prisoner."

"You savages kill, I know that," said Khalid ibn Yezid. "Go on and kill me. It's the will of Allah."

Wulf laughed aloud and shook his helmeted head. "It's not my will. And we don't kill prisoners. Our queen says not to do that."

"Your queen, your sorceress." Khalid's white teeth showed. "Your demon-obeying enchantress. I've heard about her. She must have used black magic to win today."

"If it was magic, it wasn't black magic." Again Wulf looked to where distant horsemen harried other distant horsemen. "Khalid, you call yourself. That's the name of a great Arabian champion."

"Khalid ibn an-Walid, the sword of Islam. I'm his namesake, a close relation to his family." Khalid drew a long, unhappy breath. "If you won't kill me, what will you do with me?"

He had lowered his hands to his sides; he wavered on his feet. He was young, exhausted, unhappy. Wulf walked to where Khalid's fallen scimitar lay and picked it up. It was a beautiful weapon, its blade engraved with its owner's name in Arabic, and not a fleck of blood on it. Plainly Khalid had done no serious fighting. Wulf tucked the scimitar under his arm and faced Khalid again.

"We'll go to headquarters," he said, and looked at Khalid's horse, standing with lowered head. "Get up and ride, Khalid. You can't get away. Your poor beast can no more than walk with you."

Khalid listlessly mounted the sagging beast. Wulf noted that under Khalid's rich robe was a richer coat of gold-flecked mail, and that gold tassels dangled from the toes of his handsome red boots. Wulf wiped his own big blade on the hem of his cloak, which was already blood-spotted, and swung into his own saddle. Susi joined them, leading Wulf's other horse. Wulf pointed back to where men gathered around the captured baggage camels. The Cahena's red banner rose among them.

"We'll report there," said Wulf.

Susi led the spare horse on the far side of Khalid as they headed back, and Wulf examined the captured scimitar. It balanced beautifully in the hand. "A splendid weapon," he said to Khalid, sticking it back inside his belt.

"It's mine no longer," mourned Khalid as they approached the red banner.

The Cahena directed the unloading of some of the sulky camels, but told drivers to send most of the beasts forward with their burdens. "We'll distribute some rations here, but we'll need more with the pursuit," Wulf heard her say. "Where's a messenger? Send to Lartius and Yaunis, let them look out for captured supplies. Any gold we find is to be brought here to me."

She looked up as Wulf and Khalid dismounted. Wulf knelt and touched his face to her shadow, then stood up. He knew that he was rumpled and sweaty, that his clothes were blood-splashed, that he was hardly a courtierlike figure.

"Well, Wulf?" she prompted crisply, as though they had never lain in each other's arms. "Who's this with you, a captured enemy?"

She had discarded her cloak and stood in her blue and white gown. It clung to the sweat domes of her breasts, to the lyre curve of her hips. Khalid stared at her lovely face. Then he, too, prostrated himself and kissed her shadow.

The Cahena looked down at him. "Who is he, Wulf?"

"An Arab of the Arabs, Lady Cahena," said Wulf. "He calls himself Khalid ibn Yezid, one of Hassan's officer-companions."

"Get up," the Cahena commanded Khalid in her halting Arabic. "You've picked up Imazighen manners quickly."

Khalid rose, quite gracefully. Again he gazed at her.

"Nobody told me of the Queen Cahena's beauty," he said.

She understood that, at least partially. "You're a handsome young man yourself," she said. "And a Moslem officer, an Arab."

"Of the Koreish, the tribe of our prophet Mohammed."

Narrowly she studied him. "Put him with those other officers we've captured," she said. "Maybe I'll talk to him when there's time for talking."

A guard marched Khalid away. He looked back at the Cahena. She turned her attention to Wulf.

"You look as if you've been bloodily busy," she remarked. "Are you wounded?"

"Only tired, Lady Cahena. I confess that I forgot my duties as a commander. I got into the fighting like any other warrior."

"Yes," she agreed. "You planned our fight, then you left me to direct things. Things have gone well without you."

But she smiled to say it, and how perfect her teeth were, how red her lips were. "We'll press on, all along the line," she said. "Fifteen miles east there are streams and springs, Bhakrann says, and our horses and men will need to drink. These camels will follow more slowly. Go over there with Djalout, Wulf. You and he are the wisest and best-educated men we have, and you two can make some sort of record of those supplies."

With that, she walked away, giving orders to subchiefs and sending messengers here and there.

Djalout stood with a sheet of parchment spread against the saddle of his patient mule. In one hand he held a wooden inkstand, and with a pen in the other he made lines of figures on the parchment. Wulf talked to men in charge of the camels and repeated to Djalout numbers of sacked wheat flour, roasts of beef and mutton, parcels of dried fruits. The Cahena paused beside the two of them.

"Our fighting men are moving ahead, slowly. See, it's noon or nearly; our men and horses will feel the sun. Follow me when you're done here and leave orders for these supplies and any others to follow you."

She smiled at Wulf almost conspiratorially as she rode away. Wulf looked up at the sun. It was almost overhead. Where had time gone since daybreak? He'd been too busy to notice its flight.

Djalout quickly completed his record, complaining that he had oversimplified. Wulf got on his horse and rode toward the front, with Susi and Gharna behind. The heat was oppressive, and they kept their horses at a walk. It was more than an hour before they overtook the Cahena and her aides. Ketriazar was there, briefly, to report that there was little opposition to the march of his tribesmen. The Cahena shaded her eyes with a slender palm to gaze eastward.

"We're chasing them everywhere," she said. "Find me couriers to tell the chiefs to keep the pursuit up, with men from behind to relieve the front elements and others to pick up all the plunder. Those Moslems are throwing away everything—arms, provisions—so as to ride faster. Let's keep after them, all along our advance."

"Well planned, Lady Cahena," said Wulf. "Brilliant."

She turned her smile on him. "I've listened to you and learned from you. Let's follow the battle along."

It had almost ceased to be a battle. The Cahena's warriors kept the enemy on the run, scooping in the slowest of them. At one grove of trees there was an effort to make a stand, plucky but futile. Well to the rear, patrons gathered spoils. They herded riderless Moslem horses away, loaded mules and donkeys with trophies. Other trains of camels were captured, with burdens of food and equipment.

The sweltering heat of the day passed, the sun sank away to westward. Bhakrann rode back from the front to say that twelve miles ahead was a low area, with water.

"We'll stop there tonight," said the Cahena. "Make camp, put out patrols, and pursue again at dawn tomorrow."

Messengers carried the Cahena's orders here and there. Wulf rode with her, looking eastward to what happened. The Imazighen horsemen advanced, advanced. Far in the distance were swirls of action, where Moslems tried to fight back. Guards herded leashes of disconsolate prisoners away. Several handsomely equipped Moslem officers were presented to the Cahena.

"We're not afraid to be killed," declared one gray-bearded man.

"I believe you," managed the Cahena in her halting Arabic. "But you won't die at our hands. Keep these officers together, you guards. I'll talk to them when I can find the time."

The pursuit went more slowly. The fleeing Moslems kept well away, except for some whose horses broke down. Those surrendered scowlingly, were brought back.

"What's to be done with these?" the Cahena asked Wulf.

"Keep the officers, but let the others go, the way you did when we fought them at the pass last year," he said at once. "If we keep them, we must feed them. Take their weapons, anything worth taking, and let them go. They can tell their friends we can't be beaten."

"That's good advice," she said, and passed the order along. She and her staff followed the now distant advance at a walk. Wulf rode with her, Susi and Gharna behind him.

"You're right, I don't command armies well," Wulf confessed. "It's you who have commanded well."

"I've said I've followed your general plans. You're wise and brave, Wulf, and you've done your duty. But don't ride to the front and get killed. Don't leave me to mourn you."

She smiled as she spoke, but her bright eyes were serious. They rode close together, and Wulf almost put out his big hand to take her slim one.

"You saw that I wouldn't be killed," he reminded her gently. "You told me that. My luck has been good so far."

"It will stay good," she said back. "I've seen that, I've heard it. You'll live through this war—live to be old." Again her eyes upon him. "Though not even I can see you as old."

The afternoon sun fell away behind them. They rode over dead Moslems, and vultures sailed in the sky. Here and there they were loudly cheered by Imazighen salvage parties. Some of the men had donned captured armor, captured cloaks, many had fine horses and brought along the Imazighen horses they had ridden before.

The Cahena and Wulf and the escort kept their own beasts to a walk. Here and there, men shepherded camels carrying supplies. Wulf had time to realize how tired he was. His right arm was sore from shoulder to fingertip. He had not slept or eaten since yesterday. He wondered how he himself had escaped even a slight wound. The whole day, the whole fight, had been another example of the blind toil of warfare.

"You seem to be thinking deeply," the Cahena said beside him.

"I only wish this battle was over," Wulf replied.

"It is over, more or less. When we camp this evening, the Moslems won't be waiting for us anywhere within reach."

She spoke with her customary assurance. Her voices must be telling her.

They proceeded for some three hours. Water flashed in the sun up ahead. They came to where streams and pools lay, among green grass and groves of trees. Here and there were houses with thatched roofs and clay walls, and men and women chattering at the doors. The Cahena was hailed with a deafening chorus of welcome.

"Talk to them, Wulf," she directed. "I'll see to our camp."

A hairy villager told Wulf that the Moslems had been through their little settlement twice, advancing and retreating. Nobody had been hurt, but the Moslems had driven away their cattle and sheep and goats, and the people were hungry.

With the Cahena's approval, Wulf issued generous rations of captured food, and the villagers praised him as they ate. Meanwhile, men pitched a tall Moslem tent of red and white striped cloth for the Cahena's headquarters. Wulf went to see to his own arrangements. He had three Arabian horses now, and Susi and Gharna unsaddled them and watered them from a pool, then picketed them. Wulf stripped to the waist and scrubbed himself with sand and water. As he put on his tunic again, Bhakrann strolled by.

"They've been running from us all day," he exulted, pointing. The grove-tufted plain extended for miles. Heat waves stirred above it in the afternoon light. Nothing else moved there.

"We dogged them all the way past the horizon," said Bhakrann. "*Ahi*, they ran like deer, those we didn't catch. I must have killed six or eight. How many did you kill, Wulf?"

"I don't know," said Wulf. "What's going on over there?"

Near the Cahena's tent, someone had lighted a fire. Wulf saw women dance back and forth before it. Voices rose, singing to the accompaniment of instruments. Wulf strolled that way, with Bhakrann and Djalout.

The women postured to and fro. At both sides away from the fire, groups of warriors sat and watched.

"A victory dance," muttered Djalout.

The dancers were not naked this time, though they were dressed sketchily enough. Daphne twirled and quivered there, her hair flying and whipping as though in a gale. Suddenly she stood still and flung up a hand.

"Lady Cahena!" she cried loudly, and prostrated herself. The others bowed and knelt. The Cahena walked toward them from the big tent. She wore a white robe that both swayed and clung, and around her temples was bound a narrow white fillet. Wulf wondered if these things were captured from the enemy, too.

"No," she called. "Go on with your dance. I came to watch."

"Sing to us, Lady Cahena," pleaded a woman.

"Sing! Sing!" chorused others.

The Cahena smiled. "Well, if you wish it, why not? Do I see a harp there? Let me have it."

The harp was brought. The Cahena took it, struck the strings, and listened. She tightened one, another, and again struck a chord. All waited silently.

Now she picked the strings, evoked a melody of minors. She sang, richly, tunefully:

"I hear, I hear;
Voices whisper in the shadows. They say,
Your people are strong, wise, brave.
Your enemies came to eat you up, but they flee unfed.
They worship one god, they call him almighty,
But your gods are many and great.
Your gods hold your land for you,
Make war for you to save your peace.
You will live, will prevail.
The enemy cries out, all is fate,
All is foreordained—
Their foreordained fate is loss, is flight, is ruin.
The voices say the truth,
And the truth we believe."

She muted the harp strings with her spread hand. Deafening applause rose all around, from men and women. "Sing again!" cried the listeners, but the Cahena smiled and shook her head so that the black torrent of her hair tossed.

"Let's have Bhakrann sing to us," she said. "I've heard him sing now and then, when the mood was on him. He makes good songs."

"Let me be excused from this thing," protested Bhakrann. "I can't play the harp, anyway."

"I'll play for you," said the Cahena, and struck a ringing chord.

"Wait, let me choose my words," said Bhakrann. He closed his eyes, and his bearded lips moved soundlessly. "All right," he said after a moment.

The Cahena played the tune she had made, and Bhakrann sang, harshly but with spirit:

"They came, yes!
They came to fight us, conquer us,
Their eyes and beards were fierce, their weapons were bright.

Loud they called on their god to throw us down—
And what then?"

"What then?" yelled a Djerwa warrior from where he sat listening. Bhakrann sang on, without breaking rhythm:

"Their god did not hear them.
We met them and turned them around there,
And they ran before us, frightened, in dread of death,
In dread of the death we showed them, brought upon them."

Bhakrann's voice rose, not tuneful but exulting:

"See, they run, they run, and we run after them,
Make them run faster, faster,
Make them afraid,
Make them find the shortest way back
To their own place, far far away."

He stopped and lifted his hands and bowed, and again there was mighty applause. The Cahena tucked the harp under her white-sleeved arm to clap her hands.

"Now, Wulf!" she cried.

"Wulf!" came back the happy voice of Daphne.

"Wulf!" came the deep-chested shout of Bhakrann. "I sang, Wulf! Now you sing!"

Others urged him, women and men. Wulf was embarrassed. He spread his big hands in appeal.

"But I've never done such a thing in my life," he said to the Cahena. "I've never improvised a song—"

"But I improvised, and so did Bhakrann," she rallied him, smiling. "Don't disappoint us now."

"Well . . ."

She was right, he must do it. This was the Imazighen way, and he must sing. The Cahena was strumming the harp again. He sang, because he must:

"There is also the Cahena!
Our queen, our prophetess, our chieftainess—
Who more beautiful, more wise, more strong?
War, and she strikes like the lightning;
Peace, and she smiles like the bright rising of the sun.
Splendor is hers,
Wisdom is hers,
Power, mighty power, is hers,
Our great queen, our Lady Cahena."

Then the applause, deafening cries from the women and men who had heard him. "Wulf! Wulf!" they called to him. "Sing again!"

He lifted his hands, as though in surrender, and smiled and shook his head. "Thank you, but I can't think of anything else. Let me go back and eat supper with my friends."

"No," said the Cahena, handing the harp back to its owner. "You'll eat supper with me. There's a lot to decide about tomorrow."

"A council?"

"Just the two of us. We'll give orders to the chiefs later."

He walked with her to the big captured tent. "You're a poet," she said.

"I could only sing what I thought."

"Yes, that's what poetry is."

A guard with a javelin saluted them, and they went in and closed the tent flap behind them. Carpets covered the ground inside. There was a table, with dishes of food upon it, and a brass lamp with a pale yellow flame. Fragrant perfume hung in the air.

"Eat first or talk first?" Wulf asked her.

"Eat and talk later."

Her slender hand was on his arm. She led him toward where a figured hanging curtained off a rear corner of the tent. Within the chamber it made, cushions were spread, with a coverlet over them. A soft whisper crept in the air, like faraway voices.

"But first," he heard her say.

Her hands busied themselves at the fastenings of the neck of her robe. Its fabric flowed down her, fell in a circle around her feet. The filtered light from beyond the hanging put a soft glow on her tawny-golden nakedness.

"Take off your things, too," she said.

"Daia," he spoke her name.

XVI

They loved each other, tenderly and thoroughly and knowledgeably. They knew each other's body and they thought they knew each other's heart. "Wulf, Wulf," she whispered at the height of their ecstasy, and "Daia," he said back to her, the name forbidden to all others, the loveliest name he knew. Afterward, they washed each other from a captured silver basin. She donned her white robe again, he put on his clothes, and they went out to supper in the main tent. It had grown cold but it was good—sliced roast meat with a hot sauce, a salad of cucumbers, Moslem wheat bread, olives, and raisins. As they ate, they talked of what must be done next.

A vigorous advance to press those beaten, fleeing Moslems, was Wulf's advice, with patrols of scouts to show the way. Behind the strong, steady front line would come more squadrons, ready to strengthen the van in case the Moslems tried to make a stand anywhere, and captures of all stores of food and equipment, on which they would subsist as they marched, as they fought if there was any fighting to do. But if the Moslems continued their demoralized retreat, pursue them, even all the way to the sea.

"That's wisdom," the Cahena praised him, putting an olive between her red lips. "You're a strategist, Wulf. You're a poet, too. How beautifully you sang about me."

"That was a clumsy effort," said Wulf. "As for my strategy, it's only basic. You flatter me too much."

The sun was down outside. Chill crept into the air. The Cahena found herself a cloak of blue cloth with a beaded design and gave Wulf another captured cloak, black and white wool with gold thread shining in it. Swathed in these, they went out into the night.

Fires shimmered, camping warriors sang happily. At one fire the principal chiefs gathered. Ketriazar and Daris wore Moslem garments, and their beards bristled triumphantly. Yaunis bowed low to kiss the Cahena's shadow in the fireglow. Lartius was there, in a beautiful embroidered mantle. He looked tired, but he looked smug.

"We've beaten them," he exulted. "Destroyed them."

"We've only begun to destroy them," said the Cahena. "There'll be more to do, and we'll have to do it right. Let Wulf explain."

Wulf sat and elaborated on what he had outlined to the Cahena, about a strong, advancing line with scouts in front and reserves close behind. Perhaps, he said, a concentration of force at the center. If the Imazighen could drive through the midpoint of the retreating host, that host might be rolled up to right and left and virtually finished off.

"What do we do with prisoners?" asked Lartius.

"Take their weapons and money and horses, and then let them find their way to wherever they started out at us," said the Cahena. "They can tell the story of how we can't be beaten. But keep any officers you catch; we can use them. Wulf, what became of that interesting young Arab, whatever his name is?"

"Khalid ibn Yezid," said Wulf. "He's under guard, off there to the rear."

"He took defeat gracefully, and he's well spoken," said the Cahena, almost musingly. "You others might like him."

"I don't like any Moslem," declared Ketriazar. "The only interest I have in a Moslem is where his neck and shoulders come together, the right place to put my sword."

"I want no prisoners killed," said the Cahena, an edge in her voice.

"My people take very few prisoners," said Daris from beside Ketriazar. "Very few indeed."

Djalout came up to join them. "Lady Cahena, I've been making an inventory of captured valuables," he said. "The men have been good at bringing them in, only a few Arab coins sticking to their fingers. Here, I brought this to show you."

His old hand held it out. It was a ropelike string of glowing pearls, all round and white except one at the center. That was glossy black, the size and shape of a pigeon's egg.

Lartius leaned to look. "They're worth a fortune," he said.

The Cahena took the pearls, fastened them with a gold clasp, and hung them around her neck. The black pearl glistened richly upon her bosom. She touched it with her finger.

"Let's get back to talk about tomorrow," she said. "Up at the first touch of light before dawn, everyone ready to move. Now, attention to orders for each of you."

The orders she gave showed that she had well estimated the warriors of each chieftainship, their organization, their behavior in battle. She finished and rose, and all rose with her.

"Now, I want to visit the wounded, wherever they are," she said. "Come with me, Djalout. No, Wulf, you needn't come. You've ridden hard, fought hard. Get some rest for your work tomorrow."

Away she walked into the dark. Wulf returned to his own campsite. The horses drowsed, Susi and Gharna lay swaddled and asleep, but Bhakrann rose on an elbow. "*Ahi,*" he greeted Wulf.

"*Ahi,* Bhakrann. If you're going to ask about tomorrow, we'll do more of the same. Pursuit and mopping up."

"She thinks we'll succeed?"

"She knows we will," said Wulf.

"She knows everything."

"Yes," said Wulf. "Everything."

He drew off his boots and tunic and lay on his back. He was weary, but he was happy. Thinking of the Cahena, he imagined her nestled there beside him. He went to sleep and did not dream.

When he wakened, swiftly, clear-headed, it was still dark but the stars faded in the east, a message that dawn was coming. He rose. Bhakrann was already on his feet, on the far side of the last embers of the fire.

"Come here," said Bhakrann softly. "I want to show you something."

Wulf joined him, over where Gharna lay snoring. Bhakrann pointed at the ground, and Wulf stooped to look. There in soft earth were the deep prints of divided hoofs, two and two and two, where they led away. Wulf knew those prints.

He and Bhakrann walked back together, to their side of the camp. They stood and looked at each other in the growing light.

"We'll still lose lives," said Wulf at last.

"Then you know who came and looked at Gharna, don't you?" said Bhakrann. "Wulf, I begin to understand you when you say you hate war."

"Don't tell Gharna," said Wulf.

"Of course not."

Neither of them had spoken the forbidden name of Khro.

Wulf put on his boots. Bhakrann set a brass bowl of water on the coals and fed on more wood. When the water heated, he trickled in some dried, crumpled leaves of a plant Wulf did not know. They drank the brew and ate scraps of Moslem bread. Susi and Gharna woke and shared with them. Then came the bridling and saddling of the horses, the putting on of armor. All around them, warriors were doing the same, were mounting, forming ready for action. Bhakrann went away to summon his scouts and move ahead of the main bodies.

"Ride close to me, Gharna," said Wulf, swinging into his own saddle. "I won't be in the thick of things today, and neither will you."

"Whatever you command," replied Gharna.

Dawn peeped over the distant horizon. Subchiefs yelled orders, the squadrons went forward. Wulf joined the Cahena, with Mallul and a party of aides and couriers.

"Ride with me," the Cahena said to Wulf. "Observe anything you can. What orders you give will be obeyed as though they came from me."

"All I can think of just now is to see that the enemy doesn't pull together to make a stand," he said.

"We'll watch for that."

The host moved forward and so did the Cahena's party. In the distance moved busy dark dots, an open line of them, Bhakrann's scouts. No sign of Moslems, not just then.

They left the pools and streams; they were on the dusty, tree-tufted plain. The advance was steady, all elements keeping touch at the flanks. The Cahena's party came at a brisk walk, sometimes trotting to keep in command position. Couriers constantly sped this way and that to tell chieftains what to do, what to look for.

They passed huts and clusters of huts. Hysterically joyous people came out to meet them, telling of the arrogance of Moslems as Hassan's host advanced, the demoralization of the same men in retreat. There were prostrations to kiss the shadow of the Cahena's horse, invocations of spirits and gods with names strange to Wulf. The Cahena spoke kindly to such people and ordered that captured food be given to those in need.

There was no great strew of dead bodies on the ground, as there had been the day before. The Moslems were not standing to fight. On the way, the army passed an ancient tomb structure, a cone of fitted rocks fully twice a man's height. Wulf checked his horse to look at it. There had been a closed doorway to the east, now partially opened, its loose stones scattered. Perhaps Moslems had dug there, looking for possible treasure. But they had not opened a way big enough to enter. What had stopped them? Fear? At the top of the tomb two jagged points of rock stabbed out to north and south. Horns? Like the horns of Khro? Wulf grimaced and rode on to catch up with the Cahena.

She pointed. "Action up there ahead." Wulf saw a swirl of horsemen almost a mile away, and instantly put his own mount to a gallop to get there. Susi and Gharna hurried behind him.

He heard shouts, he saw combat, javelins against curved swords. His own weapon sang out of its scabbard, and he hurried to get into the thing. Fairly flying, he was there, saw a Moslem wheel to face him, lifting a bow with arrow on string. It sang past him, and then he was close in, cutting the man into a flying fall to the ground. Wulf spared a glance to make sure that his stroke had killed, then looked behind him.

Someone else was down. Gharna.

The other Imazighen had put the surviving Moslems to flight. Wulf dismounted to look at Gharna. The blank face turned up. The arrow had struck Gharna's very heart, had driven in half its length. So close had been the range that Gharna's mail jacket had been pierced like cloth.

Susi was there, too, wide-eyed. His hand trembled as it held his bridle. "At least death was quick," he quavered. "What do we do?"

"Bury him here," Wulf ordered. "Stop a couple of men to help you; tell them I said for them to help. Find big stones to put on his grave, to keep wild dogs and hyenas from digging him up. Then come on and find me again. I'll be up ahead somewhere."

He made haste to rejoin the Cahena's party. Briefly he told her why he had stopped.

"Then you lost a good servant," she said. "I knew him, I'm sorry about him."

"He looked after me," said Wulf. "He knew about horses. But it was going to happen—there were hoof tracks beside him where he slept last night."

The Cahena glanced at him sharply. "Don't say the name."

"I wasn't going to say the name. But I think of some things I've talked about with Djalout. About gods; when people don't worship them anymore, do they become spirits of evil? Spirits that destroy? Did that happen to the hoofprint maker?"

"Please," she said, and he had never heard her use the word to him. "Don't talk about it. Let's follow on, see what's happening."

What was happening was the utter routing of the Moslems. None of them waited to meet the triumphant advance except those who were too weary, too poor in spirit, to get away. Such men grumpily held up their hands in token of surrender. Among them were commanders of companies or squadrons or battalions, recognizable by their handsome dress. The Cahena ordered these prisoners kept, and told common warriors to go east and try to find their friends.

The pursuit was hardly pursuit by now. The Moslems had scuttled away to a far horizon. Warriors of the various tribes gathered in abandoned baggage camels, whole herds of riderless horses, stacks of abandoned weapons. Wulf saw valuable spoils, too, gold and silver coins in pouches, jewelry. These were fetched together and carried along under guard. The Cahena had ordered that, and her orders were strictly obeyed.

In camp that night, the Imazighen warriors slept on their arms. The Cahena did not call Wulf inside her big captured tent. She sat outside, in the light of a small fire, and conferred with her principal chieftains. Bhakrann reported after a busy day of scouting, to speak of what they would approach.

"We'll come below Cairouan—they're abandoning it—and to the south is that place they call El-Djem," he said. "A day or so, and we'll be there."

"Thrysdus is the name," said Djalout, "where the Romans had an important garrison town, and maybe the third biggest circus in all their empire."

"If the Moslems leave Cairouan, we'll ignore it for the moment," said the Cahena. "Send squadrons to occupy, and go on to Thrysdus. I've heard of it, but I've never seen it. I'll see it now."

They watched her—Wulf, Djalout, Mallul, Ketriazar, Daris, Yaunis, Lartius. She declared her coming to Thrysdus with all her usual confidence. In a moment of silence around the fire, Wulf heard the softest of soft voices, like a mutter in a dream. Her spirits were speaking to her, telling the future. He had never learned to be used to those voices, nor to anything else about the Cahena.

"So Thrysdus is like a fortress?" she said. "We'll see."

There was more direction of the same plan tomorrow as the last two days. Let the Moslems run, unless there was some sort of stand. And let the runners go, let them run, gather in only officers.

Moslem food was brought them. Wulf relished slices of smoked fish. At last the council broke up and Wulf went to where Susi and Djalout had made camp. Susi muttered prayers for the rest of Gharna's soul, but Wulf could not make out what gods were addressed.

At dawn, yet again the advance across broad country the Moslems did not try to defend. There were no dead bodies to show where defense, if any, had been attempted. Birds twittered in trees. Great camel-loads of plunder plodded behind the advancing warriors. The Moslems had brought much equipment, much provision, with them, and had abandoned it in their flight. Wulf wondered what they ate as they ran.

The army passed a sizable sprawl of houses, large enough for a town. In its midst stood a clay-plastered church, with a clumsily made cross of rocks on its roof. People cheered them and fell prostrate as the Cahena rode among them. A pursy, flush-faced man in a swinging black robe came and bowed at her stirrup.

"I'm the bishop of these Christian people, great queen," he rolled out impressively. "Our prayers are answered. God has sent you to destroy these infidels."

"Thank you," she said gravely. "But give your own thanks to your God for my brave men, my wise chiefs, who have made victory possible."

He flourished the sign of the cross at her.

Bhakrann had been given command of the strong contingent sent to observe, perhaps to occupy, Cairouan. The main force fared on until the vast pile of Thrysdus rose on the horizon, rosy brown in the late afternoon sun. Small houses clustered around it and outside those, orchards and vineyards, spreading like dark, hugging clouds over the ground.

XVII

The towering central structure of Thrysdus, red-brown in the last rays of the sun, looked like a mountain, ruinous though it was at the top. The Cahena led her staff to the forefront of the army. A scurrying press of people rushed out past the orchards and vineyards to greet them. They fell on their faces around the hoofs of the Cahena's horse, and several talked at once.

It seemed that the Moslem garrison had fled Thrysdus without stopping to pack. All who remained were civilians—Jews, Christians, even some Moslems—who now rejoiced at the flight of their arrogant masters.

The Cahena spoke graciously to all these, but authoritatively to Wulf. "Take a couple of hundred men and ride in," she said. "Make sure that the enemy is really gone, and send word back to me."

"At once, Lady Cahena."

He chose two squadrons of Djerwa, one of them the following of poor Uchia. Several men of Thrysdus volunteered to guide him. He took his following along a street fringed with plastered huts, and straight to a broad entrance to that huge stone building at the center of everything. People were there with torches and lanterns to light them.

They came into a wide central arena, open above to the evening sky. Undoubtedly it had once been skillfully sanded, for headlong races or for combats of men and beasts, but now it was green with grass, the blades nibbled down by horses or cattle. Wulf guessed that it was more than five hundred paces long and nearly that wide, and on all sides of its oval expanse rose sloping bank after bank of seats, enough as he judged to hold all of the army that followed the Cahena. The men who had guided him swore again that the Moslems had fairly scuttled away.

"They left food cooking," declared one. "Some of them even left their wives—pretty wives, at that."

Wulf quickly sent parties to ascend on all sides of the arena and explore every corner of the building. They hastened to do this, while he waited in the arena with those who held the horses. The patrols came back to report that all was safe. Back of the seats were corridors and chambers, fountains of water from some system of conduits, disordered baths, and here and there kitchens with bubbling pots and meat roasting on spits. Wulf sent a swift rider to carry this information to the Cahena.

While he waited, he and Susi made a tour of some of the passages and rooms. Sure enough, food was on fires in several places, but Wulf did not taste it and posted guards in the kitchens to keep others from helping themselves. He surveyed with pleasure a great steambath with perfume in the air, a library of rolled manuscripts, a system of pipes with running water. He encountered several people, most of them women who simpered at him behind their veils and vowed that they considered him and his companions as deliverers.

The Cahena and her staff rode into the great open oval, having halted the main body of the army outside the houses of Thrysdus. She and Mallul dismounted to hear what Wulf had to say about the situation. Fires were lighted here and there on the arena's grassy level, to dispel the dark. The Cahena herself visited the chambers of the lower tier, and chose a spacious room with a window looking outward on the corridor. Another room opened into it from behind.

"Put my things in here," she directed. "Light a lamp. Mallul, you can choose a room close by. Wulf, what have you learned about the retreat from here?"

"That there wasn't much of an armed garrison, but a number of officials. They got out long before we came in sight."

"Bring together all those chief men we captured," she said. "Tomorrow, when we've set up full possession here, I'll assemble those prisoners to talk to."

She visited the kitchens, peered steadfastly into pot after pot, murmured over them, and then pronounced them safe to eat. Warriors found bowls and spoons and served themselves. The Cahena herself ate only sparingly. She ordered Mallul to see that the herds of horses and camels and cattle had good grass outside the houses and orchards, with guards to watch over them. Finally she went to the apartment she had chosen. Many of the warriors spread their rugs and cloaks on the stone seats of the arena and slept gratefully.

Wulf and Susi were content to find an adequate square cubicle, with a single window opening upon the corridor and a stout door with a bar inside. Susi was soon asleep. Wulf lay wakeful, pondering the army's position and the problems it must face. The dwellers at Thrysdus had welcomed the victors in; he had noticed fraternization between Imazighen warriors and townspeople. Girls and young women had been especially receptive. Indeed, some of those were cuddling up to warriors on the great stone benches. But that sort of easy acceptance might mean an equally easy rejection if a strong enough enemy force came back. Wulf knew he must make ready for any change in the fortunes of this war.

When he did sleep, he dreamed of a vast plain on which rose a sort of forest of Imazighen tombs. Among those things, he thought he saw a prowling shape as black as charred wood, near at hand but stealthy. In his dream he followed it, sword drawn, and glimpsed the curved horns on its head. Khro, he dreamed of Khro, and was glad to wake up at dawn, wash and eat, and report to the Cahena.

Hassan's captured officers had been assembled in the arena. There were something like eighty of them, enough for a squadron, all handsomely turned out in fine turbans and mantles. They drew together in a close group, and the Cahena with her attendants stood at the parapet below the lowest bank of seats. She wore her blue cloak, and her cascade of black hair was bound at the temples with a silk band of gleaming white.

"I'll speak to them," Wulf heard her say to Djalout. "My Arabic isn't of the best, and so I ask you to translate what I say." She turned to look at Wulf. "Listen to how he translates, Wulf. See that he doesn't misquote me."

"Would I ever do that?" Djalout smiled, unabashed.

The Cahena, too, smiled. Then she faced her glum audience, and raised her voice:

"You're men of importance, the officer-companions of your general, Hassan. I don't want to hurt you, I don't want to make you even uncomfortable. Swear to me now, by the name of Allah your god, that you won't try to escape while you're with us, and we'll treat you as our guests until we see how to send you back to your own friends."

Djalout translated. There was a moment of silence. Then one of the officers stepped clear of his fellows. He was tall, lean, hawk-faced. His beard was shot with gray.

"We swear to that, Queen Cahena," he said, and a murmur of agreement rose through the gathering.

"You all swear?" prompted the Cahena. "Does any of you not swear?"

None offered a denial. She looked them over searchingly.

"We'll arrange your return to Hassan," she said. "He should be glad to buy you back. We'll send one of you with a message to him. We'll offer an exchange. Each of you can buy us something we need—good horses or camels, maybe weapons, maybe gold. Is this a fair offer?"

Djalout explained.

"Fair and kindly, by Allah!" shouted back the spokesman with the grayshot beard.

"Then you are guests here," said the Cahena again. "I'll send one of you at once, to give your general our terms. Choose somebody to take that errand."

There was a buzzing conference among the captured officers. One voice seemed to protest loudly. The spokesman moved forward again to address the Cahena.

"Great lady and queen, we asked for our young companion Khalid ibn Yezid to ride on this errand, but he refuses."

Khalid moved gracefully into the open.

"Queen Cahena, I do not want to go to Hassan. I ask that you let me stay here."

She looked down at him and she smiled radiantly. "You don't want to go back to your friends?"

"I want to stay and make new friends among you."

As Khalid spoke, the others pulled away from him and stared. Still the Cahena smiled down upon him.

"You wish to turn from being a Moslem?" she asked, and Djalout translated.

"Mighty queen, I don't need to turn from being a Moslem to see that you are great and compassionate and beautiful," said Khalid, and Djalout rendered his words into Imazighen.

"Well," said the Cahena, "stay if you want. I'll talk to you later."

The other officers chose their spokesman to ride to Hassan. The Cahena ordered that a horse be given him—his own, if it could be found among the captured stock—and a water bottle and provisions. An escorting rider would go with him, to get him past whatever was happening with Bhakrann's men at the town of Cairouan.

To the others she said, "We'll find quarters for you to have while the exchange goes forward. You'll be well treated. If you want to talk to any of us as friends, I'll permit that."

The gathering murmured, as though in applause. A square-built Moslem said, "You show great mercy, Queen Cahena, and Allah, who is merciful, sees mercy when it is shown."

"Thank you," she said grandly. "Now, my people will assign you to quarters and see that you're provided for."

Turning, she left the parapet. Wulf and Djalout and others went with her. She walked into the corridor behind, and to the spacious chamber she had taken for herself. Stopping inside the door, she raised her head as though to listen.

"My voices," she said. "They speak here."

Wulf had a sense as of a hum somewhere, but could make out no words. The Cahena looked around at them.

"Fetch that young Arab, what's his name—"

"Khalid ibn Yezid," supplied Wulf.

"Fetch him to talk to me. I take it that those others aren't particularly glad that he said he wanted to stay with us." She looked around again. "Have someone bring wine, good wine if we brought it along. We've captured lots of food here, but the Moslems don't drink wine, at least they say they don't."

Obediently Wulf went to find Khalid, who still waited in the arena. They went back to the Cahena's door. The others had left, and at her beckoning gesture Khalid entered and she shut the door, with Wulf still outside. He frowned. Would she be safe alone with Khalid? Probably. She knew how to read minds, whether to trust those minds or not.

A hand touched the sleeve of Wulf's tunic. He turned. There was Daphne, bunching her cheeks to smile.

"You think it's good here, Wulf?" she chattered to him. "My father's going to take over a forge here, one deserted by the Moslems, but he wants things brought from his Tiergal place. He's joining a party riding back there, and he's left me to look after things this end."

Her smile grew wider; it was almost conspiratorial. "Our new forge, the place where we'll live, is below here." She pointed down. "If you come visiting, you won't miss it."

"Thanks," Wulf said. "Just now, I have about eighty details to look into."

She pouted as he turned away.

His first detail was to attend to the captive Moslem officers. He went down into the arena, where they still stood together as though waiting for dismissal. Susi went for a horse for the one who would take the Cahena's message to Hassan. Then Wulf explored here and there for living quarters for the others. There were plenty of chambers, and he assigned them two to a chamber. He spoke in Arabic, and several replied in friendly fashion.

"Your great queen is merciful to us, but you weren't," said one. "I never saw a champion strike such blows as you struck. You should be a Moslem, one of us."

"If I'd been one of you, I'd have been on the losing side," said Wulf, smiling. "Maybe killed, if I'd have been chosen to be killed."

"Chosen?"

"Something in this country chooses men to die in battle. Something with horns."

"An ifrit, a djinn," said the Moslem. "A creature of Satan."

"Undoubtedly," agreed Wulf. "Maybe we'll talk more about djinns and ifrits while you're here."

He went to busy himself in organizing a patrol system for guarding Thrysdus, bodies of armed men to range through and around the place to observe in all directions, with subchiefs in command of each. He told himself that the Djerwa would be best at such a duty, and that Lartius's men from the Cirta district would be poorest. He finished his duties for the day by assigning camp areas here and there outside the arena, with quarters inside it for the chieftains. Finally he went to a steambath, which refreshed him greatly. When he dressed and came out, he was told that the Cahena invited him and her other lieutenants to an evening meal.

Her spacious lodgings had been decorated with figured hangings and set with cushioned furniture. Wulf found himself in company with Ketriazar, Yaunis, Lartius, Daris, Mallul, Djalout and Khalid. The Cahena introduced Khalid as a new ally, an adviser to whom she listened with profit.

"My voices said we would profit by our battle," she said, "and Khalid is the profit. I've heard wisdom from him, great wisdom from a man so young and modest."

"You flatter me," said Khalid, his slim hand to his trim young beard. "I've said only things I thought were obvious."

The Cahena smiled. "Repeat them for my chieftains."

Her women fetched in the dinner, soup of couscous and olive oil and pungent seasonings, followed by roasted birds and wheat bread and an assortment of dried fruits. Again she told Khalid to talk, and he touched his hand to his brow in salute and did so.

"I told our queen about Hassan's troops," he said. "How he had gathered them from here and there. His companions, his officers, are chiefly Arabs, but most of the others come from everywhere. A great many from Egypt and Libya and these countries hereabouts—new converts to Islam, rude and even savage peoples."

To Wulf this remark seemed fairly sensible. The Cahena put her hands together, almost applauding. "You feel that this is significant," she said.

Again he touched hand to brow. "Very much so, Queen Cahena. I called these people converts, but they're hardly converted. Most of them declared Islam so as to join what seemed the winning side. And they marched with Hassan, not to spread the faith of Allah but to find plunder in your towns, your cities."

"Cities like Cirta," remarked Lartius, putting a grape in his mouth.

"If they want gold, we don't have gold mines," put in Djalout. "We only get gold by caravan, many days across the southern deserts, or by trade from the east."

"Or by capture," pointed out Yaunis. "Maybe enough to be worth stealing."

"And there are your women," went on Khalid, his brilliant eyes upon the Cahena. "Hassan has told his men that they will find women like the houris of paradise."

Everyone seemed to think, and not to like the thought. At last Wulf spoke: "I'll remind you that we've kept our women so far, and that we'll fight to keep them if Hassan comes again. Will he come, Khalid?"

"That depends on whether Caliph Abd al-Malik keeps him in command here. I can't read the caliph's mind and wishes, but we should soon learn what happens to Hassan."

"We'll find out," said the Cahena confidently. "We'll have contact with Hassan, and I have voices other than our contacts. Those voices have always helped me," and her eyes lingered on Khalid, whose gaze met hers, and again his hand sought his brow.

The council broke up, but the Cahena put her hand on Khalid's arm and he stayed to talk. Wulf went out and met Susi in the corridor. Susi proposed a retainer to replace the dead Gharna. This man proved to be a sturdy young Djerwa who had been a spearman in the front rank of the great battle. His name was Smarja, and he was almost as tall and broad as Wulf, with brown hair and beard. He had done some blacksmithing and horse training, and Wulf engaged him on the spot.

The Cahena had declared that Thrysdus would be her new headquarters, and sent messengers to invite all residents of Tiergal to come and join her. Wulf found Jonas at his new, well-appointed forge and metal shop in a chamber of the arena. Jonas mended mail and sharpened weapons, and Daphne rejoiced in this new home.

"The women here are friendly and interesting, more interesting than most of those at Tiergal," she said. "They say flattering things to me, say I'm pretty, wonder why I don't have lovers."

"Why don't you?" Wulf asked her.

She looked at him long. "Maybe I'm hard to please."

That evening, another council in the Cahena's great sitting room. Djalout said he had organized a signal system to the west, a series of manned stations where fires could send up columns of smoke to warn of possible Moslem threats and summon all of the Imazighen to battle. Daris and Ketriazar heard this and expressed a desire to go back to their homes, there to wait for any orders. Yaunis and Lartius, who enjoyed the luxuries they had found in Thrysdus, said that they would delay any return to their own towns. As for the Cahena, she announced that she would make a tour to the northward over the territories wrested from Hassan, and added that town after town sent invitations.

"It will be like the progress of a mighty queen," said Khalid from where he sat beside her. "A queen like Cleopatra of Egypt, like Dido of Carthage. I'll ride with you and see your glory."

"And I'll come," promised Lartius, "And I," said Yaunis.

"I'll stay here," said Djalout. "I've found some interesting documents in Arabic and Latin, even a few in Latin. I want to study them. Wouldn't you like to see them, Wulf?"

"Wulf will come with me," said the Cahena. "Let people everywhere see him and speak his name for his courage."

The council broke up, and the chieftains headed for the door. Wulf, on the threshold, saw that Khalid still waited, and turned to look.

Khalid and the Cahena stood close together, almost touching, gazing almost raptly into each other's face.

"I've never seen a man more beautiful than you," she said, and Wulf heard every word. "You're brave—wise. I'll take you to my breast, Khalid, to be my son."

"Yes," said Khalid eagerly. "Yes."

Wulf went out and closed the door behind him. He sought his own quarters and sat down on the shelf against the wall that did duty for a bed. A crockery jug was at hand. He poured wine from it into a cup and held it in his big clenched fist.

He remembered when the Cahena had summoned him to her, had put her swelling breast to his mouth. He remembered what had happened afterward. Now that would be happening again, with Khalid.

He had been the Cahena's lover, eagerly she had given him love. She had said that he was sent to her by whoever spoke to her with disembodied wisdom and guidance. Now she talked like that to Khalid.

He felt as though he sat in a soggy, chilly mist that soaked to his bones.

The lover of Daia the Cahena, how had Wulf been that? She had always sent for him to make love with her. Never, he reflected, had he made the first move. She had sent for him to come to her, and he had come to her, and there had been deep ecstasy. Now . . .

Now, and what about now? And what about other things, for that matter?

Had she had other lovers before Wulf, lovers mystically recommended to her by those voices she knew? Other men welcomed, accepted, possessed, and later superseded? Had that happened with her? Wulf had never wondered about that before. And no point in wondering now. She had taken Khalid to her in there, and Wulf was alone out here.

A noise at his half-open door. Somebody had peeped in at him, and as he looked up the somebody slipped out of sight. It had been a woman. Who? Certainly not the Cahena.

Scowling, Wulf drained his cup of wine. His hand closed fiercely on the stout earthenware, and it shattered in his grip. He reached for another cup and filled it from the jug.

XVIII

Wulf had vague, fitful dreams that night. One was of Khro, bull-horned and gigantic and ungainly, looming over him with a fanged mouth. Others were of the Cahena, her smile, her caressing hands. He rose early, dressed and ate bread and dates, and went out into the corridors.

He completed organization of the guard. Each troop of fifty riders would serve for a day and a night, and then be relieved by another. Arranging this took all morning. In the afternoon he toured the whole great arena-fortress. There were levels above levels of the wide corridors, with all sorts of chambers for living and storage. The inhabitants he met were shyly friendly. At last Wulf resorted to the baths. He soaked in a steaming-hot tub and let a barber trim his hair and cut his beard to a point. In the evening he dressed and came out again.

The Cahena met him outside his quarters.

"The principal chieftains will eat with me tonight, in my council chamber," she announced. "We'll have some plans to approve."

"I've eaten already," said Wulf. "A Moslem woman grilled me morsels of peppered mutton, on a skewer with pickles and onion slices."

"A Moslem woman?" she repeated.

"My servant Susi found her. They like each other."

"Wulf," she said, "you seem distant."

"I only try to be respectful, Lady Cahena."

She pursed her beautiful lips. "You're displeased with me."

"Would I dare be displeased?" He looked levelly at her. "I'm your servant, your man-at-arms."

"Why are you bitter?" she asked.

"You can answer that yourself. I'm not so much bitter as chilly—put out in the cold."

Her frown deepened. "You mean Khalid."

"It's you who said the name, Lady Cahena."

"Daia," she said, as if to correct him. "If I speak to Khalid, have I rejected you? Too much has passed between us to be forgotten."

Wulf shrugged. "Lady Cahena, I don't know how to go half shares on anything. I doubt if Khalid would."

"Oh, be sensible," she snapped. "My voices ruled me with Khalid, as they did with you. Come to the council, whether you eat with me or not."

She walked rapidly away. He heard her giving orders to servants.

For an hour he looked into trifles of administration. At last he joined the others in council. They sat on cushions, Khalid next to the Cahena, Mallul next to him, and Djalout, Ketriazar, and Daris opposite. The Cahena motioned him to a seat beside Djalout and asked him about his arrangements for guard and garrison at Thrysdus. He explained in detail, and asked about supplies.

"I've attended to those," Mallul said. "People fetch in grain and dried vegetables and goats and cattle. We pay them with our captured treasure."

Ketriazar then spoke of surveying pasture lands for both the herds from Arwa and the beasts left by the fleeing Moslems. He and Daris thought that crops could be sown.

"Meanwhile, what will Hassan do now?" the Cahena wondered. "What do you think, Khalid?"

"That depends on the Caliph Abd al-Malik, Commander of the Faithful," said Khalid. "How he considers Hassan's defeat. Whether to keep him in command or put someone in his place."

"All I know about Abd-al-Malik is that he became caliph about fifteen years ago," said Djalout. "What's he like?"

"I've seen him at his court in Damascus," said Khalid. "He's middle-aged, learned, and devout. Frugal, too—some call him a skinflint—and he believes in signs and omens and dreams."

"What will he dream now?" was Djalout's next question.

"Probably about whether to keep Hassan in command," said Khalid, his slim hand stroking his beard.

"We'll find out," declared the Cahena, sipping wine. "We'll be in communication with Hassan, about exchanging his officers. As soon as we know we hold this region, I'll travel to Cairouan and other towns." She sipped again. "To Carthage," she added.

"When do we go home?" asked Daris.

"I'll arrange that for whoever wants to go," the Cahena replied. "I'll stay here, bring the Djerwa here. This place is a fort, where we can meet any Moslem advance."

"They won't dare advance, after that whipping we gave them," offered Ketriazar. "How many did we kill? That whole country, all the way to Arwa, is planted with their dead. It should be fertile for years to come. The farmers will thank us."

Khalid sank his head, as though he did not like that. Other details were discussed, and finally the Cahena dismissed the council. But Khalid stayed beside her as the others left.

Days passed. Bhakrann sent word that the people left in Cairouan were quiet, cooperative, but that the water supply was scant. A messenger came with a letter from Hassan, now far away toward Egypt in the east. Hassan promised to pay ransoms for his captured officers. All the while, the Cahena efficiently consolidated her position at Thrysdus and spent hours apart with Khalid. Now and then she spoke winningly to Wulf, who made restrainedly courteous answers. She did not invite him to a private meeting. He wondered if he would come if she asked it. He did his best not to think about her.

Plans went forward for the triumphal march to Carthage. The Cahena chose an escort of veteran Djerwa horsemen, and Wulf and Mallul and Khalid as staff officers. Yaunis and Lartius would bring their contingents on their way home. Ketriazar and Daris would garrison Thrysdus with their men, and Djalout would command there. From the east came word that Hassan and the remains of his army were building a line of fortified castles.

"They think only of defense," decided the Cahena. "Form for the march."

It was an impressive column of horsemen and supply camels. The Cahena rode at the very front with Mallul and Khalid. Wulf and Smarja followed, and Lartius joined them to clatter happily about the victory. "Hassan won't come against us now," he said.

"If he's in command, it will be to fight us again," said Wulf.

"If they fight us again, we'll whip them again," said Lartius confidently. "It was pleasant at Thrysdus, wasn't it? I approve of the baths there, and of some of the women. I'd like to see more of that armorer's daughter, what's her name?"

"You mean Daphne."

"Yes, Daphne, like the nymph who changed into a laurel to get away from Apollo. I don't want her changing into a laurel."

"Then don't press her with your attentions," said Wulf, and Lartius blinked and rode away to talk to Yaunis.

They came to Cairouan, a town with lofty walls and minareted mosques, forested with trees outside. Bhakrann greeted them at the gate, knelt to kiss the Cahena's shadow, and roared welcome to Wulf.

"We'll have a banquet in the palace yonder," he promised. "They like me here. They don't know I killed Okba—I don't even wear his sword here. What are the Lady Cahena's orders?"

She gave them—no townspeople to be roughly handled or insulted. Her followers might buy things, but must not steal, and mosques would not be entered. A trembling imam thanked her for that.

At dinner, Bhakrann said that he had ordered the digging of more wells to relieve the water shortage. A number of influential Moslems had said they would obey the Cahena's rule. And no enemy were reported, all the way eastward for thirty-five miles to a great bay.

"Well done, Bhakrann, and thanks," said the Cahena. "You come with me to Carthage. Who can we leave in command here?"

"Why not Zeoui?" said Bhakrann, pointing to his friend beside him. "He's a tried scout; he knows the enemy."

"Very well," granted the Cahena. "Let's rest early tonight. It's a good three days of riding to Carthage."

They were on the way at dawn and camped two nights in open country. At sunset the third day, they came to shattered Carthage.

People still clung to makeshift shelters along the ruined streets, and came out to applaud the Cahena's entry. Khalid spoke of how she was like Dido in the ancient capital city. Dido—Daia. Had Khalid been told to speak her secret name? Undoubtedly.

Wulf visited the house where he had lived before the fall of Carthage. It was no house, only a pile of rubble. Wulf remembered a pretty, mock-demure girl who had served him and wondered what the Moslems had done to her.

Some big palaces, temples, fortifications still remained. Wulf found Lartius surveying there. "We seem well liked here," said Wulf.

"For the most part, yes," said Lartius. "But somebody showed me a sort of poem, on parchment. It was in Hebrew, and I had to get a translator. It's doggerel. Compares the Cahena to Nebuchadnezzar, to Hadrian."

"Nebuchadnezzar?" repeated Wulf. "I don't understand. She hasn't set up any golden idol to be worshipped or cast anyone into a fiery furnace, and certainly she doesn't go around on all fours eating grass. As for Hadrian, he wasn't cruel as conquerors go. He did build a wall up north in my English country, to keep out the Picts and Caledonians, but down here it's Hassan who builds defenses."

"How educated you are," said Lartius. "I don't understand, either, but we seem to have enemies."

They lingered one day at Carthage and went east to Bulla Regia, where throngs scattered spring flowers before their horses. Another banquet that night, with Khalid seated at the Cahena's right hand. She beckoned Wulf to come to her left.

"I have an important assignment for you," she told him. "Go on east from here, bring back news of all the towns and peoples, how they stand as our friends. Take Bhakrann along."

"How far do we go?" Wulf asked.

"Ride for, say, thirty days—six hundred miles or so. You needn't go as far as Tinga—that's a stronghold of the Goths." She mused for a moment. "There's a place they call the Tomb of the Christian Woman. I hear strange stories about it, but I've never been there. Go survey it and come back to Thrysdus."

"Whatever you say," assented Wulf.

She turned and talked to Khalid. Wulf sought Bhakrann, who said he would look after provisions for their journey. They chose two horses each. Bhakrann would take Cham along, Wulf would take Smarja. In the morning, the Cahena gave each of them a purse of silver coins.

"You'll be a hundred and fifty miles along when you go north of Cirta," she said. "From above Cirta, another hundred miles or so to Cuicul. I have been there; it's a half-ruined town, but its people are vigorous. Some followed Lartius with us. And then go on, go on to that Tomb of the Christian Woman." She smiled. "Be wise and diplomatic, Wulf. I'll wait for your report at Thrysdus."

In the gray dawn the four of them rode away. The air was warm and dry. Behind them rose dust, and within its cloud showed the dark head of a mounted column. They slowed their pace and let the leaders catch up. Lartius was one, and he said that his warriors were returning to Cirta. He invited Wulf and Bhakrann to come with him and be entertained.

"Pretty women there." He snickered. "Too many, really, for me to notice as they deserve." But Wulf declined with thanks, saying that he was ordered to keep to the coast.

Two days of riding, two nights of camping, before Lartius led his men off on a trail to the southwest. Pursuing their own way, Wulf and Bhakrann visited a string of small villages, where they were entertained with fish dinners, bathed in the sea, and heard exultations over the Cahena's victory. They turned inland to a sizable town called Cuicul, perhaps two hundred and fifty miles west of Bulla Regia and a hundred beyond Cirta. Here, once-sturdy walls were more or less tumbled down, as was a large circus oval outside them, but the inhabitants were hospitable. A genial old chief said that Cuicul had once been a Roman legion's garrison town, that the legionnaires had married native girls and prospered, and that a series of attacks by Imazighen raiders had half ruined the defenses and houses. News of Hassan's defeat had come there. A number of Cuicul's warriors had been with Lartius on the campaign. These would be returning to tell of the fighting.

"Maybe they'll bring plunder," said the old chief. "How much plunder was taken? Gold, jewels?"

"Here's a sample," said Wulf, giving him a broad gold piece. For that, Wulf and his party were given supplies of smoked goat's flesh and flaps of barley bread and raisins. They went north to the seacoast again. After a week or so of camping among pleasant orchards and vineyards, they reached Tipaza.

This was a town with a harbor and fishing boats. News of the great battle was little more than rumor there, but the people of Tipaza knew about the Cahena, her military skill and the strange voices that guided her. What sort of place was Thrysdus? Wulf found it hard to explain in terms they could understand. Was the Cahena as beautiful as report said? More beautiful than that, replied Wulf. Would the Moslems invade again? If they did, Wulf predicted, they would be defeated again.

The party was quartered in a hut within sound of beating waves. Bhakrann ate shellfish and counted on his rough fingers.

"This is our twenty-third day, and I judge we've come better than five hundred miles," he said to Wulf. "When do we turn back?"

"The Cahena told me to go to something called the Tomb of the Christian Woman," replied Wulf.

"People here talk about that, and not good talk," said Bhakrann. "They say there's an evil spirit. Stray sheep get torn to pieces. A pair of lovers wandered there one night and were found with their throats ripped out. I didn't hear the Cahena's orders, so I don't have to go there. Don't you go there, either, Wulf."

"I heard her orders, and I'll go."

Five more days of journey brought them to another seaside village, where they had supper of couscous with scraps of salt fish in it. Their hosts said that the Tomb of the Christian Woman lay an hour's ride westward, and added that it was a place of blackly ill omen. Bhakrann and Cham and Smarja frowned as Wulf rode out alone under the sinking sun.

The way was rocky, fringed with thorn bushes and occasional grim-looking trees. The moon came out, round and pallid. By its light, Wulf saw what must be the tomb. He rode close, dismounted and tied his horse to a tree, and looked.

It was a great round structure in the moonlight, its domed roof tufted with coarse grass. He walked to it, his sword drawn. It was more than a hundred feet high as he guessed, and considerably more than that in diameter. It was built of ancient-looking cut stones, dark and light, spaced about with pillar-like columns set into the wall. Wulf wondered if he heard a moan of voices somewhere, inside or out. He paced along the circumference and came to where steps led down in the glow of the moon. He walked down. There was a stone-faced door. It opened under his hand, with a dry groan of movement. Sooty darkness inside.

"Nobody here but me," he said aloud, for the comfort of his own voice.

"Am I nobody?"

She stood within, a woman in a long dark cloak. Her short, curly hair seemed ivory pale. Her face was round, her dark lips full. She held a lamp, and now she blew on it, and up rose a murky flame. Her eyes on him were bright and silvery pale, like two coins.

"You've come here, too," Wulf said to her.

"Come here? I live here."

The lamplight showed that she was amply symmetrical in her loosely folded cloak, deep-breasted, wide-hipped, mature but not old. Some would think her appetizing.

"Who are you?" he asked.

"My name doesn't matter. What's yours?"

"Wulf."

"I know your name; it's come all the way to me, here in these parts. You fought those invaders off there to the east, you won the Cahena's battle for her. I know her name, too. Come in."

He stepped into the entry. The air was stuffily close. "Tomb of the Christian Woman," he said, looking into her pale eyes. "It seems older than Christianity."

She smiled. "I'd call it more than eight hundred years old. It was built for a king named Bocchus."

"Bacchus?"

"Bocchus," she corrected him. "Powerful Bocchus, warlike and stern."

"You sound as if you knew him," said Wulf, and her full lips parted to show small, sharp teeth.

"What if I said I did know him?" she half mocked. "Knew him so well that he put a curse on me when he died, told me to live forever in his tomb?"

If it was a joke, Wulf didn't understand it. He smiled back at her. "You don't seem anything like eight hundred years old," he said.

"Come, let me show you the inside of this place."

They went together into an inner corridor. She carried the lamp high, and Wulf saw that the walls were of rough, rocky make. He heard a noise as of breathing. He counted the paces he made on their journey—about thirty, say something more than seventy-five feet. Then they were in a central chamber, rectangular, stone-floored. Against the far wall was what looked like a sort of dark couch or pallet.

"Here," she said, and led him to stand beside the couch. Stooping, she set the lamp on the floor and straightened again to look at him. Her eyes shone pallidly.

"Wulf," she half whispered, "do you know what love is?"

"I know, to my sorrow," he said, resting his sword point on the stones of the floor.

"To your sorrow." She leaned toward him. She seemed to have grown taller. "Love has been pain to you."

She smiled. Her teeth looked sharp as needles.

"Your Cahena, Wulf," she said. "She's beautiful, isn't she? Wise, isn't she?"

"You know about her," said Wulf, not liking the idea.

"I know about lots of things. I lie all day, numberless days, and all I do is think and know. Your Cahena is guided by voices. What if I sent those voices, what if her wisdom comes from me, to ruin her at last?"

Wulf scowled and clamped his hand on the hilt of his sword. "Ruin her?" he said. "Why ruin her? Are you jealous of her?"

"Perhaps I only envy her. She's there, with all that power and worship, and I'm here alone, not understood, not spoken to. Do you love the Cahena, Wulf?"

He kept his voice steady. "I think that any man who sees her wants to dare to love her."

"Do you dare love her?" she asked.

Wulf was losing his temper. "How I feel about the Cahena doesn't come into this conversation."

"Then you do love her." The teeth showed again. "Shouldn't we love?"

He poked with his sword point at the dark pallet. Then, quickly, he stepped well clear of her and passed the sword so that his other hand held its broad blade. He lifted the cross hilt almost into her face.

"That's earth in your bed," he said, quite levelly. "It makes me sure of what you are."

"Don't!" she suddenly wailed, and fell back before the cross hilt. She put her back against the wall, flung out her arms.

"So," said Wulf, "it's true that your sort can't face the shape of the cross. You wouldn't tell me your name. Shall I name you? Shall I call you Lamia?"

She squeaked like a bat, so shrilly that his ears tingled.

"Lamia," he said, "I wish you a quiet, hungry evening."

She writhed. Wulf whirled and strode back into the darkness of the passage, his left hand on the wall to guide him.

"You can't go!" she cried behind him, but he went. He did not run, but he went swiftly. He was at the door and through it. He sprang upward into the night with the moon swimming overhead. He ran toward where his horse waited.

"No!" her voice beat at him from behind. She must have followed him to the door. The horse whinnied in recognition of him. He ripped the bridle from its tether, mounted, and rode away at a swift trot that he urged into a canter.

He had known what that woman, that devil-woman was. She had been a peril to him, but he had warded her off, had thrust aside the spell she had tried. She had spoken of love. Love had wounded Wulf, but love could not destroy him. Certainly not the kind of love that Lamia had meant to give him.

XIX

Back at the hut where his party had been lodged, Wulf turned his horse over to Smarja and went in. Bhakrann sat up in a corner.

"You look as if you'd seen a ghost, Wulf," he said.

"I've seen worse than that," growled Wulf. "Somebody bring the chiefs of this place here. I'll tell them about it."

Cham hurried to fetch back three men and a gaunt, gray woman. They sat cross-legged on the floor. Wulf stared at them.

"A woman's there at that tomb," he said. "She isn't a Christian woman, not exactly a woman." Scowling, he sought for words. "Maybe she's called that because, lifetimes ago, Christianity was an ugly word here. The Goths and Vandals could be unpleasant—but let that pass."

"Then what is she?" asked the old woman, who was a sort of priestess of a belief Wulf did not know. "Is she dead or alive?"

"Not truly one or the other," Wulf told her. "A demon, if you like to say that. The Greeks called such a thing a lamia, sometimes a mormo, sometimes an empusa. When I was at Constantinople, Huns in the cavalry told me about creatures along their river Dana, what the Romans call the river Danuvius. At night, such a being rises from a bed of earth and drinks living blood. Blood of animals if that's all it can get, but blood of men and women if it can get that."

They all goggled nervously, even Bhakrann. "You're sure?" prompted the priestess, huddling her mantle around her.

"Yes, and I'm also sure that she can be done away with," said Wulf. "She's terrible at night, but she's powerless by day. We'll go there tomorrow at sunrise to destroy her."

"Not I," vowed one of the listeners. "Not for anything."

"I'll go," declared Bhakrann. "I shouldn't have skulked here last night. Do you know how to kill her, Wulf?"

"Yes. Sunrise tomorrow, then. But for now, I've said enough and more than enough. I want some sleep."

For Wulf was tired. He had seldom been so tired in his life.

At dawn, Wulf found a stout length of hardwood, and with his dagger sharpened it to a lean point. "Do we have any garlic?" he asked.

"Lots of it," said Cham, fetching a handful of cloves from a saddlebag.

"Bring it along and let's go."

They saddled up, Wulf and Bhakrann and Smarja and Cham. Of the villagers, only the gaunt priestess dared join them. They rode to the great domed tomb under a murky rising sun, dismounted, and left Smarja to hold the horses. Wulf led the way, carrying his sharpened stake. The others drew back as he descended into the entry and shoved the door open.

She lay just inside, jumbled in her cloak. Her half-opened silver eyes brooded. Her teeth showed. Wulf hooked a hand in her armpit and dragged her out and up into the open. She lay flaccidly on her back. The others stared.

"Give me the garlic," said Wulf, and Cham put it into his hand. Wulf dragged the limp jaw down and stuffed the garlic into the mouth. A sound as of retching came from somewhere.

"Pick up that big stone, Bhakrann," directed Wulf, and set the point of the stake to her motionless breast. "Now, hit it the hardest blow you can. Drive it in."

Grim-faced, Bhakrann lifted the heavy stone high in both hands and brought it down with all his strength. The point went deeply in, as into muddy soil, went through flesh and bone. The blank face writhed, she squeaked like a bat. Then she went slack all over.

"It killed her," said Bhakrann, staring at a trickle of thick dark blood.

"We'll make sure, the way I've heard in stories," said Wulf, and dragged the body to level ground. "Pick up wood, lots of it. But stay here, you priestess. Say your best prayer to ward off bad magic."

The priestess trembled as she chattered something. Wulf and the others ranged after fuel. Then they laid a pyre and dragged the body upon it. More wood went on top, and more, as high as a man's waist, with handfuls of dry grass poked in here and there. Bhakrann scraped flint and steel, his hands steady at the scraping. The grass flared up, a flurry of flame burst out of the wood.

They stayed clear of the heat and smoke, the priestess muttering all the while. Wulf did not know the gods she called by name. Once they all went to fetch more wood. At last—and it was midmorning by then—the pyre had burned down to black ashes and glowing embers. Among the embers they saw bits of charred bone.

"Your village can visit this tomb safely now," Wulf told the priestess. "Let's go back and have breakfast. I'm hungry."

Breakfast was eaten in the presence of a stream of visitors, loudly thanking Wulf, praising him. He bade them take example of the dead she-devil's defeat and the tomb where she had ruled, told them not to fear fear, to face fear, to make fear be afraid. He and his friends packed their gear, turned their horses eastward again, and rode away with the villagers staring worshipfully after them. Bhakrann rode beside Wulf.

"I never killed a woman before," said Bhakrann. "Did you?"

"Don't say that it was a woman. Say that it was a lamia."

"Do you feel all right about it?"

"I feel free," said Wulf. "Just free. When we camp tonight, let's have a swim in the sea."

They swam in the moonlight, and ate fish that Cham and Smarja speared in the shallows. Wulf slept soundly, the soundest since they had left Bulla Regia, and did not dream. Some sort of peace had come upon him. Riding next day, he tried to explain that peace to himself.

"You're serious," observed Bhakrann, ambling beside Wulf. "You think."

"Often I think," said Wulf. "Just now, I'd better think about how we'll report on all these people, and on what happened at the Tomb of the Christian Woman."

"*Ahi,* you think we destroyed an enemy there."

"Yes." Wulf nodded.

And perhaps he had defeated an enemy within himself. The Cahena had made one of her enigmatic decisions. As once she had drawn Wulf to her, now she had drawn Khalid. She could cast spells, as the Lamia creature had tried to cast a spell on Wulf and had failed. Maybe he could be free of the spell of the Cahena, the dream of the Cahena.

Day after day they traveled. The weather grew warmer, and sometimes there was rain. At every town they revisited, the people hailed them as friends, as triumphant warriors. They reached Bulla Regia and turned south to come at last to Thrysdus. The Cahena herself came to the main gate to greet them, smiling radiantly. To Wulf she looked as beautiful as she had looked the first time he had seen her. At her side walked Khalid, turbaned and rich-robed, with a great gold rosary at his neck. He salaamed low to Wulf. "I'm glad to see you back safe and in good health," he said.

The Cahena led them to her council chamber. Ketriazar and Daris were there, and Djalout. Wulf told of their journey, of the general friendliness of the seacoast settlements, and described in detail his adventure at the Tomb of the Christian Woman. They heard him with earnest attention.

"I take it this Lamia, as you call her, frightened you," said Ketriazar when Wulf had finished. "It's hard to think of you being afraid."

"The unknown can terrify," put in Djalout. "Things like the thing Wulf met and destroyed aren't so rare in the world. Both Jews and Arabs wear charms to keep them away. Lilim, they're called—is that another name for Lamia? And the Lamia has been reported in Libya, not so far away from where we're sitting."

"I don't want to meet one, by whatever name," said Daris.

"She talked to you about love, Wulf," said the Cahena, her eyes brilliant.

"The love she talked was greedy. A love that drank blood. A love that would kill."

"Is love like that?" the Cahena asked.

"Not with me," Wulf replied, meeting her gaze. "I won't die for love. I'd rather die in battle."

He felt uncomfortable. Perhaps it was his sticky, sweaty tunic. He would change it soon.

"You say that she knew about me," the Cahena reminded.

"Yes, and she said she might overthrow you," said Wulf. "Well, she can't do that now. We burned her to ashes."

Khalid tweaked the point of his beard. "What might have happened to her spirit?" he wondered. "We Arabs call such things ifrits, demons."

"Let's change the subject," said the Cahena. "Khalid"—and a caress came into her voice—"you've suggested a policy to me. Tell this council your thoughts."

Khalid looked from one to another of the group, as though thinking what to say. Finally he spoke:

"I'll remind you that Hassan himself, and most of his officers, are Arabs who have been Moslems all their lives. But this army of his comes from everywhere, from conquered tribes, many of them here in Africa. It's made up of men who make a loud pretense of being Moslems, but they were converted with swords at their throats."

"True." Djalout nodded.

"They follow Hassan because they want to conquer and plunder."

"True," said Djalout again.

"Here in this land, the Imazighen have cities and property," went on Khalid. "Herds, orchards, fields of grain. These hordes that Hassan commands, they want those things." Again he looked around at them. "Loot is what they're after. What if there was nothing for them to conquer and steal?"

He waited for somebody to say something.

"What you mean is to leave them no loot," said Daris at last.

"That's just what he means," declared the Cahena. "Level our towns, lay our fields waste, leave nothing. We can do it. The Imazighen have been wanderers, have lived lifetimes in the wilderness. It sounds like good wisdom to me."

"And to me," said Ketriazar weightily. "My people live in tents. They can move wherever they like—camp one place, camp another. If I said to do it, they'd do it."

"My tribe would do the same," Daris seconded him.

"What about Lartius?" wondered Djalout. "What about Yaunis?"

"They'll have to do what I command," said the Cahena. "I follow Khalid's advice here, leave the Moslems no profit in another invasion." She lifted a hand in dismissal. "That's all for now, you may go. But stay here with me, Wulf."

The others departed. Khalid looked back at Wulf once. Wulf sat opposite the Cahena and waited. When they were alone, she smiled radiantly.

"We haven't seen much of each other lately," she almost purred.

"I've been away for two months on your orders, Lady Cahena."

She pursed her mouth. "You won't call me Daia?"

"I don't think I should."

"Suit yourself. But tell me more about this thing at the tomb, the one you call Lamia."

He told her his adventure, in detail. She nodded as she listened.

"And she said those things about me, as if she knew me," the Cahena said when he finished. "Said she helped me, but she didn't say she liked me. Was she an enemy, far away there at our backs?"

"Not anymore," said Wulf. "She's nothing but ashes now. She doesn't exist in this world, maybe not in the next."

The Cahena leaned toward him. "Wulf," she said, "what about us?"

"I do my best to carry out your orders."

"Have you forgotten—"

"I've forgotten nothing."

She leaned closer, as once she had leaned to him in the days before Khalid came.

"Love," she said softly. "You've said that you loved me. Shouldn't love make us wise, make us sensible?"

He did not lean back to her. He frowned silently for a moment. The Lamia, too, had spoken of love, had offered it. At last he said:

"I don't agree that love does that. When you're in love you need to be wise and sensible, but it doesn't work like that. Love confuses you. You're blinded by lightning flashes, you're deafened by rolling thunder. Your blood races, your heart beats like a drum, you believe dreams and not realities. You're not rational."

She was quickly on her feet, and so was he. Her splendid eyes glittered fiercely.

"You're irritating," she said between set teeth.

"You asked me a question about love and I answered it as well as I could."

She motioned at the door. "Perhaps you'd better go."

"Perhaps so."

She prodded his back with her eyes as he left. At his quarters, he stripped off his travel-fouled garments and put on a dark red Moslem robe and slippers with turned-up toes. He went to the bath and lay for long minutes in a steaming tub, scrubbing himself thoroughly. The bath attendant trimmed his beard and cut his hair. Then Wulf returned to his room and sat on the cushioned bed-shelf. He poured himself a cup of wine, and thought.

Whatever the Cahena had meant to do with him, she had not done it. Had not shaken him, defeated him. What would happen between them now he did not know, did not care to know.

The heavy door murmured open. Someone peeped in, then came in. It was Daphne, in a long gown of black and silver, draped close to her plumply curved body. Her hair was bound with a lacy fillet. She closed the door and the latch fell into place, with a click like a dagger going into its sheath.

"There, I've locked us in," she said. "I wanted to see you. I've missed you."

"Will you have a drink with me?" he asked, and filled a cup. She sat on the shelf with him and they drank. The wine was sharp, strong. It made Wulf's nose tingle.

"How do you like Thrysdus?" he asked her.

"We're getting used to it." Her eyes crinkled with a smile. "My father's busy making swords. Everyone wants a sword now, along with his javelins. You've taught our warriors about the sword, Wulf."

"I wish nobody needed a sword," he said. "Fighting gets tiresome."

"Yes, doesn't it?" She drank and put her plump little hand on his wrist. "What do you need to make you happy?"

"Peace, I think. For everybody."

"Maybe a little stir of action now and then?"

Her face was almost against his. He kissed her mouth.

"Oh," she whispered.

His arm slid around her of its own volition. There was nothing under her gown, nothing but Daphne. She kissed him strongly.

"I've wanted this," she said, close to his ear. "Wanted it since the first day at Tiergal, when you came for your mail coat."

He said nothing. For a moment, the Cahena was out of his angry mind. He put down his cup and slid his hand inside her black and silver gown. She was made snugly, silkily. She sighed, and she was feeling inside his robe, too.

Down she sank on the cushions, holding him tightly to her. He shrugged out of his robe and drew her garment open. Her body was paler than the Cahena's body, it was an abundant body, it welcomed him. As he covered her, she lifted her loins to his.

It was long before they were finished with each other.

XX

Afterward, Wulf wondered if the Cahena could know, she who knew so much. Perhaps she didn't bother to know, in her preoccupation with Khalid. As for Daphne, she comforted Wulf. They met again and then again. She always came to him when nobody would disturb them. She soothed him like wholesome bread, where the Cahena had stirred him like strong wine.

The Cahena sent for him one evening and received him alone in her chamber. She motioned him to sit opposite her. "I've an important errand for you," she said.

"What errand, Lady Cahena?"

No faint whispers in the room, no half-heard music as in times before. Wulf heard only her voice.

"You know what's been decided," she said. "We'll make a desert here, leave nothing for those invaders to steal. Carry my orders to Lartius and to Yaunis, out there in the northwest."

He frowned. "What if they don't like those orders?"

"They'll have to see wisdom," she said, sternness in her voice. "I want their towns razed to their foundations, I want their groves and orchards cut down. Tell them I said so. You heard Ketriazar and Daris agree."

Still he frowned. "Ketriazar and Daris are used to the wild, roaming life. These others are different. They won't understand."

"They don't have to understand." Her fine teeth showed. "All they need do is obey." She studied him. "You'll obey, too."

"I'll go and give them your orders," he agreed. "When do I go?"

"Start tomorrow. Is that agreeable?"

"May I take Bhakrann?"

She shook her head. "Bhakrann handles our exchanges of their officers and gets back ransoms—weapons, camels, horses, gold, and so on. And he watches that life of castles Hassan is building. Take someone else."

"I'll take my man Susi, yes, and Cham. Cham has scouted all those lands."

The Cahena nodded permission. "And you go tomorrow, I say. Will you eat here with me? Talk with me?"

Her voice sounded winning, but Wulf rose and bowed.

"With your permission, I go make ready."

She pouted at that. "We should be better friends, Wulf."

"I'm your warrior and your errand runner, Lady Cahena."

"You don't call me Daia."

"How would I dare? Give me leave to go."

He stooped to kiss her shadow, and went.

At early dawn Wulf and Cham and Susi rode away on their best horses, leading a pack mule with provisions. Cham showed them a trail to the northwest, not a good one but plainly marked. There were wells here and there, and occasional hamlets of a few huts apiece. Sometimes women held important posts in those places, as chieftainesses and priestesses. When the party stopped for a night, they were gladly entertained, were sung to and praised as conquerors of Moslems. Wulf told of the Cahena's plan to blot out villages and farms, and his hearers listened soberly but did not protest.

Reaching Cirta at last, they were hospitably greeted by Lartius, who gave them a fine supper, served by his sketchily clad maidservants. Wulf set forth the Cahena's orders of destruction. Lartius knitted his black brows. "Destroy Cirta? You'd need thousands to do that. Cirta is a fortress, a treasure city. Cirta has been here for centuries."

"I'm here to tell you the Lady Cahena's orders," said Wulf evenly. "She wants to deny the Moslems any plunder, any profit or provision or shelter."

Lartius shook his head. "If we destroyed our town, there would still be this height—Cirta's a natural fortification. Wulf, I don't follow your advice."

"It's not my advice, it's the order of the Cahena."

Lartius munched a fig. "Whose advice is it, then? Khalid's?"

"Yes, Khalid's advice," Wulf felt obliged to say. "He points out that Hassan's followers are mostly new, half-converted Moslems, who want spoils of war." He gazed at Lartius. "All right, she'll be waiting for your answer."

"I'll have to think, it needs thinking," said Lartius unhappily.

"Do I take that back for your answer?"

"Yes, tell her that." Lartius managed a smile. "Let's change the subject. Do you fancy any of these nice girls waiting on us? Pick one for your bedfellow tonight."

"Thanks, but I'll leave early tomorrow to visit Yaunis, and I don't want to start out feeling jaded."

"That's wisdom, anyway." Lartius clapped his hands, and a eunuch came to them. "Show Wulf where he'll sleep."

At dawn Wulf's party headed westward. They came to where Yaunis kept his place, a busy village somewhat similar to the Tiergal Wulf had known. Yaunis soberly heard Wulf's report on the Cahena's policy of destruction.

"I never heard such stern measures," vowed Yaunis. "We settled here I don't know how many lifetimes ago. How can we go wild, the way she orders?"

"Ketriazar and Daris will go wild," Wulf reminded him. "So will the Djerwa."

"But they've always been tent dwellers and hunters," said Yaunis. "I'll have to call in my subchiefs and wise men and women, hear what they say about this."

"The Cahena thinks she's the one to say, about everything."

"I'll confer with my people and send my message to Thrysdus."

Wulf led his party back the way it had come. He reported to the Cahena, who sat with Khalid beside her and tightened her lips as she heard what Lartius and Yaunis had said.

"So they balk?" she snapped. "Weigh my orders before they obey? Maybe I should go up there and do the destruction myself."

"What if they rebelled?" suggested Wulf.

She tossed her head, stirring her black cloud of hair.

"They wouldn't dare. I'm their queen. I saved them from the Moslems and I'll save them again, in spite of their objections." She looked at Khalid. "Would you lead a force to tear them down?"

"I'd obey any command from you," said Khalid, bowing.

"We'll see," she said. "Thank you for that news, Wulf."

He sought his own apartment. As he entered, Daphne slipped in behind him. He closed and barred the door. She threw her arms around him, pressed herself to him.

"Welcome home," she whispered against his cheek.

Time went on. Bhakrann and his scouts took one Moslem officer after another eastward to Hassan and brought back weapons and horses and gold. Bhakrann said that Hassan's line of forts neared completion and that new swarms of Moslems gathered there.

"They look like another army of invasion," Bhakrann said in council.

"Invasion and plunder," said Khalid from beside the Cahena. "If they find anything worth taking."

"They won't," declared the Cahena. "I'll see to that."

She told Wulf and Khalid and Mallul to stay while the others left. Stooping above a flicker of fire in a corner of the room, she whispered rhythmically. She strewed dust from an embroidered pouch on the fire, which blazed up pale blue. Again she whispered. Finally she turned back toward the three men.

"I don't understand," she said, almost plaintively.

"You don't hear your voices?" asked Wulf, and her eyes glittered at him.

"I know where to turn for counsel," she said, and looked at Khalid, who made his graceful bow.

"I know what to do, and I'll see that it's done," she said. "Are you rested, Wulf? Then go to Ketriazar and Daris. Say that I order them up yonder to Cirta, to see that it's laid waste."

"I'll go tomorrow," said Wulf. "I'll take Susi and Cham."

Daphne slipped into Wulf's room that night, barred the door, and fairly leaped into his arms. Again she was a solace to him. She left at midnight. At dawn Wulf gathered his party and rode away westward.

He found Ketriazar's Medusi living in tents, happily hunting deer and wild hogs. Ketriazar greeted the visitors with a dinner of big snails stewed in highly seasoned olive oil. When Wulf repeated the Cahena's orders, Ketriazar smiled in relish.

"I'll come with you to see Daris," he said.

Daris's people, too, had taken readily to a tent-dwelling nomad life, and Daris chose his best cavalry squadrons to join with those of Ketriazar. Almost two thousand strong, these forces rode northward on a mission they seemed to relish in advance.

Back at Thrysdus, Wulf met Bhakrann. Bhakrann had been busy returning the last of the captured Moslem officers to Hassan and bringing back goods and gold for ransom. His first question puzzled Wulf:

"You've been out in the west. How are things? I mean, did you see any odd shapes or hear any odd noises?"

"Why no, nothing like that," said Wulf. "Nothing strange."

Bhakrann shrugged. "Nothing strange in these parts, either. That's what's strange about it. No appearances, voices, little happenings out of the ordinary. Not even with the Cahena."

"Not even a glimpse of Khro?" said Wulf, and Bhakrann glared.

"Didn't I tell you, don't say that name?"

"Why not say it?" Wulf flung back. "I know it means death. But I'm not afraid of death. I've been so close to death, time after time, I could see the flash of hell's flames. Death doesn't bother me. Let death come, any day and any hour."

Bhakrann's glare became a blank stare. "You must be lost in your heart."

"Don't bother about my heart, old friend."

He sat down in his apartment to drink wine. He was drinking a considerable amount of wine these days. A diffident scratching at the door, and he went to open it and in came Daphne.

She looked plump and pleasant, caught up in one of the captured Moslem garments she liked. Wulf smiled down at her.

"What's on your mind?" he asked.

"What's usually on my mind?" she asked back, and flung the garment from her bare body. She was an opulently toothsome sight like that. Wulf caught her in a hug so powerful that she gave a bubbling gasp.

Quickly, eagerly, they had each other. Wulf wondered why he did not truly love Daphne for her gladness, her passionate acceptance of him. He almost forgot the Cahena at the supreme moment with Daphne—but not quite. The Cahena could never be forgotten. Never never.

Crops grew and farmers brought them in for trade. Word came from Ketriazar about events at Cirta.

Lartius had protested, had resisted. He had mustered warriors to face Ketriazar and Daris, and there had been a skirmish of sorts. Two of Ketriazar's Medusi killed, two of Daris's Nefussa, and maybe twenty of the

Cirta force. Lartius had retreated up his height to go on the defensive, and the men of the expedition had gleefully set fire to grain fields, chopped down big orchards, had laid the land waste for miles around Cirta. From there they had gone to seek Yaunis, but Yaunis and his people had left their settlement to live in tents and gather what wild food they could. Ketriazar and Daris had burned their houses and destroyed their crops, had done the same thing elsewhere. The coastal territories in those parts, once pleasantly fruitful, were becoming the desert the Cahena had commanded.

Djalout and Wulf talked about it.

"I can't publicly challenge her plan," said Djalout. "I can only deplore it in private."

"She's trying the loyalty of her chieftains," said Wulf. "Surely she didn't make such a move at the bidding of her spirit voices."

"It was at the bidding of the very human voice of Khalid." Djalout stroked his beard thoughtfully. "Once we heard the echoes of those who spoke to the Cahena. But things are becoming distressingly workaday—dully logical, don't you think?"

"Now that you mention it, yes," said Wulf. "I've missed a strangeness in the land, the air. The last really extraordinary business was at that Tomb of the Christian Woman."

"Where you destroyed that Lamia." Djalout nodded. "Has it occurred to you that her destruction may have had its effect on all this land?"

"She was evil," Wulf said. "She claimed to know all about the Cahena, said she influenced the Cahena, would eventually see her defeated. I'm glad she's gone."

"Something's gone with her. All sorts of strange somethings. How shall we fare without them?"

"A lot of that depends on Hassan, gathering his new forces," said Wulf.

"He'll come at us again," said Djalout. "I don't pretend to hear prophesying voices, I only observe events. Meanwhile, the Cahena acts on the advice of Khalid."

"Do you approve of laying the land waste?" Wulf asked him.

"My approval hasn't been sought, and neither has yours. Come, I want you to meet somebody."

They went down to the lower level and out in the great open arena, where horses of the guard details were picketed. Djalout led the way to a sort of makeshift tent of striped cloth, pegged against the wall. Before it sat a small misshapen man, cross-legged, scanty-bearded, staring at them.

"This is Shua, Wulf." Djalout made the introductions. "He's been in Egypt, he's watched Hassan's preparations, and he can tell us some interesting things."

Shua got up. His thin legs were bowed, his back rose in a hump almost as high as his head. His dark, wrinkled face looked like a fuzzy raisin. His eyes were so bright that they almost bit.

"You're welcome here, Shua," said Wulf. "Where are you from, and what's your calling?"

Shua stamped crookedly to where a horse stood tethered. Like Shua, it was brownish black and, like Shua, it was misshapen. Its legs were grotesquely knuckled, it was deeply swaybacked under its old saddle. Its head on its scrawny neck was as blunt as a melon. Shua groped in a saddlebag and brought out a gleaming round crystal.

"I'm from Ethiopia," he growled. "Your Moslem troublemakers haven't come there yet. By trade, I'm a soothsayer."

"We hope you can say sooth," said Djalout politely.

Shua squatted at his little tent. He was almost as tall sitting as he had been standing. He glared at his crystal ball.

"Say sooth?" he repeated. "I wanted to see what sooth you say here. I've heard of the wisdom and power of your Queen Cahena, of all the gods you worship. I came to find out, and I find nothing."

"You think we haven't any skills," suggested Wulf.

"Maybe you had them once, but where did they go from you?" flung back Shua. "I made my journey, I wanted to learn and profit. But nothing I do has any response. Look here."

He held out the crystal on his palm. "Look at it. Think of the future, what it may hold. Look hard, think hard."

Wulf studied the shining globe. Bright motes seemed to stir in it, to form a pulsing cloud. Wulf looked. The cloud grew dim, melted away.

"You see?" grated Shua. "No, you don't see. There should have been a figure, somebody with a broom, sweeping to make ready for a vision. And after that—" He clamped the crystal in skinny fingers. "No good, not here! You don't have any gods or spirits or angels or devils. Nothing!"

"It makes things pleasantly uneventful," said Djalout.

"I'm a scholar, a soothsayer, looking for truth," yammered Shua. "Truth—what is truth?"

"Ah," said Djalout, "that question was once asked by a Roman official named Pontius Pilate, of a troublesome agitator named Jesus. Pilate didn't wait for an answer, which might have been illuminating." He smiled down on Shua. "What do you plan to do, now that you're disappointed in us here?"

"I'm leaving, but not for Ethiopia just yet," said Shua. "I want to go to that Tomb of the Christian Woman I hear about, see the nature of things there. I'll leave tomorrow morning."

"Good," approved Djalout. "Come and eat with us."

At dawn Shua loaded his patient, deformed horse with a bundle of supplies, hoisted himself astride, and rode away. Djalout and Wulf watched.

"I want to hear of his adventures when he comes back," said Djalout. "If he does come back, that is."

The Cahena called a council to consider all reports of Hassan and his line of fortresses where, said Bhakrann, reinforcements kept trickling in. Ketriazar told how he and Daris had fought and driven Lartius's men and had destroyed fields and orchards there and elsewhere along the coast. "It's a desert up there now," Ketriazar said happily. "Those soft city people can find out how to live in the wilderness. It'll toughen them up."

"We ran them like rats at Cirta," added Daris. "You should have been there, Wulf, with that big old widow-making sword of yours."

"I'm glad I wasn't," said Wulf, and the Cahena turned her brilliant eyes upon him.

"Why are you glad of that?" she challenged.

"Lady Cahena, I get sick of killing," he said. "War has been my trade ever since I was a boy, but I see that war gets nobody anywhere. I wish we could stop it, among ourselves and with the Moslems."

"I thought that war was your great study in life," she said.

"More or less, but I've studied other things, and wish I'd studied them better."

The Cahena listened to more reports of how the northern country had been laid waste, and frowned over Lartius's defiance. "Well," she said at last, "he may hold on top of his mountain, but his crops are ruined. He'll have to leave Cirta, and we'll move in and raze it. How about Yaunis?"

"He didn't like to obey, but he did," said Ketriazar. "Packed up his people and went away with their herds and their tents. I tried to talk to him, but he didn't listen."

"Let him sulk until he sees my wisdom," said the Cahena. "Or, should I say, Khalid's wisdom."

"You flatter me, Lady Cahena," said Khalid, with his smile.

"Wulf, you and Bhakrann will scout to see to the destruction of the crops," went on the Cahena. "Go tomorrow morning, and get a good rest tonight."

Wulf rested only part of the night, because Daphne came stealing in to him. So tenderly she treated him, so passionately, that he felt guilty again that he did not utterly love her. She was so good.

XXI

Wulf was busy in the months that followed. The Cahena sent him northward to the seacoast, where details of Ketriazar's and Daris's men busily destroyed trees and crops and dismantled fishing villages. The inhabitants scowled but did not dare resist.

The land parched and grew bare. Smaller settlements obeyed the Cahena. They told Wulf that they would harvest one more crop of grain, pick the last fruit from their trees, then destroy everything and wander. They knew the hunting life.

Wulf talked to various wise men and women, who missed wonders they had known. They could not guess the weather, could not foretell what hunting parties would bring back to eat. When the Cahena heard his report, she was more or less pleased. He talked to Djalout, over cups of the good wine Djalout always found for them.

"What do you think of all this?" Djalout asked.

"I think nothing, I just obey orders. The Cahena tells me what to do, and I do it."

Djalout stroked his beard. "I wonder what voice she hears these days, other than the voice of Khalid. What do you think of him?"

"He has the ear of the Lady Cahena."

"Is that enough for you, Wulf?"

"It has to be enough."

Djalout smiled creasily. "Well, maybe the Moslems will come back and starve in a starved land. If that happens, if we can turn them back, maybe we can grow food and have towns again. I don't presume to forecast."

And there was Daphne, always Daphne. She came to Wulf whenever she could. He made love to her and wished he could talk to her. But she was not like the Cahena in talking. Or like the Cahena in lovemaking. There had never been one like the Cahena, in anything.

He had much to do. He drilled the men in various formations with javelins and stabbing spears, lest they grow rusty. He saw to bringing in supplies from far to the south, and paid for them. By now the Cahena had set up relays of riders to bring reports from all regions of the lands she ruled, and Wulf heard messages from Daris and Ketriazar; their tribes adjusted well to the old roaming, hunting life. From Yaunis came querulous complaints—his people did not like being primitive. From Lartius at Cirta came no word at all.

"Lartius is sulking," said the Cahena. "Let him sulk until he sees the wisdom of what we're doing."

"Yes," agreed Khalid, his eyes upon her.

Shua the Ethiopian came drifting back to Thrysdus, grotesque on his grotesque horse. Wulf and Djalout entertained him and he grumbled to them.

"I've been to that Tomb of the Christian Woman," he told them, scowling into a cup of Djalout's wine. "It's empty. The people graze their flocks around it and tell tales of whatever it was you managed to kill there. I take it that life isn't so interesting in those parts, not anymore."

"Not any more," Wulf echoed him.

"The women, for instance," resumed Shua sourly. "A traveler wants women to divert and refresh him. Don't stare, I've probably had more women in my time than the two of you together. But out there in your burned-over desert the women try to do old magics, old rites, and nothing comes of that. They complain about how they live. When the last grain is gone from the last harvest, what will be left to eat? Love, they say, isn't worth talking about. Their love gods don't appear. Maybe their love gods have vanished somewhere to a place where wonder still abides."

"Ah," crooned Djalout. "Any woman I may have once loved is now grown old and probably boresome."

"I've had my successes, in places where my magic worked." Shua's eyes glittered. "Love is magic, it must have magic to exist. Now, there's your Lady Cahena, as beautiful a woman as I've ever seen. Does she love? Wulf, you've been a close companion to her, does she love?"

"How should I know?" Wulf parried the question.

"What about that pretty young gallant of hers, Khalid? Do they love?"

"He advises her, and she takes his advice," said Djalout. "It was on his advice that she scorched all the land, destroyed the towns, to leave the invaders no plunder anywhere."

"That was bad advice," said Shua. "The people don't like it. They scold the Cahena's name. I gather that some of them have sent messages to the Moslems, hint that the Moslems would be welcome. How's that for news?"

"Sad news, but not totally surprising," said Djalout gravely. "I daresay that Wulf isn't totally surprised, either."

"Wulf seems to obey your Queen Cahena in everything," said Shua. "Maybe he loves her and doesn't dare say so."

"You've been arguing that love is dead here, like all magic," Wulf reminded him. "I wonder if you think that the death of that creature at the Tomb of the Christian Woman brought all this new aspect of life."

"It helped, it helped," growled Shua. "Now, my friends, I want to go back home to Ethiopia, where we can still have magic."

"Ethiopia," said Wulf. "It's an old country, a proud one."

"Yes, we're proud," Shua told him. "Our kings are descended from Solomon and Queen Balkis. Shabak came from Ethiopia to be pharaoh of Egypt. We've a right to be proud."

Wulf and Djalout found supplies for Shua's journey and bade him goodbye and good luck.

"He left in comparative good humor," commented Djalout. "He liked you, Wulf, your philosophies."

"You think I've become a philosopher?"

"I think you've always been a philosopher. Well, Shua's gone, but yonder I see Bhakrann, back from one of his hostage-trading trips." Bhakrann greeted them gloomily, but brightened when Djalout poured him wine.

"Good," said Bhakrann, smacking his lips over the cup. "Those Allah worshippers give you good things to eat, but nobody has wine except maybe in secret. And Hassan gets hard to bargain with."

"For hostages?" asked Wulf.

"He'll pay, but he wants to pay what he wants to pay. I asked him for swords, and he had none to spare." Bhakrann gritted his teeth. "None to spare? Why, he has bundles of swords, tied up like faggots of firewood. He won't let them go."

"He wants them for his own men," suggested Djalout.

"Yes, and he has lots of men. They crowd his string of forts. More men, I judge, than he had when we fought him and whipped him. He'll come against us again. A woman defeated him, and he wants revenge."

As Wulf pondered this, a messenger came to say that the Cahena summoned him to discuss an assignment.

She sat in her chamber with Mallul and Khalid. "You're to visit Yaunis and other peoples to the west," she said. "To see how they obey me. If the Moslems come again, I want them to starve wherever they invade."

"You'll see to that," put in Khalid. "Speak plainly to the people. Explain our reasons and remind them what will come of disobedience."

Wulf stared at him. "You're giving me orders, are you?"

"His orders are my orders," said the Cahena.

Wulf shifted his gaze to her. "I obey orders from you, not from Khalid or anybody else."

"Then obey my orders," she said bleakly. "Ride out tomorrow."

"Tomorrow," Wulf said after her. "Yes."

Daphne was with him that night, enveloping him with caresses. She wanted to go with him on his mission, and pouted when he said that that was out of the question. Between kisses, she said that she had been drilling archers in a field outside of Thrysdus, teaching them a harrow formation to send blizzardlike flights of arrows.

"But they're not the best archers," she complained. "Archers should be trained from when they're children. Those bowmen from Cirta are better."

"Cirta doesn't approve of what we're doing," said Wulf.

"Doesn't approve of what we're doing? You mean, like this?"

Her arms were around him. She laughed as he responded. She was so good.

Wulf left next morning. He took half a dozen Djerwa riders along, including Cham and Smarja. As they left Thrysdus, another man rode at a lope to join them. It was Mallul.

"I want to come with you, see what happens," he told Wulf.

Wulf wondered if Mallul would be a spy on him. "Did she send you?" he asked.

"No, I said I wanted to join you, and Khalid thought that was good, so I was given permission."

Wulf gazed off toward distant knolls. "Khalid gave you permission?"

"He suggested it, and my lady mother granted it." Mallul, too, stared away for a moment. Then: "Don't you like Khalid?"

"Do you?" parried Wulf.

"We get along well together. He knows so much. He and I talk in Arabic, and he's been teaching me to write in Arabic, too. Yes, I like Khalid."

The party crossed great expanses of what once had been good farmland. It was bare now, dusty now, and a spell of hot weather made it bleakly ugly. When they camped at the sides of streams, they filtered the sluggish, murky water through a cloth before they drank it. Here and there they found encampments of people, small family groups. Men seemed meditative, women were shy, children looked gaunt. Mallul talked to these people, eloquently assured them that the Cahena had their interests at heart. They heard him and said little in reply.

Wulf came to where Yaunis and his people lived. They had returned to their town, rebuilding huts and tending crops. Yaunis greeted Wulf courteously and answered questions by Mallul.

"You don't seem to be obeying orders," said Mallul.

"Wait until the Moslems come," Yaunis said. "If they should get this far, we could set fire to our homes, our grain, destroy everything within hours. As well wait till then as do it now."

"You wouldn't be here to see to it," reminded Wulf. "If the Moslems come, you'll be with us in the east to fight them."

"You don't have to tell me that," said Yaunis impatiently. "I've never turned my back on my duty. But it's hard to destroy all your own food and shelter. Lartius feels the same way at Cirta."

Wulf looked Yaunis up and down. Yaunis wore a handsomely patterned tunic and a jeweled chain. His beard was carefully trimmed to a point. Wulf remembered how Yaunis had talked of visiting Carthage, appreciating Carthage, the Carthage that again had been destroyed. After a moment, Wulf asked, "Is that the word you want me to take back to the Cahena?"

"Yes. She'll understand."

"She may understand much better than you'll like," said Wulf, and departed.

Wulf's companions protested as he led them by the southern trail toward Tiergal, and liked it even less when he ordered camp made at the palm-fringed spring where once the Cahena's escort had been aware of strange voices and appearances. They kept watch that night, in pairs, but no disturbance came. The haunted spring was haunted no more. The magic of the whole country had vanished.

He turned his march eastward and reached Thrysdus. The Cahena heard what Yaunis had said, and frowned over it.

"He's slow to obey, and I'd have expected better of him," she said. "It's not so strange that Lartius isn't trustworthy, but Yaunis—I'll have to bring him back into line. Where's Khalid? Bring him here, I want his views on this."

Wulf left her talking earnestly to Khalid, and found Djalout and Bhakrann idling among the horses grazing in the arena. He told them of his interview with Yaunis. Bhakrann scowled.

"Yaunis has always wanted the city life," he said. "It would do him good to live in the open, chasing deer and picking up snails. Will he stay with us?"

"I'm not sure," Wulf confessed.

"Which means you suspect he won't stay," said Djalout. "If he and Lartius desert us, there will go nearly half of our fighting force. And the Moslems will be coming again."

"My scouts say that more men show up almost every day at Hassan's line of forts," said Bhakrann. "And he collects big mountains of supplies—food, weapons, everything. Maybe making this land into a desert won't starve him. He'll bring along his own lunch. How do we fight them, Wulf?"

"It'll take some doing," said Wulf. "I must think about it."

"We must all think about it," said Djalout. "Thinking is difficult—that is why so few people do it. We try to consider the nature of reality and then the nature of wonder."

"And sometimes we find both those natures the same," said Wulf, and Bhakrann blinked at him.

"The things you say are strange things until you say them," he vowed.

"Maybe he associates with me too much," said Djalout, with one of his rare laughs. "Or *can* he associate with me too much?"

The Cahena summoned Wulf, to tell him to make a new survey of the land, to see if people obeyed her. Obediently he set out, with Susi and Cham. Daphne begged to go, and Wulf hugged her close and would not permit it.

The year out there was a dry one. The felling of orchards, the burning of crops, had had their effect. Wulf found bands of people haunting old farming areas in hopes that volunteer stalks of barley would grow and be worth reaping. Again, women looked tired, children looked unhappy and hungry. Men hunted every day, and brought back little.

"The world's dead out here," said one.

"If the Moslems come, they'll find it so," Wulf replied as he knew he must, and the man grinned mirthlessly.

"I wish they would come," he said. "We could capture their food."

"At least they wouldn't get food from us," said Wulf, and the man narrowed his eyes.

"Nobody can get food from us," he grumbled. "Not even us."

An arid winter came. Wells and streams dried up. People wandered here and there, for water and for what wild food they could find. Those who fared best were Ketriazar's Medusi and Daris's Nefussa, with their traditions of roaming and hunting. Coming back to Thrysdus with his findings, Wulf met the Cahena and saw that she was almost hysterical with worry.

"It's Khalid," she said. "He's sick, lies on his bed and won't eat, won't talk. And I can't make him well."

Wulf went with her to Khalid's quarters. Khalid did not seem to be in a desperate condition. He drooped languidly on a couch draped with embroidered silk, nibbled at a fig, and drank clabbered camel's milk. He seemed petulant when the Cahena asked him how he felt. "Only tired," he said. "Only bored."

"Bored?" she cried, as though that were a particularly dire symptom. "Wulf, why can't I cure him? You've seen me heal the blind, stop the flow of blood from wounds. This is strange."

"It was strange when you healed the sick," said Wulf. "This is natural, no magic in it. If you let him alone, maybe he'll get better."

"Maybe!" she echoed. "Maybe! What can we do?"

Djalout answered that. He came and peered at Khalid, felt his forehead and the pulse at his wrist, then went to fetch back an array of dried plants to brew in hot water. Khalid drank this, complaining at the bitterness, and then Djalout wrapped him in heavy rugs until sweat streamed on his doleful face. At last Khalid deigned to sit up and say that he felt stronger, would have some food. The Cahena brought a basin of mutton soup and spooned it to his mouth with her own hands.

When Khalid was well, the Cahena spent hours alone with him. Yet again she sent Wulf on a long journey, with Mallul to accompany him, all the way to Cirta. Lartius received them, but complained about the Cahena's orders.

"How can we destroy Cirta?" he challenged them. "It's a natural fortress on this dome of rock. If we had food enough, we could hold off all the Moslems who would come, but we don't have food enough. Your men have wrecked our orchards and fields and driven our cattle away to be wild. Tell the Cahena we're not happy."

"I'll take that to her as your message," said Mallul. "I'm her son, I can do that."

Wulf and Mallul rode away, dissatisfied. They went on westward to the village near the Tomb of the Christian Woman. The old priestess gave them a welcome that was not much of a welcome.

"Nothing happens here," she told Wulf. "I can't advise these people, can't cure them when they're sick. Some of them go out to that tomb and mope around the place where you killed her and burned her. Maybe they ask her for help. If so, she doesn't give any. What was it you called her?"

"Lamia," said Wulf. "Do you think she had all that power and that when her power went, all the magic went?"

"I only know it's gone. And I wonder if what you did was a good thing for us."

"At least nothing drinks your blood," Wulf reminded.

"I wonder about that, too."

Wulf and Mallul went back to Thrysdus.

Things went on like that, all the year and into spring of the next. Scouts told that the Moslems mustered, mustered, all along their line of forts. The Cahena held councils. Khalid did a great deal of the talking. When Hassan made his move, he said, let the Imazighen choose a good ground of battle, meet the Moslems with spears, counterattack with horsemen, score another victory.

"We've good ground to the north of here, where they'd have to tire their horses, advancing up a long slope," said Wulf.

Bhakrann, away from his scouting to attend the council, squinted at Khalid. "You count yourself one of us," he said.

"My Lady Cahena has made me one of you." Khalid smiled. "She granted me mercy, let me kiss her shadow. She trusts me."

"I trust you," said the Cahena, with music in her voice.

It was summer. Trusty scouts roamed through the great Moslem force, pretending to be volunteers. They estimated that Hassan had assembled sixty thousand warriors, from every Moslem nation from Persia to Egypt, and that he had swarms of camels to bring along supplies. Hassan seemed to know how the Cahena had destroyed farms and dispersed herds so that he could not count on capturing rations. It was Bhakrann who brought news that the enemy was marshaling for an advance. The Cahena called Wulf and Mallul and Djalout to hear this.

"The most men and horses and camels I ever saw," Bhakrann reported.

"I've sent swift riders to call Ketriazar and Daris," said the Cahena. "For Yaunis and Lartius and every man they can bring."

But a visitor from Cirta said that Lartius had sent messages to Hassan, had offered to go and capture Carthage for the Moslems. The Cahena's eyes blazed.

"Lartius has signed his own death warrant," she said to her council members. Before the Cahena lay a great tray of sand, such as diviners used to read the future. She drew in it with her forefinger.

"Where's Khalid?" she asked. "I want his viewpoint."

A messenger hurried to Khalid's quarters and hurried back.

"He's not here," he said breathlessly. "They say he rode away early this morning, on the best horse he had. That he carried food and water for a long journey."

"Which way did he go?" demanded Wulf.

"To the east."

They looked at each other, all of them.

"Back to Hassan," said Djalout.

XXII

The others sat and looked at Wulf. Not at the Cahena, whose hands hid her face. It was at Wulf they looked, all of them.

"He's deserted us," said Djalout. "And I'm not really surprised. Should I be?"

"He meant to spy on us and betray us," said Mallul. "He'll tell our plans to Hassan."

"And Hassan will profit by his mistakes in the other battle," added Djalout. "What must we do, Wulf?"

"Make new plans," said Wulf at once. "Where is Hassan starting, Bhakrann?"

"From about ten days away toward Egypt," judged Bhakrann. "What's your word, Wulf? Change our position from that high ground?"

"No, some of us must wait to bring him there. And others, our best riders, can head north and then come back, strike his right flank. Hit him, roll him up like a rug."

The Cahena stared. Tears shone in her wide, wounded eyes. "When did you think of that?"

"Right now," said Wulf. "It'll need lots of organization. We'll clarify it while we wait for Daris and Ketriazar to get here—say five or six days. Then, if we move the right way and strike the right way, perhaps we can bring it off."

"Desperate measures," muttered Mallul.

Djalout nodded. "In a desperate situation."

"You take command, Wulf," said the Cahena, fighting to steady her voice. "I put you in command—you'd never betray us."

"Of course not," he said. "Let me go away and think."

In his quarters he mused frowningly. He thought of the men, the horses, how he must depend on them. He thought for hours. At last Daphne stole in at the door and cuddled beside him.

"They say a battle's coming," she said. "Will I be in it?"

"Everybody will be in it," he said, his arms around her, and they made love.

"I've been training some of us in archery," she said afterward. "Mostly boys, big boys who can draw strong bows. They'll help."

When she was gone, Wulf lay long into the night, thinking, pondering. In the morning he fetched Bhakrann for a talk.

"I'll tell my plan to nobody but you," Wulf said. "It'll be secret between us. Khalid's gone, but there may be other spies. I'll take a strong, well-mounted force off and around the Moslem flank, with another force here to meet their advance. You know this country better than I do—how should we move?"

They found a tray of sand, such as the Cahena had once used to read the future. Bhakrann set a pebble to represent Thrysdus and modeled a landscape with the slope to the north of town and, back of that to westward, a succession of ridges and plains and valleys. Here and there, he said, were ponds and water holes, and he marked them with the point of a twig. A march could advance in those hollows, out of sight of any observers to the east.

"How far can we go there?" asked Wulf. "Forty miles, two days of riding? We'll need to do that; they'll have an extensive front."

"We can come to here and head out over this height," said Bhakrann, pointing. "With luck, we'll flank them."

"Luck," repeated Wulf. "Nobody can live two minutes without luck."

"Your plan's good," Bhakrann said. "So far as I can see, it's our only chance, and we'll have to take it."

Yaunis rode in that evening. He had no more than two dozen hard-faced companions with him. His usually neat beard drooped. He joined a council summoned by the Cahena.

"My people turned traitor," he announced bitterly. "The subchiefs voted to stay neutral—not go over to the enemy like Lartius—but they won't join us. I have only these few true men."

"You're welcome, Yaunis," the Cahena said. "What's that you say about Lartius?"

"He's heading for Carthage, to hold it for the Moslems."

"That's not where we'll fight them," said Wulf.

"Where, then?" asked the Cahena. Her confusion at Khalid's desertion seemed gone, or at least conquered. She spoke like a queen.

"I'm going to divide our forces," said Wulf.

"Divide?" repeated Djalout. "Is that good tactics?"

"It's desperation tactics," replied Wulf. "I won't go into details now. Wait for our loyal tribes to get here, and I'll explain."

He went to talk to warriors and subchiefs, to examine horses. Days passed, and Ketriazar came, with his best riders. The rest of the Medusi would follow, and behind them Daris's Nefussa.

"What's the condition of your horses?" was Wulf's first question to Ketriazar.

"Good," was the reply. "We came on the best mounts we had. There hasn't been much straggling."

"We'll make a long march, almost at once," Wulf told Ketriazar. "When Daris gets here, he and I and you will talk about it at dinner with the Cahena."

Daris arrived. His squadrons and Ketriazar's made camps outside the walls. "Now," said Wulf, "I'll tell you everything at dinner."

Bhakrann, too, came to the Cahena's big room. It was a simple meal, roast mutton and barley cakes and a flagon of wine passed from hand to hand. In a subdued voice, the Cahena called on Wulf to explain his proposed campaign.

He spoke simply. By now, Khalid would have told Hassan of the plan to meet the Moslems on high ground. Part of the Imazighen force would take that position, resisting but falling back. Meanwhile, the best riders would slip north and behind the enemy flank, striking hard. All listened intently.

"How long a march?" Daris asked Wulf.

"Bhakrann thinks two days, maybe part of a third, and a hard fight at the end of it."

"How many men?" was Ketriazar's question.

"Maybe twelve or thirteen thousand, depending on what men are trustworthy and what horses will last."

"What chiefs?" asked the Cahena, who had not been talking much.

"Ketriazar and Daris, to command their tribesmen," Wulf replied. "Bhakrann will guide us. Lady Cahena, I'll leave Yaunis with you, and most of Bhakrann's scouts, and some ten thousand warriors."

"What do we do on that slope above here?" she prodded.

"Face them, stick them full of javelins, and fall back. Don't close with them. Pray that our flanking movement succeeds."

"Pray?" she repeated. "To what gods? The gods don't answer prayers anymore."

Wulf said nothing, but he felt that she spoke the truth. He himself would put no reliance in any god he had ever heard of. He'd trust only in himself, Wulf the Saxon, prone to errors, limited in vision, but himself. All he had to trust.

He and Ketriazar and Daris went out to speak to men and examine horses. They chose those who seemed fit for the march and the battle. They wound up with more than twelve thousand, and organized them in troops and squadrons, under petty chiefs. From the stores of Thrysdus were issued rations of smoked meat and barley bread and dried fruits. No wine, said Wulf flatly. Each man would sling two leather water bottles to his saddle. Susi would lead along the best of Wulf's spare horses, with his mail jacket and helmet and shield hung to it.

Daphne came, begging to go along. Wulf shook his head. "Command your archers here," he said. "We'll meet again when the fight's over."

"If we're still here." She hugged his neck and kissed his bearded face. He took off a gold chain he wore. "Here," he said. "This will bring you luck."

Bhakrann reported no evidence of enemy in the region. At dawn, Wulf ordered his following into four columns of fours. Someone came to where he stood by his horse. It was the Cahena, blue-robed, white-coifed.

"Yaunis will help me command here," she said. Her face was drawn, her eyes deeply circled. "How will you fare, Wulf?"

"That's all to find out. Pray for me."

"I can't pray, I can only hope. Wulf, I haven't been fair to you. Forgive me for being weak. Think well of me."

"Of course," he said evenly.

She went away. He mounted and gave the command to march and heard it echo along the formations.

The close-drawn columns moved a hundred yards or so apart. Each man carried a sheaf of javelins. Many wore captured Moslem swords. Scouts strung out a mile or so to the right. Bhakrann rode with Wulf, pointing the march to low land with sparse grass. Ketriazar and Daris joined them. Both were eager for the venture.

"Where will they strike?" wondered Ketriazar.

"Our spies report that they're passing Cairouan to concentrate on the area where they expect us," said Wulf. "Khalid will have told them about that."

"Bring me in stabbing distance of Khalid," grated Daris.

"Or in stabbling distance of Lartius," said Ketriazar. "I'd like that. He never was a true man and not much of a fighter, either."

Three hours of marching brought them to a string of ponds. They watered the horses, squadron by squadron. When they left again, Wulf sent along an order for the men to walk and lead their mounts. Everyone was in good spirits as they went behind a sheltering range of hills far to the right. At noon they stopped to eat and rest. Wulf conferred with Bhakrann and Ketriazar and Daris.

"We can camp tonight in a valley with streams and good grass," promised Bhakrann.

"A valley," repeated Wulf. "That means high ground to both sides. We'll bivouac a strong force on the right. I hope we have enough food."

"We started with enough, but some of the men were eating as they rode," said Daris. "I spoke unpleasantly to them."

After an hour, all mounted again. Bhakrann guided them, and scouts still struck out to the east. That evening they camped among more scattered ponds. Wulf ordered that no fires be lighted and told the subchiefs to set up a series of watches. The men ate and talked. Some of them sang. When they lay down to sleep, muffled in their cloaks, they were scattered over acres of ground. How many acres, Wulf did not try to guess. He commanded a considerable host. But Hassan's numbers would be much greater.

Again a conference with Bhakrann and Ketriazar and Daris. They had accomplished something like twenty-five miles that day, and the horses seemed to be in good condition as they slouched in their picket lines. Bhakrann explained the next day's route, with more hills to screen them from possible enemy observers. They speculated on the way Hassan would approach. Probably some Moslems would occupy Cairouan. Hassan could leave a garrison there and still march to a main battle in tremendous numbers.

"If he heads for the high ground where the Cahena and Yaunis will be, he'll be close by midafternoon tomorrow," said Bhakrann. "We can move about fifteen miles eastward and get to close quarters. There'll still be hours of light to die by."

"Let's get some sleep and start early," said Wulf.

He lay down with his head on his saddle. Almost at once he slept and dreamed of the Cahena. Of her bared skin softly golden, her hair like a black banner, her face close to his. Her voice murmured his name, her hand was on his arm so strongly that he woke. But it was Bhakrann's hand, shaking him.

"Word of the enemy," Bhakrann said. "Cham came with it. Our scouts have ridden for hours to bring it."

Wulf scrambled to his feet. "Bring Cham here, and send somebody to wake Ketriazar and Daris and fetch them."

Cham came to salute the chieftains. He described how two scouts had spied the Moslem host as it went into camp less than a day's journey from Thrysdus. Relays of other riders had brought the news. The Moslems advanced in a great line of battle, close-drawn, miles in extent. Wulf thanked Cham and gave orders.

"Everybody up and in the saddle before dawn," he said. "We'll ride as soon as there's light to ride by. Columns again, but as we get close to them we'll spread for a charge. A line of squadrons in front, more in columns close behind. When we get to where we can hit them, I'll signal and whatever trumpets we have will blow. Any questions? Then go do as I say."

Bhakrann lingered with him. "You seemed happy while you slept. I hated to stir you up, but I had to. Maybe you were having a good dream."

"It was just a dream," said Wulf, and thought again of the Cahena, her last words to him when he mustered for his march. Could she have meant to call him back to her? But no time to think of her, or of Daphne, or of anything but fighting tomorrow.

Bhakrann went away. Wulf paced among sleeping warriors in the dark. He was glad they slept soundly. Many might never sleep again. But someone else moved among them.

"Who's that?" he called softly, and walked toward the shape. Tall, ungainly—he had seen it before, with its horns that curved like a dark crescent moon.

"Khro?" he challenged, and closed in, hand on his sword. The shape drew away, lost itself in the night. At least Wulf wasn't being chosen. But many would be killed tomorrow. Wulf stared after Khro. Not all magic was gone from the land. Here prowled the most baleful magic of all, the chooser of the dead.

He went back to where he had left his cloak and saddle. He sat down and shivered, from a chill that was not of the night air. He stretched out and put his drawn sword beside him. Again he slept.

He woke in the first gray dawn. Bhakrann was up, too, and Daris and Ketriazar. They and the subchiefs got the men on their feet to gobble a cold breakfast and saddle up. The host formed on Wulf's orders of the day before and moved eastward. Bhakrann and a wide scattering of scouts pulled out far in front. Then came a line of squadrons in close order, and behind that the others in columns.

They traveled over a land of dry grass and clumps of thirsty trees. Here and there showed cindery remains of habitations, destroyed by the Cahena's orders. Bhakrann led them along a succession of valleys chained with hills far to the east. No signs of an enemy, though scouts gazed into the distance. Again Bhakrann found pools of water, somewhat stagnant, for the noon halt. The sun was hot in the sky. Wulf mopped his face and wrung out his damp beard.

"All right, where are they?" Ketriazar prodded. "My men want action."

"They'll get it, sometime this afternoon," said Bhakrann.

They pressed on, under the glower of the sun. The men pulled up their hoods against its rays. Wulf rode here and there, studying the horses, glad that they bore up well. Bhakrann moved ahead to talk with scouts who rode in, then out again. At midafternoon he joined Wulf and pointed to a hilltop where a horseman showed.

"Enemy in sight," Bhakrann said.

The distant rider held a javelin crosswise above his head in both hands. Peering, Wulf saw the javelin raised to arm's length, then drawn down and raised again and again.

"Enemy in sight," Wulf agreed, "and in large numbers."

Susi brought up the spare horse with Wulf's armor. Wulf wriggled into his mail jacket and set his helmet on his head. He slid his left arm into the loops of his shield. Then he beckoned to Daris.

"Hold our main body where it is," Wulf said. "Come on, Bhakrann, let's ride up there."

They loped to where the signaler waited. A jumble of big rocks crowned the ridge. They dismounted and peered past the rocks.

On a great expanse of plain beyond, the whole world seemed flooded with riders. In close formations they moved purposefully southeast. Wulf had never seen such a great armed gathering.

"Do you know where they are now?" Bhakrann asked him. "They're moving toward that height where the Cahena is."

"And we're past their flank, we can get behind it, and they don't know it," Wulf exulted fiercely. "Signal for our main body to come."

Bhakrann gesticulated. Men of the forward elements turned in their saddle to repeat his signal. The squadrons advanced in formation.

"Ride back there, Bhakrann," directed Wulf. "Let them be at a trot when they reach here, and when they cross this ridge, charge."

"Where will you be?" demanded Bhakrann.

"Right here. I'll lead that charge in person."

XXIII

They hurried up behind Wulf, and he kicked his horse's sides and galloped ahead. Hoofs drummed like thunder. A yell went up:

"There is also the Cahena!"

They howled her name, they believed in her. Wulf's sword swept from its sheath, he laid it flat on his thigh. Up there ahead, enemy riders drew rein, looked uncomprehendingly on a rush of men they hadn't suspected. Almost at once, Wulf was there.

"I am Wulf the Saxon!" he brayed his name, and cut a man out of the saddle. He drove into the press of Moslems. He heard a mighty shock of sound, horses driving against horses. Another enemy slashed at him. He blocked the blow with his shield and drove his point into a mailed chest. "*Ahi!*" he heard a voice he knew. Bhakrann was at his work, with the sword once borne by Okba. All around Wulf, everywhere, the fight was joined.

They're five to one against us, he thought grimly. Each of us has to kill five. He himself had accounted for two. A Moslem rode against him. Their horses jammed flanks. The Moslem's blade rang deafeningly on his helmet, glanced away, and Wulf slashed hard at the neck and sent the man sprawling from the saddle. Three now. He sought another.

He'd live through this. Khro had chosen men to die, but not Wulf. Again he slashed, parried, thrust. Bhakrann rode past, skillfully transfixing an enemy. Just here, the Moslems were in disorder. The Imazighen were killing them, driving them into a great disorganized jumble.

"*Allahu akhbar!*" That was an officer on a gray horse, with flashing gold worked into his cloak. He tried to rally his men, he rushed at Wulf. Then, abruptly, he reined away.

"It's Shaitan!" he shrieked. "The devil!"

He was afraid. Wulf rode for him. Others came between, barred the way. Wulf's own men were there, too, stabbing with javelins. Wulf headed into the thick of the churning press.

They faltered before the Imazighen attack. The Moslems had gone into a disorganized muddle, retreated, trying to get away. They hadn't expected this, didn't like it. Wulf's Imazighen shoved at them, holding a line of sorts. Suddenly, almost in a moment it seemed, the Moslems scuttled far away, leaving rumpled bodies strewn on the dry grass. To Wulf's either hand, the attackers paused as though by mutual consent.

Wulf drew a deep breath. He was sweating; he had fought hard. He rode along his line, shouting praises, encouragements. Then somebody yelled and pointed. The Moslems had rallied, were countercharging in a close line of their own.

"Javelins, close range!" thundered Wulf.

Bhakrann called out the same order. It was repeated by subchiefs. The men sat their horses, poised their javelins. They grinned in relish, they knew their own skill. Just now they felt like winners. They had killed and driven their enemies. Wulf hoped to win. Something must be done and he, Wulf, must do it.

The enemy came at a trot, rending the air with war cries. "*Allahu akhbar!*" A storm of javelins soared at them. Horses and men went down. Back came the yell of the Imazighen:

"There is also the Cahena!"

More javelins flew. More Moslems fell. The Imazighen line rushed forward, as though on an order Wulf had not given. Almost at once, the two forces were together, stabbing, hewing.

Again Wulf chopped a man out of his saddle. They seemed to come at him and go down. Another was there, but Wulf's bigger horse struck the smaller, made it stumble, go sprawling. Beyond, yet another foe wheeled and dashed to the rear.

"I am Wulf the Saxon!" Wulf yelled his name loudly. He saw his men striking with swords, thrusting with javelins. Some of them fell, but Moslems fell, too. Again he thought a Moslem attacked is less terrible than a Moslem attacking.

Almost as he thought that, the Moslems had fallen back for more than a hundred yards. He flourished his sword high and rode to the front, and his warriors came with him.

"There is also the Cahena!" they bellowed.

Wulf reined his horse to let the squadrons go past him. He had been wrong to fight mindlessly, like a common warrior. He was supposed to be the general here. He shouted and beckoned to half a dozen riders, and they came.

"You'll be my couriers, carry my orders," he said. "You on the red horse, go there to the left. Tell whatever subchief you find to hold his men and let fresh fighters pass him. Say to gather up javelins and throw them again."

The man hurried with the message. Wulf rode behind the line where fighting had started again. He rejoiced grimly that the Imazighen had the better of it, that the Moslems faltered back from them. Ketriazar hurried to him.

"We're winning!" exulted Ketriazar. "We've killed some of their leaders, and leaderless men are lost. Look to the far right!"

Off there, the Imazighen seemed to be encircling a flank of the Moslems.

"Here!" Wulf called to a courier. "Ride there fast. Tell our chiefs to advance carefully, look out for a counterattack!"

He did well to order that. A cloud of enemy came cantering back, somewhat organized. It was met with a murderous flight of javelins, and then there was more fierce hand-to-hand fighting.

Wulf and Ketriazar rode toward the thick of the encounter, with a score of others. Bhakrann was there before them, was into it, yelling like a fiend. Wulf saw him hurl a javelin and fetch down an enemy, then hew with a sword. Wulf struck and slashed. He was panting, his arm and shoulder felt tired. His horse was splashed with the blood Wulf had drawn—how many had he killed? His ears rang, he struggled, but he did not glory in the fighting he did so well. He hated it.

It went like that—clashes, lulls, clashes again. Wulf ordered up fresh squadrons and more fresh squadrons, and the Moslems seemed never to be ready. Behind his own line, Wulf saw that his Imazighen were fiercer, deadlier. Their javelins sang to the mark, felling horses and riders. At close quarters, they won flurried duels more often than the Moslems. So many were dying. Vulgar deaths, unknown to fame—Homer had said that, somewhere in his *Iliad.* And always shattering noise. Buffets of horses in contact, clashes of metal, the oaths and shouts of warriors—these shook the sky that was getting to be an evening sky. How long had they fought?

The Moslem host still blackened the land. Wulf had hurt them on the flank, had nibbled the flank away, but there were still overwhelming numbers of them who had not yet been in battle. Suddenly he called for his couriers to ride everywhere and command a withdrawal. He himself rode away toward the right, and met Ketriazar.

"Our men don't want to pull away," said Ketriazar. "We've fought them hard, fought them well, killed more of them than they've killed of us."

"Where's Daris?" asked Wulf, reining around to watch the retirement he had ordered.

"Killed," snapped Ketriazar.

Bhakrann came to them. "Those Moslems aren't pressing our retreat," he shouted. "We've been too harsh for them. What now, Wulf?"

"Get clear away, head back to the north of Thrysdus," said Wulf. "Join our friends there if we can find them."

The three trotted their horses together. Their warriors had changed their line of battle into a heavy column. They moved to the west, where the sun had dropped low. That fight had gone on for hours. Wulf looked at the horses of the column, and was glad that most of them seemed in good shape. Horses had endurance. He had known horses to travel all day and part of the night without collapsing.

The loud din of battle had died away. There were only murmurs, chorused hoofbeats. The throngs of the Moslems were there, not pressing in great numbers. But three of them rode out, glittering men on richly decked horses, waving their curved blades and shouting.

"Champions," said Wulf. "They're challenging, daring any of us to come out for single combat."

"Why keep them waiting?" said Bhakrann, and turned his mount away from the Imazighen column.

"Come on, Ketriazar," called Wulf, and also rode forward. Opposite him, a Moslem in a brightly striped cloak roared at him and waved his sword.

"I am Wulf the Saxon!" Wulf yelled back, and drove in close. Their shields rang together. Wulf parried the other's scimitar and sliced at the turban-bound headpiece. The man went tumbling to the ground and slumped on hands and knees. Wulf caught the reins of the riderless horse and looked down to where the Moslem staggered erect. He had dropped his weapon. He glared up at Wulf.

"Oh, I'm not going to kill you," Wulf said to him, "but I'll keep your horse. It looks like a good one."

He cantered back to his own men. They hailed him with hoarse applause. Bhakrann came back, too, his sword dripping red.

"I killed my man," he told Wulf. "I knew him—he was one of those officers we held for ransom. How did you fare?"

"I spared my man's life."

"Spared his life?" cried Bhakrann. "Why?"

"I just didn't feel like killing him. But this horse of his is a fine one, worth taking."

Wulf dismounted from his own weary animal and vaulted aboard the captured one. It was nervous, but he stroked its neck and spoke to it in Arabic and it subsided. Ketriazar, too, was back, wiping his blade on the mane of his steed. Over opposite the close-drawn Imazighen formation, the Moslems hung back. The fate of their champions had daunted them. Wulf sent along orders for his own squadrons to move clear of the vast enemy horde, to head westward and seek for the warriors who had stayed with the Cahena.

They headed for the red blotch of the sinking sun. Wulf took time to check on himself. He had a slight wound on the cheek; he did not remember getting it. He was thirsty and drank from a leather flask, swirling the water in his hot mouth. He was tired, too. His big chest heaved, his face dripped sweat, his sword arm ached. He sent more orders for a complete detachment from the enemy, for seeking out their friends and joining them, perhaps to share in more fighting.

Twilight was upon the land. The great clutter of Moslems was not easy to see anymore. Wulf and Ketriazar and Bhakrann rode along the column, speaking to wounded men, asking about the resolutely enduring horses. Bhakrann's scouts searched in front of the march, leading toward where the Cahena must have made her stand.

Night came, and half a moon gave them some light on their way. Wulf found bread and figs to eat. Ketriazar came to ride at his left.

"How do you think we fought?" Ketriazar asked.

"Pretty well, but we didn't do what we came to do," Wulf said. "There weren't enough of us; it was five to one against us. I was mistaken in what I tried."

"We had to do something," argued Ketriazar. "If every man of us was a man like you, we'd have chewed them up and spit them out."

"Since we didn't really win, we lost," said Wulf. "And I mourn for our friends who died in that useless fight."

"I mourn Daris. I wonder who'll be chief of his Nefussa."

They rode into the night. At last Wulf sent word along for a halt beside some ponds. They rested for an hour, then back in the saddle, marching on toward the west. The half of the moon climbed. The hours passed. It became the shadowed early morning.

From the head of column rose a din of voices. Wulf trotted his horse there. He could hear Bhakrann yelling at the men.

"No, let him alone, he's one of us," Bhakrann was shouting. "He was left back here with the Cahena. Wulf, look who's here—Zeoui!"

Zeoui it was, on the weariest of horses. His mail shirt was chopped and blood-spattered. He saluted Wulf listlessly.

"We got beaten," he said in a wretched voice.

"I suppose so," said Wulf, his own voice unhappy. "That army of theirs reached for miles and miles. While we fought them on one flank, the other flank reached you and fought you. What exactly happened?"

Zeoui made a helpless gesture. "They charged us and charged over us. Those of us who didn't run out of there are lying dead on the field."

"The Cahena—" Bhakrann started to say.

"She got away. We made her run. Somebody grabbed her bridle and hurried her off. And Yaunis got killed. He charged into the thick of them to give the Cahena a chance."

"How many did your party lose?" Wulf asked.

"I can't say how many. A lot. The Moslems gobbled us. Those poor archers—just boys, most of them—they did some killing, but they were wiped out."

Wulf felt a chill. "Daphne?" he asked.

"They killed her, and her father, Jonas."

Wulf sank his head. She was dead. Daphne was dead, Daphne who had loved him so much, and he had never quite loved her. Dead. She was better off dead than captured by those invaders.

"I see," Wulf said after a moment. "Come on, let's move ahead and join the Cahena. Guide us, Zeoui."

Silent again, he rode along. Bhakrann came to his side.

"Too bad," Bhakrann said. "Too bad about Daphne. She was a fine girl, a brave girl."

"She was so good," said Wulf, striving against his tears.

Bhakrann glanced keenly at him in the night. "Yes," he agreed.

XXIV

The bloodred sun glowed in the east from which they had fled when they came to the campground of the Cahena and her surviving followers.

It was a disorganized camp, men hunched around little fires, gnawing at scraps of food. Some of them told Wulf about what had happened on the height above Thrysdus. The Moslems had stormed up and killed and killed, until those who escaped the killing ran. As for Thrysdus, women and children and other noncombatants had fled earlier, nobody knew where. The Moslems had taken Thrysdus back, would call it El-Djem again, would revel in its plunder.

While Bhakrann and Wulf listened, a messenger came to say that the Cahena summoned Wulf. He followed the messenger, leading his horse. Her red banner drooped limply. She rose from beside a little blaze of twigs.

Inside her blue robe, her figure was noble. Under her white scarf, her face looked drawn, plaintive. "Wulf," she greeted him.

"Lady Cahena." He knelt to kiss her shadow.

"Sit with me," she said. "Have you eaten? I have some fruit here. What happened with you and your men?"

"We failed," he replied shortly. "We crumpled their flank a little, but we didn't turn it enough. While we tried, their main force tackled you, miles away." He scowled. "We failed. I didn't do what I set out to do."

Her head bowed. "Such hosts of Moslems," she whispered.

"Too many for us."

"My fault." She looked up at him again. "I drove my people away with my mad order of destruction. If I hadn't, we could have kept Lartius, kept all those other deserters. Enough fighting men to drive the enemy back into Egypt again."

Her hand was on Wulf's arm. It trembled there.

"You're all I have left," she said. "I've lost. I don't hear voices, see visions. All the gods are gone, except maybe Allah—he came here with the Moslems. Should we put trust in Allah now?"

"We'd better trust ourselves." He gazed here and there across the camp. "They must have killed most of you."

She took her hand back and cupped her chin in it. "They killed lots of us, but lots more just wandered off, trying to hide."

Mallul came and sat down with them. "What now?" he asked.

"What now?" repeated the Cahena.

"We keep retreating," said Wulf. "Get to Arwa. That's a rough part of the world, all ridges and hollows, but we know it and the Moslems don't. If we can get to where they can come at us only a few at a time, maybe we have a chance."

"Not much of a chance," said Mallul. "They fight like devils. They think if they die fighting for Mohammed, they'll go to paradise, all among their beautiful houri concubines."

Khalid must have told Mallul about that, but Mallul had not mentioned Khalid, not before the Cahena.

"I'll talk to you in private," the Cahena said to Wulf, and Mallul got up, bowed, and walked away. The Cahena gazed at Wulf. Her eyes were weary, darkly circled.

"What if I said I'm sorry?" she asked. "Sorry for being weak, for what I believed, what I did?"

"You did what you thought was right," said Wulf. "Maybe you've changed your mind, but at the time you thought it was right."

"Sorry," she said again. "I've lived long years without saying I was sorry for anything."

"You've ruled well," said Wulf.

"Until I listened to a false voice." Her slim, tawny hand was on his great, dinted one. "There's been talk about that creature you destroyed and burned, up there at the Tomb of the Christian Woman. That maybe magic left the land when she died. But magic left when I turned away from voices I knew and listened to a voice that lied."

"Khalid," Wulf decided to say at last.

"He turned against us, after all he said and did to make us think he was with us." She took her hand back and clenched it until the knuckles turned white. "I wish he was dead."

"If I get within reach of him, he'll be dead," said Wulf evenly.

"Wulf!" she cried his name. "Do you remember what we were to each other? Back in Tiergal?"

"How could I forget?"

"I was deceived. I was foolish. But can we again—"

"Lady Cahena," he interrupted, "don't talk of it now. We'd better keep retreating. If what followers you brought this far are rested, if their horses can travel, head for Arwa. I'll keep my own men here for another hour and then follow you like a rear guard. Up yonder, we'll find another campsite."

"How wise you are," she said caressingly. "How good and strong you are. Why didn't I remember that? I almost lost you."

"You and your men had better get started."

They both rose. He kicked dirt over the fire. She seemed as though she would say something more, but he bowed and walked away. He looked back to see Mallul carrying the limp red banner.

Among his own men, he talked to Bhakrann. Some of the command had drifted away—deserters, Bhakrann called them. Cham was there, and Zeoui. What had happened to Tifan nobody knew, but Cham thought he had died in that assault on the Moslem flank. Wulf waited an hour before he ordered the squadrons to follow the Cahena as a rear guard.

Rain came up suddenly, drenching cloaks. The march fared on and away from that rain, and again the sun was hot and bothersome. On they strove, with only brief rest stops, and in the afternoon they caught up with the Cahena's followers. Ketriazar and Bhakrann rode on either side of Wulf. Both scowled gloomily.

"When will we see those Moslems, and how will we fight them?" Ketriazar wondered.

"Let's hope we'll be on Arwa by the time they come," said Wulf. "Be on ground we know and can use to our advantage. We'll be badly outnumbered."

"A lot of our people feel they've beaten already," said Ketriazar. "They keep slipping away. I hate that. I'm staying with the Cahena—it's too late for me to do anything else."

"Too late for almost anything," said Bhakrann. "But if we die fighting, that's a good death and a quick one. I've expected it ever since I was a boy." And the red glint was in his beard.

"I'll say that, too," said Wulf. "But I haven't seen Khro skulking anywhere near."

"Don't say that name," warned Ketriazar.

"Why not say Khro's name? Why not remind him?" demanded Bhakrann. "I'm like Wulf—I'm past being afraid of him."

Djalout came on his mule to speak to Wulf. He sagged in his saddle, his beard looked limp. "Who could have predicted this disaster?" he asked. "I couldn't, and usually I predict better than most."

"Predictions are in short supply with us," said Wulf. "Maybe the Moslems are better at those than we are."

"They leave everything to *kismet,*" said Djalout. "To fate. Which just now seems to favor them. Here, will you have a swallow of wine? I brought a good article away from Thrysdus."

He passed a leather bottle across to Wulf, who drank. Djalout was right, it was good wine. Ketriazar and Bhakrann had mouthfuls, and Djalout took the bottle back and drank in turn. How gray his face was, how hollow his eyes.

"It seems shorter, going back," he said. "If we get back."

They marched until sundown and dismounted where the ground rose away westward toward Arwa. Water was there, and stretches of grass fit for grazing horses. The Cahena's standard was planted, a sort of tentlike structure of cloaks and saddle blankets was put up on poles. Messengers summoned Wulf,

Bhakrann, and Ketriazar. The Cahena sat by a little fire, a mantle drawn over her blue robe. Djalout half crouched at her left. She motioned Wulf to the place at her right. Mallul came also, and several subchiefs.

"Thank you all for standing by me," the Cahena addressed them, clear-voiced. "Though maybe my thanks isn't much anymore. Wulf, we look to you for advice on what to do now."

"I'd say, seek some point where the enemy will have trouble closing in," offered Wulf at once. "A rocky height where we can make our defense."

"Lady Cahena, we're a day or so ahead of them," said Djalout. "Isn't that right, Bhakrann?"

"So I hear from my scouts," Bhakrann replied.

"That's time enough to find proper ground," said Ketriazar.

"Why meet them at all?" asked Djalout. "Why not go over Arwa, off to the Atlas mountain country? They wouldn't even know where that was."

"No," said the Cahena flatly, and her eyes glowed like chips of jet.

They stared. Wulf wondered who had come to stand behind her, what tall shadowy thing.

"No," she said again. "I'm through running like a lost sheep ahead of wild dogs. I won't run any farther than where we are now."

Wulf got up. That shape behind the Cahena, it was towering, its head wore horns. He knew what it was.

"I'll be back in a moment," said Wulf, and took a step. The horned one drew away into a scrub of eucalyptus. He moved after it.

"Khro," he addressed it in a whisper. It did not wait. He moved through the eucalyptus after it. In a clear space beyond, it retreated.

"Choosing those who'll die, Khro?" Wulf asked. "Do you choose me?"

Khro vanished, like smoke. Wulf came back to the gathering around the little fire.

"I thought someone was listening," he said.

They all waited for the Cahena to speak. She spoke:

"Maybe some of my sight of the future has come back. All of you can run if you want to. Go to the Atlas, go anywhere and leave me alone here. I've been a queen. I've ruled the Imazighen, the Christians, even the Moslems here and there. I've lived as a queen. I'm ready to die as a queen. They can kill me. I'll make them kill me."

Was Khro back? A shadow flitted. Wulf could not be sure.

"Maybe the Moslem god, their Allah, is here now," said the Cahena. "So go on, leave me here alone."

"Leave you?" repeated Mallul.

"You, my son Mallul, ride back and meet those Moslems. Tell them to explain their faith to you, say you'll be a Moslem like them. Ride fast, carry a white cloth in your hand for a sign of truth. That's an order, Mallul. I order you to join them."

Mallul got to his feet. "When?"

"Now. At once. There's enough of a moon to show you the way. Get your horse and go."

Mallul shrugged. "Good-bye," he said to all of them, and walked slowly out of the group.

"You, Wulf," the Cahena said. "You go, too."

He actually laughed. "Do you think that they'd accept me? After they've watched me kill so many of them? No, Lady Cahena, I stay here. I'll die here, if it's my time to die."

"I'll die here, too," said Djalout from where he sat. He crossed his arms on his updrawn knees and put his face down on them. The Cahena gazed into the coals of the fire.

"How many men do we have left?" Wulf asked.

"I don't know exactly, but not very many," said Ketriazar. "They've been drifting away from us all the way here. Riding off one by one, or in little parties, thinking they can pretend to be simple, peaceable native people if they run into any Moslems. The ones that are staying are mostly my tough old Medusis, they're used to trouble."

"Used to trouble," repeated Bhakrann. "So am I."

"You men will need rest," said the Cahena. "The enemy will be here tomorrow. Go get some sleep. Wulf, will you wait?"

The others got up, all but Djalout, who sat where he was, his head bowed. They went away to wherever they were camped. The Cahena moved to the hanging that made a flap to her makeshift tent.

"Will you come in, Wulf?" she asked him, half shyly.

He followed her. Inside was only the faintest wash of light. She stood there, almost against him. He heard a whisper of fabric as she dropped her mantle.

"Wulf, shall I ask your forgiveness?"

"Who am I to forgive you?" he said. "I've loved you."

"Loved!" she half wailed the word. "Loved—that means you don't love me anymore?"

"It seemed to me that I had your permission to go."

"You have my permission to come back. Wulf, we've condemned ourselves to die at the hands of the Moslems. But now, tonight—can't we live?"

Her slender hand drew his big one to her. She had opened her robe. She put his palm to the swell of her naked breast. The nipple rose tautly. She breathed deeply.

"Wulf?" she whispered. "We're alone here. The others went away when I sent them."

"Djalout didn't go. He's still sitting, just outside."

"Go see why he's waiting. Then come back."

Wulf went. Djalout sat where he had sat, his head on his arms. Wulf stooped above him, spoke his name. Djalout did not stir. Wulf put his hand on Djalout's shoulder, then took it away and turned back to where the Cahena waited, expectantly waited, at the door of her shelter.

"Tell him to go," she said.

"Djalout won't be going," Wulf told her. "Djalout has died."

XXV

Wulf found Bhakrann, waked him, led him to where Djalout sat so motionlessly. They straightened Djalout out to lie on his back and folded his arms across his chest. Then they dug a shallow grave with their daggers. The Cahena stood and watched. They lowered Djalout into the hole and spread his old cloak over him and scooped back the earth. From here and there they fetched big rocks and set them like a pavement over the grave, to discourage beasts of prey.

"Something ought to be said for him," said Bhakrann. "A prayer, maybe."

"I've forgotten all the prayers I used to know," said Wulf, sheathing his dagger.

"I'm afraid that I have, too," confessed Bhakrann.

The Cahena came to join them beside the grave. "Let me speak," she said. She gazed up into the night. Her face looked amber-brown.

"Our friend has died," she said slowly. "He knew that he was going to die. He wasn't afraid. He was able to die in peace, not in battle."

"Yes," said Bhakrann. Wulf could barely hear him.

"He was good," said the Cahena. "He was faithful. He was wise—much wisdom has died with him. Peace to him as he rests."

Bhakrann and Wulf sat down and looked at the array of stones. The Cahena sat with them. Wulf gazed off to where a shadow moved, a tall shadow. Did it have horns? It faded away.

Wulf sat with his knees drawn up, his arms crossed upon them. He was bitterly tired. At last he lowered his face upon his arms. That was how Djalout had sat at the last. Wulf slept.

He woke in the dark. The stars told him it would be two hours before sunrise, there in the east from which enemies would come marching. He got up, stretched his arms and legs, and walked among sleepers. A couple of sentries squatted there. Looking at those who slept, Wulf reflected that Ketriazar was right—these were veterans, with gray in their beards. They had followed and worshipped the Cahena for so many years that they knew no other worship. They were with her at the last. They would rather die with her than live under the rule of Moslems.

Bhakrann came tramping. "What now?" he asked. "What's waiting?"

"Nothing will be waiting. Those invaders will be coming," said Wulf. "I told you once, Hassan heard that he must defeat the Cahena before he could conquer this land. She beat him once, and now he wants to destroy her. He'll get here sometime today, will make a forced march to do it."

"Thirsty?" Bhakrann offered a wine flask and Wulf took a swallow. "That was Djalout's wine," said Bhakrann. "I took it. He's past the need of it. I'm going to miss him."

"Not for long," said Wulf. "At the end of this coming day, you and I will be on his trail. I predict that we'll die in battle."

Bhakrann drank and wiped his mouth and laughed. It was a short, ugly laugh.

"I hope it's a quick death. It ought to be an adventure, seeing what comes after death."

"Does anything come after death?" asked Wulf. "Who knows?"

"Who knows?" Bhakrann echoed him. "I never heard anyone say, except a bunch of priests and magicians."

"How does anyone know?"

"We'll find out, my brother. Remember when she said you and I were to be brothers? We've been brothers, Wulf."

Bhakrann's broad, hard hand clapped Wulf's shoulder.

Wulf glanced at the stars. "It's moving toward morning," he said. "Maybe we should eat. Is there anything?"

"I have some couscous. Let's make a fire."

Wulf gathered dry branches and scraped flint and steel to kindle them. They blazed up, then died down to make red coals. Bhakrann filled a brass dish with water and set it on stones to heat. When the water stirred and muttered, Bhakrann trickled in handfuls of couscous. Wulf scraped a clove of garlic into powder over the dish. They watched the cooking. A dark figure loomed. It was Ketriazar.

"If you'll let me join you, I have a bit of smoked pork," he said.

He drew his dagger and cut the meat into shavings to mix into the couscous.

"What food will the men have?" asked Bhakrann.

"They're lucky," said Ketriazar. "They found some camels last night and slaughtered them. I hope they divide it evenly."

Bhakrann stirred the couscous with a twig. "It's done," he reported, and gingerly twitched the bowl from the fire. "Let it stand until it's cool enough to eat."

The Cahena approached, with her mantle over her robe.

"What are you doing here?" she inquired.

Bhakrann stooped to kiss her shadow in the firelight. "We're making breakfast, Lady Cahena. Will you have some? And here's wine—it was Djalout's."

"Djalout." She sat beside Wulf. "I couldn't sleep. He's buried so close to where I lay." Her shoulder, her knee, touched against Wulf. "It's strange, being without him. He was my councillor for so long."

"He died because he felt it was time." Bhakrann nodded, studying the bowl. "This can be eaten now, I think."

Ketriazar and Bhakrann dipped into the dish with their fingers to roll balls of the couscous to swallow. The Cahena took only small pinches.

"You don't eat, Wulf," she said.

"I'd better eat, to face what's coming," he said, and helped himself.

"To face what's coming," repeated Ketriazar.

"Death is coming," said the Cahena.

"Death is always coming, to everybody," said Wulf. "We sit here expecting it. But the best death is what's unexpected."

Bhakrann looked up quickly. "Somebody who could write ought to put down these wise things you say."

"That's been written already," said Wulf. "Plutarch quoted Julius Caesar."

"Who was Plutarch?" asked Ketriazar.

"A Roman who tried to write the lives of everybody," said Wulf.

The Cahena almost snuggled against Wulf. "You're a comforting talker," she half crooned. "Even about death."

"Are you afraid to die?" he asked her.

"No. It should be restful, like sleep. Djalout knows by now."

They finished the bowl of couscous, down to the last grain. Bhakrann passed the leather wine bottle. Somewhere far to eastward showed the faintest wash of gray, dawn coming. The Cahena got up and so did the others. Her hand took hold of Wulf's wrist.

"Where do you go now?" she asked him.

"Here and there among the men, to see how they fare. Last night, we talked about where the Moslems were. I expect them to make all the speed they can, get here by midafternoon, try to finish us."

"How do we die, Wulf?"

"Like a brave dog, with its teeth in a throat," he growled, and her hand let go of him.

"Well said," declared Bhakrann. "How do we form for battle?"

Wulf pondered for a moment. Then: "Back of us here is a steep, rocky slope, too rough for horses. I advise we go up there. We'll fight on foot, and they'll have to do the same, at whatever point is narrowest. We'll be past needing horses, needing anything but to line up and face them."

"I'll be next to you," the Cahena said at his ear. "We're all agreed that death is coming. Let's meet him together."

"Meet Khro?" he said, and she flinched. "Don't be afraid to say his name. I've said it right to his ugly face. I've tried to get close to him, and so far he's always moved away."

"But he's here. He's the only god left here."

"God?" Wulf said after her. "With those horns, he's more like what I was told about Satan when I was a boy in England. Maybe we need evil spirits around us, to help us understand life and death. Maybe there were evil spirits before there were good ones. Maybe men feared spirits before they worshipped them."

"Maybe," she said.

"Now, I'm going back among the men. They'll be waking up."

They walked together here and there, to where sleepers stirred and rekindled fires. Wulf asked again and again if there was food. Most groups had something to eat, not much. One or two warriors seemed happily excited, spoke of beating the Moslems. If anybody was afraid, he did not say so.

As the sun showed its bright rim to eastward, two men galloped in. They were Cham and Zeoui, who had scouted far to the rear, and now they reported that they had ridden all night to say that the Moslem host pressed grimly after them.

"They marched even after their evening prayers," said Cham. "There's a whole world of them, all mounted, all full of fight. It looks like a sure way to death."

"You're right," said Wulf cheerfully. "They that take the sword will perish by the sword."

The Cahena widened her brilliant eyes. "Bhakrann's right, you say witty things."

"That saying is attributed to Jesus," Wulf said.

Bhakrann gave Cham and Zeoui what food he had, stale scraps of barley cakes.

The sun climbed. It was afternoon when more scouts came back, to say that the enemy was following. In the distance, Wulf and the Cahena saw a far-flung darkness that moved on the land. Hassan's army.

"How do you order us, Wulf?" she asked.

"Up that rocky height behind," he said. "The horses can't go up, for us or for those people coming. Up above, arrange our line, two deep, and wait for them to come into close range before we throw javelins. We'll signal for that. Have we a trumpet?"

"Here's one we captured from them," said Bhakrann, showing the instrument.

"A blast on that for the javelin throwing." Wulf gestured to his companions. "Let's get them started up there."

They scrambled up through the rocks, and the formation was quickly drawn up at the top, one line in open order and a second line behind. The men had sheaves of javelins. They stuck them into the earth within quick reach. All glared toward where the Moslems approached. Wulf walked along his double line. The Cahena paced beside him, and Ketriazar and Bhakrann followed.

"Where shall we take position?" the Cahena asked. She had taken the trumpet from Bhakrann.

"More or less at the middle, where their main charge will come," Wulf said. "There's still time for you to try to escape from here."

"Would you come?"

"Not when the battle's almost here."

"Then I won't run, either."

The vast formation flowed on the level ground below them. Wulf could see individual men and horses. They came at a slow trot—they had marched far that day, and must fight now at the end of the march. A concerted shout rose among them. Wulf came back to the center of his own position. He slung his shield to his left arm and loosened his sword in its sheath. The Cahena breathed at his side. She bore a javelin in her right hand, the trumpet in her left. Her eyes shone. She was ready.

The Moslems had halted their close-drawn approach. They were dismounting, a great swarm of them. Some held the horses, the others moved into a close line, with another line and another line behind. In front of these paced officers. There were shouted orders, and a deafening cry of *"Allah!"* and the great press of men moved forward and upward on the rough ascent.

Wulf stood at his own forefront, tense and gazing. Up they came from below. Blades flashed, shields poised. Nearer, nearer. He measured the distance with his eye. He looked at the Cahena.

"All right," he said. "Sound that trumpet."

Its note blared out, strident, penetrating. The men in Wulf's line raised their own cry:

"There is also the Cahena!"

And the air was full of whizzing javelins. Men of the charging phalanx went down. Others shoved forward to take the places of the fallen. More javelins, a flying flock of them, and more men going down. The Moslems strove against the storm. Here they were, bristling beards, glaring eyes.

"Everybody get a man!" bawled the voice of Bhakrann, and Bhakrann rushed forward. The sword that had been Okba's made deadly play against the blade of an enemy. Another Moslem rushed to his comrade's aid and went down under a slashing blow. But yet another buried his point in Bhakrann's chest, and Bhakrann, too, went sprawling. All that in swift seconds, as Wulf leaped into the fight.

Everywhere the clash of combat, javelins, swords, loud voices shouting war cries. Wulf faced a man in a white turban, a man with teeth clenched in the darkness of his beard, a curved sword upflung. Wulf beat the descending steel aside and thrust to the throat, cleared his point as his man almost somersaulted away. He engaged another swordsman, when a javelin darted to transfix the man's chest. The Cahena was there to strike that blow, even as a dozen Moslems drove upon her and Wulf.

A blow struck shatteringly on his face. He heard the crunch of bone. He slammed to earth, and did not feel it come up to meet him.

XXVI

Consciousness came back to Wulf, laggingly, uncertainly, as though it was not quite sure of the way. First he could hear something, voices above him. Then he could feel, he ached and quivered. He opened his eyes, and he had blurred vision. Bearded, turbaned men leaned above him. One stooped and touched his face.

"Can you stand up?" asked the man, not unkindly. "Our general wants to talk to you, if you can talk."

Wulf spat out a mouthful of blood. "I can talk," he managed. "Let's see if I can stand."

He drew a deep breath. It hurt, but he judged that he had no broken ribs. He managed to sit up. Hands were upon him, helping him to rise. He stood with feet braced wide. His head throbbed like a gong. He drew another breath, another.

"All right, take me to him," he said.

One of them pointed the way. The others, five or six, thronged around Wulf, their hands on the hilts of their crooked swords. The evening sun beat down hotly. Corpses lay everywhere. Wulf took staggering steps, then his legs grew steadier. He let himself be escorted to where other men stood, fifteen or twenty.

To the front of that group stood Hassan ibn an-Numan al Ghassani. He wore chain mail, with a checkered cloak over his shoulders. His turban was green—of course he had been to Mecca—swathed around a steel-spiked helmet. His sword hung sheathed at his side. His white beard had a fleck of blood at his left jaw.

Beyond Hassan and his companions, the land was full of the victorious Moslems. Some seemed to be tending wounded men. Wulf looked past Hassan. Mallul was there, his head swathed in a Moslem turban. With Mallul stood Khalid.

"Your name is Wulf, they told me," said Hassan, in Arabic.

"I am Wulf the Saxon."

Hassan stroked his beard. "Stand away from him. You planned these battles and you fought in them, fought very well indeed. You're too brave to die."

"Nobody's too brave to die."

"Are you thirsty?" asked Hassan. "Give him water."

A listener thrust a skin bottle into Wulf's hand. Wulf drank eagerly. The water spread inside him, seemed to heal him a little. His hand to his face felt half-dried blood. His nose was smashed flat.

"I admire bravery," Hassan was saying. "You should be one of us. You should be a true believer and strike those hard blows to the glory of Allah."

"I believe in nothing," said Wulf.

Hassan frowned. "They told me you were a Christian."

"I was."

"A Christian." Hassan shook his head slowly. "But there is no god but Allah, the giver of mercies. See"—and he gestured. "The Cahena's son has accepted the true faith."

"Mallul," said Wulf. Mallul stood motionless.

"His new name is Abdar-Rahman," said Hassan. "Wulf, do not say, there are three. Repeat after me: There is no god but Allah, and Mohammed is his prophet."

"There is no god," said Wulf, and drank water again.

Hassan's companions surged forward, muttering. Hassan lifted a gaunt hand to quiet them.

"Perhaps you worshipped the Cahena," said Hassan. "But she's dead. Her head was cut off. Show him."

To one side lay something under a bunched cloak. Wulf had not seen it before. An officer leaned down to twitch the cloak away.

There lay her severed head. The skin was ashy pale, the eyes were closed. The hair tumbled, gleaming black. It was as though she lay asleep, peaceful, trusting. Hassan looked, too.

"She must have been the most beautiful woman in the world," he said. "Like a houri in Paradise."

"You'll send her head to your caliph in Damascus, won't you?" said Wulf. "He can thank his Allah that she's not a threat anymore. You found out her secrets, you tricked her people into deserting her. Even then, you had to kill her because she wouldn't run. The only way to beat her was to kill her."

Again the grouped men around Hassan snarled, but Hassan did not snarl.

"That's true, by Allah," he told Wulf. "Cover her head up again, you. She fought me, once I had to run for my life. She drove me and took prisoner eighty of my companion train."

"I was there when it happened," said Wulf, gathering strength from his rising fury. "You and your army ran like deer. I helped capture your officers. We sold them back to you, two or three at a time—sold them all except Khalid." He gazed at Khalid. "Let Khalid fall on his face and kiss the ground," he said. "Her shadow is still on this ground."

"In the name of Allah, let's kill this prisoner," said one of the listeners.

"Wait," said Hassan; and to Wulf, "Words like that can condemn you to death."

"All right, kill me."

"Don't die an infidel," Hassan almost pleaded. "Live among us in the true faith, be great among us. Say after me: There is no god but Allah, and Mohammed is his prophet."

"There is no god," said Wulf again.

Hassan smiled. It was a wry smile. "What if we kill you, then?"

"I'd be dead and out of your reach."

"Unbelievers are cast into hell."

"Agh!" Wulf spat blood. "Don't try to tempt me with heaven or frighten me with hell. I'm tempted by nothing, I'm afraid of nothing, I believe in nothing. I'm wounded. I don't have so much as a knife." His voice rose. "Let your men kill me. If I had a sword or a club, not one of them would dare come within my reach."

"You're as bold a speaker as I've ever heard," said Hassan, "and I think you're a true speaker with what you said just now. But you know they call me the Good Old Man, and I'm going to try to deserve that. Where's my physician?"

He beckoned to one of his officers.

"Take Wulf away and treat his wounds and bandage them," Hassan ordered. "If he can travel, give him a horse and set him free. He couldn't raise ten men to fight us now."

"With ten men I'd fight you," said Wulf.

Hassan looked at him with gentle eyes. "Go with Allah," he said. "Go with whatever god you want to worship, you whose life I've spared."

The physician came and took Wulf's arm to lead him away.

"Take your hands off of me, I can walk," Wulf snapped at him. And to Hassan he said, "Thank you for nothing. My life is nothing."

He walked away with the physician.

When old Wulf the Saxon finished his story of love and war, midnight was long past, black and chill, in the camp of the Franks outside the little village of Tours. The fire in Charles Martel's tent had burned down to pale-red coals. The great horse had settled in sleep. The big wine jug on the table was nearly empty. Charles Martel stroked his mustache and gazed at Wulf.

"So you loved her," he said.

"I did," said Wulf. "Maybe there at the last, she loved me again."

"This Khalid," said Charles Martel. "Did you ever cross his path afterward?"

"Yes, he was leading some riders up a mountain pass in Granada. I had men enough to surprise him and wipe him out."

"Killed him, did you?" prompted Charles Martel.

"Khalid was easy to kill."

"And that son of your Cahena, you said the Moslems named him Abd-ar-Rahman. Is he their general here?"

Abd-ar-Rahman's not an uncommon name among Moslems, but I've thought this one was once Mallul. I can't be sure."

Charles Martel poured the last of the wine into their cups, and they drank.

"Anyway, you and a few followers got across those straits somehow, and kept fighting," said Charles Martel.

"Fighting," growled Wulf. "Senseless. I've been sick of it for years."

"But I'm going to profit by what you've said about fighting," Charles Martel assured him. "If they want battle tomorrow, they'll get it. I'll wake up my officers and give them orders. We'll use your plan—form a long line of big men with big lances in their hands, to break up a cavalry charge. And behind that line, mounted men, for a countercharge. It's a simple-sounding thing, but it has to be explained, the way you've explained it."

"Yes," said Wulf.

"We've had a long night of it," said Charles Martel. "We ought to get what rest we can. You may lie down here. Take some of these cloaks and furs and make yourself up a bed."

"Thanks, I will."

"But one thing more. You've been helpful beyond measure, and I'm indebted to you. Tell me what I can do to repay you."

"You said we'd fight them tomorrow," Wulf reminded him. "Fight at close quarters. Just put me up to the front, where the fighting will be hottest."

Charles Martel blinked at him. "Where the fighting will be hottest? Look here, Wulf, where the fighting's hottest will be hot, or I miss my guess. That's just the place where you could get yourself killed."

Wulf set down his empty cup.

"I know," he said.